PRAISE FOR *SHARON LYNN FISHER*

Grimm Curiosities

Recommended by *The New York Times* in "Holiday Romance Novels to Make Your December Merry and Bright"

"Fisher has penned a haunting, romantic tale."

—*Booklist*

"Fisher allows the suspense to build slowly even as the romance burns quickly. Romantasy readers will be hooked."

—*Publishers Weekly*

Other Books

"Fans of *Jane Eyre* will go feral for this mysterious, historical fantasy retelling of their favorite classic read."

—The Everygirl on *Salt & Broom*

"Readers of Brontë's original will appreciate this character-driven, romance-filled mystery."

—*Booklist* on *Salt & Broom*

"Fisher's loose retelling brings a gothic fairy tale vibe to the classic and adds some twists that will keep even those familiar with the original guessing."

—*Publishers Weekly* on *Salt & Broom*

"A pleasant, atmospheric romp that fantasy or romance fans will enjoy. There's no need to be familiar with Brontë's novel to enjoy this one."

—*Library Journal* on *Salt & Broom*

"Fisher has a fantastic voice—crisp, magical, and crystal clear."

—Darynda Jones, *New York Times* and *USA Today* bestselling author

"Magical and brilliant! A fast-paced romp that expertly weaves two different worlds into an adventure not to be missed. Sharon Lynn Fisher crafts clever dialogue and creates characters to fall in love with."

—Lorraine Heath, *New York Times* and *USA Today* bestselling author, on *The Absinthe Earl*

"The environment is lush and imaginative, with everyone appearing to hide their own seductive, dark secrets. It's a world that comes alive with mysterious, foggy moors, dangerous peat bogs, and gorgeous green hills . . . Irish mythology and folklore are where Fisher's writing shines."

—*Kirkus Reviews* on *The Absinthe Earl*

"This is quite a wonderfully dizzying mash-up of a historical setting, time travel of a sort, and the fae. If you're a reader drawn to historical fantasy and magical Regencies, definitely give this series a try."

—*Book Riot* on the Faery Rehistory series

"This is a really fun sci-fi romance . . . Very cool setup and characters that I couldn't put down . . . The twist at the beginning will really hook you in!"

—Felicia Day, actress and producer, on *Ghost Planet*

TEA & ALCHEMY

OTHER TITLES BY SHARON LYNN FISHER

47North

Salt & Broom

Grimm Curiosities

Faery Rehistory Series

The Absinthe Earl

The Raven Lady

The Warrior Poet

Science Fiction

Ghost Planet

The Ophelia Prophecy

Echo 8

Erotic Fantasy Shorts

Before She Wakes

TEA & ALCHEMY

SHARON LYNN FISHER

This is a work of fiction. Names, characters, organizations, places, events, and incidents are either products of the author's imagination or are used fictitiously. Otherwise, any resemblance to actual persons, living or dead, is purely coincidental.

Published by 47North, Seattle
www.apub.com

EU product safety contact:
Amazon Media EU S. à r.l.
38, avenue John F. Kennedy, L-1855 Luxembourg
amazonpublishing-gpsr@amazon.com

ISBN-13: 9781662528699 (paperback)
ISBN-13: 9781662528682 (digital)

Cover design and illustration by Story Wrappers

Printed in the United States of America

For Selah, who knew I had a vampire novel in me.
For Talia, who's always up for bingeing Twilight.

Her light step would appear wandering amidst the underwood, in quest of the modest violet; then suddenly turning round, would show, to his wild imagination, her pale face and wounded throat, with a meek smile upon her lips.

—John William Polidori, *The Vampyre*

AUTHOR'S NOTE

The setting for this story is based on a real village and very old chapel in Cornwall, England. Search "Roche Rock," and you'll easily find it. I visited on impulse—we'd unintentionally arrived in Cornwall during the first weekend of a spring school holiday, and I was looking for less-frequented attractions. The place made my jaw drop, and I knew immediately I had to put it in a book.

If you'd like some additional visuals to complement your reading experience, you can visit my Pinterest inspiration board (username "sharonlynfisher").

And for music that inspired the story, you can find playlists for my books on Spotify. Click the "Profiles" button below the search bar and type "Sharon Lynn Fisher."

Lastly, a note of caution—the alchemical medicine created in this story is fictional and sometimes contains toxic plants. Okay for supernatural creatures but not people.

PROLOGUE

Harker Tregarrick

Roche Rock, Cornwall—September 27, 1854

Pushing open the casement, I bent close and breathed the moist air rolling in off Goss Moor. We'd seen the last of the long, sun-drenched days that had left me parched as harvest stubble.

Though the English Channel lay some seven miles to the south, my finely tuned senses sifted the seawater tang from the gentle movement of air. They also made me painfully aware of something much closer—a scent that had tormented me almost daily for the last two years.

A woman was walking along the road that divided the village of Roche from my family estate. A towering wall of granite and a thorn hedge screened her from me, but I could hear her shoes lightly striking the packed earth.

I knew neither her name nor her face. Neither her age nor her station in life. Only that she walked to town most days and occasionally took a footpath across the rocky, uneven heathland that sloped down from my stone fortress.

Roche was a small hive of activity that supported the surrounding farming and mining communities, and many people traveled that road.

But this woman . . . she smelled of meadowsweet. No floral essence or apothecary-formulated scent, simply her own delectable smell.

Sweet almond and light musk.

The scent was strongest in the mornings. In the late afternoon, when she returned home, it had been muted by village smells—horseflesh, coal fires, pipe smoke, tea.

Yet behind this ever-evolving perfume, I could always smell her blood.

Everyone who passed along any boundary of my land smelled of it. But none of the others tempted me away from my "vital essence" as she did.

I swung the casement shut, for all the good it would do. Fitted to the fifteenth-century window opening, it sealed out drafts about as well as you might expect.

My fortress was a chapel, constructed from the same type of stone that it rested upon by my ancestor John Tregarrick (originally Tregarrek, Cornish for "homestead of the rock"). He had intended it for a gift to the church but then moved in with his family when a fire destroyed the manor.

So the place was a "chapel" in name only. The black quartz schorl walls, which looked like a natural outgrowth of the high outcrop on which they rooted, enclosed the *un*holy. They shielded Roche's inhabitants from my ancient family, and vice versa.

Here I grew up, half orphaned from the day I emerged from my mother's womb.

The strange tragedy of the place, and the secrecy of my family, had long generated lore in the parish. Some said religious zeal had caused John Tregarrick to withdraw here. Others, that he'd contracted leprosy. The idea of an old hermit in the chapel persisted, though a new heir took possession every century or two. Almost as if the villagers believed there had only ever been one master of the estate. They weren't far wrong.

Other, darker tales of the place were still told, especially in the autumn and winter months, when the nights grew long. They warned of a "Wolf of Roche Rock," mad and murderous. Fantastic tales in this bright new age of science and industry. Believed only by superstitious fools.

Yet some of the old things were best not forgotten.

I had made it my long life's work to ensure the good folk of Roche village—including my anonymous tormentor—could rest safely in their forgetfulness. I had studied the condition passed down from father to son. My studies had led me to alchemy, which helped me to understand my physical body's lack. The reason for my deadly thirst.

Alchemy, too, had provided a kind of treatment. My alchemical vital essence was a substitute for the natural vital essence that flowed through the veins of every living creature.

Though an aqua vitae ("water of life") in more ways than one, my vital essence was no cure. Alchemy had not transmuted me into a normal man any more than it had transmuted base metals to gold or yielded the secret to eternal life.

I was grateful for what it *had* given me. A lessening of the fear that at any moment my true self could break free, reviving old terrors among my countrymen. Unleashing the ancient evil.

A *lessening* was all it could be.

THE MAGPIE

Roche village, Cornwall—October 2, 1854

"Mina," said my employer, ruddy cheeked, as she carried a tray of teacups into the kitchen, "could you clear that last table while I get started on the washing up?"

"Of course, Mrs. Moyle." I emptied coins from my apron pockets onto the worktable before going back out to the tearoom.

Things were quieter now, thank heaven. Such a rush of workers came to Roche for the harvest that Mrs. Moyle and I could scarcely draw breath. Like the clay miners, the grain reapers were mostly the kind who preferred the frothy pints, hearty stews, and rough brown bread at The Wolf's Head, but we caught the overflow and filled them with tea, scones, and pasties. (The strongest drink on offer at The Magpie was a dark cup of Assam.)

I made my way to one of the tables by the windows. I recalled a man had sat there alone, eating scones with Mrs. Moyle's home-made strawberry jam and clotted cream while reading a newspaper. I hadn't taken much notice of him; he'd been polite, quiet, and neatly dressed. I didn't think he was from Roche, but we saw a lot of his sort. Probably a clerk working for one of the china clay companies or tin mines.

He'd left his newspaper behind, and I tucked it under my arm for Mrs. Moyle. "Being a woman is no excuse for being uninformed" was a favorite slogan of hers. More than a slogan, for my employer had taken it upon herself to teach me reading and writing (beyond what little I'd learned from my mother), saying I wouldn't be of much use to her if I couldn't read a list for market or write down a customer's order.

While I supposed these were good reasons, I also thought she was lonely. We had that in common.

I carried the man's dishes to the kitchen, brushing crumbs from the plate and emptying the tea strainer before setting them next to the washbasin. Upon opening the teapot to remove the leaves that had stuck inside, I froze.

The Magpie had been a welcome change for me in every way but one. Emptying all those pots, I had begun seeing *shapes* in the clumps of leaves. Everyday things like candles, or flowers, or crescent moons, but now and then a crown, or sword, or castle.

Sometimes after seeing a thing, I'd hear a bit of gossip that seemed related to it. Like the time I saw a ring in the teapot at a table of young ladies, and after a few days I heard one had become engaged. Another time, the sodden leaves formed a line across the bottom of a large teapot, and a month later we heard that the family was setting sail for America. But once I'd seen a sickle shape in old Lady Rundle's cup—right before she suffered apoplexy.

I'd chided myself for paying heed to it, yet it kept happening. And try as I might, I could no more *not* see those shapes than I could *not* smell the gin on my brother, Jack, when he came home from the clay pits (and the tavern) in the evenings.

In *this* pot, I saw a magpie, plain as day—tea leaves forming the black feathers, the glazed clay of the pot forming the white. Magpies were news bearers, and Mum used to sing an old nursery rhyme about them:

One for sorrow,
Two for joy,
Three for a girl,
Four for a boy,
Five for silver,
Six for gold,
Seven for a secret never to be told

One for sorrow. Near the magpie was a narrow, pointy shape that I couldn't see as anything but a knife. Or, by its handle, more like a dagger.

"That's the last of it, then?" asked Mrs. Moyle, turning from the washbasin, the red in her cheeks deepened by the steamy water.

Blinking away the worrisome thoughts, I replied, "It is, ma'am."

The skin pricked at the back of my neck as I stuck my hand in the pot and dug out the wet leaves before handing it to her. My fingers trembled as I picked up the towel to begin drying.

Let it go.

But I couldn't.

"Mrs. Moyle," I said, trying to keep a lightness in my tone, "did you know that fellow who sat alone by the window this afternoon?"

My employer didn't miss much, and she looked up sharply. But she answered mildly enough. "I've never seen him before. I imagine he was just passing through. Seems we see more strangers in Roche every day."

"That we do." Roche had grown with the clay mining in the years since Mrs. Moyle had opened The Magpie using money from the sale of her late husband's livery business. It was why I'd found work here.

She studied me as I dried a saucer patterned with dog roses. "I'm always dreading the day a young man will catch your eye and steal you away from me, but this one was old enough to be your father."

I laughed, feeling the color in my cheeks. "Nothing like that, Mrs. Moyle."

She handed me the clean teapot to dry. "What then? I can see you working something over in your mind."

I rubbed the pot's gleaming surface with the towel. "You'll think me a fool. I think it myself."

"I've met fools aplenty, Mina, and I've never counted you among them."

Sighing, I set the pot on a shelf next to the window. Outside, mist gathered low along the ground in the garden, snaking slowly among the dried-up stalks. Most of Mrs. Moyle's flowers had withered in the heat of the last couple of weeks, but the red roses still bloomed, and a few sweet, creamy woodbine blossoms dotted the vines growing along the hedgerow in back. The birds were at the haws, and we'd have to pick them soon if we were to have any for jelly.

"Sometimes," I began slowly, "I see things in people's teapots. Shapes, or likenesses. It often seems as if those shapes are trying to say something to me."

"You're a tasseographer," said Mrs. Moyle in wonderment.

I raised my eyebrows. "Tassy . . . *what?*"

Her blue eyes were full of interest. "Tasseography! I've read about it but never knew anyone who could do it."

"What *is* it, ma'am?" I asked, finding some comfort in the idea that the things I was seeing had a name.

"The reading of tea leaves. They form shapes that are symbols of certain outcomes—births, deaths, marriages, and the like. Did your mother read them, by any chance?"

I frowned. "Not so far as I know."

"There are women who earn money by it; it's a kind of fortune-telling. Once, a customer left a copy of *The Times* that had an article about it. There's a school for young ladies on an estate in Yorkshire that *teaches* it." She smiled. "My grandmother always said women with red hair could divine things, especially freckled ones like you, my dear."

My mother's hair had been dark, but now that I thought of it, we'd had strangers in the house sometimes for tea. Only when Da was at the mine. Mum sat with them, and she'd send Jack and me outside to hang laundry or peel potatoes. After they'd gone, Mum would tell us not to pester Da by talking about the guest, and she'd give us a bit of bread with jam. Once when I sat down to eat it, I saw her pluck a sixpence coin off the table.

"I think I might be wrong about my mother," I said.

Mrs. Moyle gave me a knowing nod. "I daresay some would call it the devil's work, and maybe she thought it best to hide it. Not that *I* set any store by such ideas." She eyed me more keenly. "Did you see something in that gentleman's cup? Is that what made you ask about him?"

"I did. I saw a magpie."

She frowned, thinking. "I know some people believe a magpie's bad luck, but my grandmother believed that magpies bring news from the spirit world, and that they're a sign we should pay attention."

I swallowed. "I saw a dagger, too."

Now her brow clouded. "I can understand why that would worry you. I wish there was something I could say to set your mind at ease, though I expect all will be well." More cheerfully, she added, "We may see the man in here again. People don't forget my scones."

I smiled. "No, they don't."

"Why don't you go sit in the front room, and I'll make you a cup of tea. Take the chill off your thoughts before you go out into the fog."

"That's all right, Mrs. Moyle," I protested. "You'll want a rest yourself."

"There's plenty of time for that when the house is quiet this evening." The tearoom was in an old cottage with fresh thatch and a door painted the color of grass shoots. Mrs. Moyle slept in a small bedroom upstairs. "You can continue reading about young Catherine Morland's adventures," she said. "I'm anxious to hear what you think of her!"

My employer wouldn't have it otherwise, so I went out and settled in one of the armchairs in front of the coal stove.

The Magpie was about the coziest place I'd ever been in. The cottage had last been home to a bookshop. Mrs. Moyle had removed most of the bookcases and filled the space with odds and ends of battered tables that she'd whitewashed for both "uniformity" and "practicality"—her idea being that white tables meant she could do without white cloths, which would always be tea stained.

The white furnishings against the old house's dark flooring and wood paneling reminded me of the light and dark feathers of the bird the place was named for. Mrs. Moyle had chosen the name well, as I doubted more gossip was exchanged anywhere else in the village.

She had made the room cheery by hanging colorful paintings against the white plaster above the wainscot. She arranged flowers from the kitchen garden in little vases on the tables—fresh in the spring and summer, dried all the rest of the year. The money she saved on tablecloth laundering she spent on pretty lamps and fine white candles for the darker days of autumn and winter.

She'd filled the few remaining bookcases with her own collection. Novels of high adventure, gothic terror, and romance, and books on things like flowers and birds that were filled with pretty illustrations. Some customers even read them, and Mrs. Moyle was kind enough to loan them out if anyone asked. I read them myself when business was slow. Jack said working at The Magpie had made me a different person, and I had to admit it was true in some ways. But I thought the books were as much to blame as the job itself.

I opened a small drawer in the tea table next to my chair—my favorite hiding place for the books I was reading—and took out *Northanger Abbey*.

A few minutes later, Mrs. Moyle joined me with a pot and two cups. We sat quietly, me with my book and her with the customer's newspaper, until I realized the room was growing dim.

"Heavens," I said, starting up. "I better get on before I'm walking home in the dark."

"I quite lost track of the time myself," replied my employer, also rising.

She picked up a basket from a nearby table and held it out to me. Under the linen cover, I knew I'd find scones left from the day's business. Jack had come to take them for granted and was vexed when there weren't any for his supper.

"I'll see you in the morning, dear," she said. "Keep safe on your way home."

I went to the kitchen for my bonnet and shawl and slipped out the back door. The path through the garden led me between rows of tall sunflowers, nearly spent, their heavy brown heads drooping like a congregation in prayer.

At the path's end, a low white gate with crooked slats opened onto the road that ran alongside the old Tregarrick estate, with its dark moorstone chapel (which everyone just called Roche Rock). It was an unnaturally quiet old place. People said there'd once been a manor house as well, but it had burned down a long time ago. The cottage I lived in with Jack lay just beyond the estate, in the hamlet of Carbis.

At this hour, and with the close of the grain harvest, the road seemed almost as still as the graveyard. One lonely hay cart passed before I was left to haunt the twilight alone in the gathering mist.

A thick hedge, going to golds and yellows now, mostly blocked my view of the estate until I was closer to home. But a narrow gap showed a path climbing toward Roche Rock, first rounding the edge of an oak wood on the right, then winding up through overgrown grasses, clumps of heather, and large stones.

One of the family still lived here, in the chapel itself. I'd never been anywhere close to the old, dark tower, nor known anyone who had, but sometimes I crossed the heath that spread below it down toward Carbis. I always paused to study the high moorstone ridge and its fortress, black against the green of the hilly grounds. Sometimes I fancied a face looked out at me through a window, though it was too far to see such a thing.

On my way to and from work, I often wondered about the master of Roche Rock. I'd never glimpsed him, nor any of his relations or servants. I'd never learned his Christian name. I didn't know how old he might be, though I'd pictured him wrinkled and gray, wearing fine, outdated clothing, like some of the paintings in the tearoom. No one else seemed to know anything about him, either, but when people mentioned Roche Rock, they crossed themselves.

Though the place made me uneasy, especially after dark, it also made me curious. My mother had always said the heath belonged to the fairies, and that was why the estate had gone to ruin. It had no business being built there.

About halfway to the cluster of whitewashed miners' cottages, the hedgerow ended and an old tumbledown stone wall took over, running along the heath toward the estate's eastern boundary. No animals were kept on the property, and no person was ever seen tending it. Other folk besides me ignored the boundary, hopping the low wall and crossing the heath on the way to the holy well at Coldvreath. I'd often seen boys collecting rabbit traps from a silver birch coppice on the estate's southern edge. Poachers, to be sure, but no one ever made any trouble about them. Could be that the master of Roche Rock was both old *and* infirm.

As I reached the spot where hedge gave way to wall, a small movement caused me to stop, and I spotted a yellowhammer in the brambly tangle. The hedges were always thick with birds in early autumn, feasting on the haws, brambleberries, and hazelnuts. They usually kept quiet and out of sight at twilight, when I'd seen many a fox skulking about. The bird gave a few short, high chirps and dove deeper into the hedge.

I was starting toward home again when another movement—this time just the other side of the wall—caught my eye. There was a kind of hollow here and the mist was thicker, but I thought I'd glimpsed something slipping from wall to hedgerow. Something like antlers, so probably I'd startled a deer.

As I strained my eyes in the fading light, the mist shifted, and I noticed an unfamiliar shape on my side of the wall. It looked like nothing more than a low pile of stones—plentiful on the estate—but I'd passed this hollow many times and hadn't seen it before. Curious, I stepped off the road.

A tingling sensation traveled up the middle of my back as I drew closer. It was almost dark, and I knew I should hurry home. I could satisfy my curiosity in the morning on my way to work. But I was nearly there already, and maybe the thing wouldn't *be* there tomorrow.

Likely a dropped cloak or coat, nosy miss.

When I was within a couple of yards of the thing, the almost-full moon peeped its bright face out from the clouds.

My heart bounded up and nearly out of my body.

Not a cloak, but a *man* lying there. Still as stones.

A BAD END

"Sir?" I knelt beside him, setting my basket on the ground. "*Sir?* Are you all right?"

Sniffing the air above him, I caught no scent of drink. Still, it was the most likely explanation. I'd found Jack like this once on the side of the road in front of our cottage; thankfully I'd managed to rouse him before any of our neighbors noticed.

The man lay on his stomach, head turned to one side, his hat crushed and half covering his face. Heart thumping, I reached out and gently lifted the hat.

I snatched my hand back with a gasp, upsetting the basket of scones. The whites of the man's eyes—open and staring—glowed in the silver light of the moon. Something dark smeared his cheek. *Blood?*

Holding a fist to my chest, I struggled for breath.

Then it struck me that I *knew* this man. The customer with the newspaper. *The customer with the magpie in his teapot.*

Before I could recover enough to think what to do, I noticed another movement beyond the wall.

"Hello?" I called in a reedy voice. "Is anyone there? Please help!"

No answer came. A curtain of cloud fell back over the moon, leaving me alone in the dark with a dead man.

I darted up, lifted my skirt, and ran—stumbling, tears streaming down my face—back to The Magpie.

Settled in front of the stove again with another cup of tea—this time with a blanket, too, and no mind for reading about a girl who dreamed up imaginary terrors—I tried to attend to the constable's questions.

Fetched from his supper table, Mr. Hilliard sat in the armchair across from me, his own cup of tea untouched. He was about the age my father would have been and more well-to-do, his dark hair and mustache groomed and greased with care, skin grayed from the shock he'd received this evening.

"You saw no one else in the area, Miss—er—" He looked down at his pocket diary, where he had scribbled a few notes. "Miss Penrose." Glancing up again, he said, "There are Penroses aplenty on and around these moorlands, but with that hair I reckon you must be kin to Jack Penrose."

Mr. Hilliard was one of the bosses from Wheal Enys, Jack's mine. "Yes, sir. Jack is my brother."

He nodded and leaned forward in his chair. The door of the coal stove stood open, and firelight glinted in his keen, dark eyes. "So you saw no one else in the area where you discovered the body?"

Pulling the blanket tighter around my shoulders, I shook my head. "Just a stag on the heath."

His lips curved down. "Indeed? You're certain that's what it was?"

"Fairly so. I saw antlers."

Mr. Hilliard blinked a couple of times, thinking, then jotted something else down in his diary. "And you say you don't know this gentleman?"

"I don't, sir. But as I mentioned, he was here in the tearoom this afternoon."

"How did he seem to you, then?"

I exchanged a look with Mrs. Moyle, who stood behind the constable. She nodded her encouragement.

"He seemed all right to me. But I didn't speak with him other than to get his order. He just read his newspaper and drank his tea."

"Didn't mention his name?"

"Not to me, sir."

"Mmm." More scribbling.

When Mr. Hilliard first arrived at The Magpie, he'd been sour-faced—grumpy, no doubt, about missing his supper. He'd asked me where to find the body, and he'd left straightaway, warning me to stay put so that he could question me. Half an hour later he returned, sour mood turned sober.

"You don't believe anyone's *killed* the poor man, do you, Mr. Hilliard?" asked Mrs. Moyle.

"Something certainly *has* killed him, ma'am, but I think an animal of some kind is more likely. The wound is ragged, like it was made by teeth rather than a weapon." I shuddered, and Mrs. Moyle's cheeks lost their rosy color. "We'll have a better idea once he's been examined by Mr. Perry."

Mr. Perry was Roche's surgeon. He'd seen to Da when he was dying with the miner's lung sickness. Then Mum when she started coughing, too, though from a different cause.

The front door swung open, and a younger man came in. Like Mr. Hilliard, he was dressed for office work, and he carried a leather case.

"What've you got there, Gibbs?" asked Mr. Hilliard.

The man held up the case. "I found it on the heath, sir."

The constable stood. "Let's have a look, then."

Gibbs set the bag on one of the tearoom's white tables. Mr. Hilliard joined him and opened the bag's clasp. Reaching inside, he drew out a handful of papers, then held them close to the lamp resting on the table.

His eyes moved over one paper, and then another. "Tregarrick," he said at last.

I sat up and Mrs. Moyle gasped. "The master of Roche Rock?" she said.

Still squinting at the papers, Mr. Hilliard said, "Looks like the fellow was his solicitor. One Henry Roscoe. You said you found this on the heath, Gibbs?"

Gibbs nodded. "Just the other side of the wall, sir."

Mr. Hilliard looked at me. "You said you didn't go straight home after work, Miss Penrose, but sat awhile with Mrs. Moyle?"

I nodded. "For a couple of hours."

"Doing what, may I ask?"

I was about to answer "reading" when I recalled the tea leaves, and my conversation with Mrs. Moyle. My heart sped up as I glanced at her. Should I tell him? He was bound to think it strange, or worse. *Some would call it the devil's work,* my employer had said. But what if it could help him figure out what had happened to poor Mr. Roscoe?

Mrs. Moyle spoke up first. "We're a widow and a young woman whose only relation works in the clay pits. Which means we're *lonely*, Mr. Hilliard, and we keep each other company sometimes."

He pondered this a moment. "Well, two hours would have given Mr. Roscoe time to meet with his client. After that he may have set out for Carbis—maybe to the inn there—which would have put him on your route, Miss Penrose." He looked at Gibbs. "We'd better go and have a word with Tregarrick."

The man's eyes opened wide. "Roche Rock? Tonight, Mr. Hilliard?"

The mining boss raised one brow. "We aren't talking about poachers, Gibbs. His solicitor's been killed less than half a mile from his door. Tregarrick might have been the last person to see the fellow alive. Moreover, if some rabid animal is on the loose, he could be at risk himself."

Gibbs swallowed. "Yes, sir. Only I don't think they welcome visitors there."

Mr. Hilliard heaved a sigh. "For the love of God, man. Stay here with the women and the fire, then, and I'll see to it myself."

If this taunt was intended to stiffen his man's backbone, it failed entirely. Gibbs looked hugely relieved, and Mrs. Moyle offered him a cup of tea.

Mr. Hilliard picked up the leather case and turned to me. "After I see Tregarrick, I'm going to fetch your brother to walk home with you. Where might I find him?"

I knew Jack must still be at the tavern, else he'd probably already have been to The Magpie looking for me and his supper. I didn't like saying this to one of his bosses but couldn't see a way around it. "I reckon he's at The Wolf's Head, Mr. Hilliard."

His grunt suggested he wasn't surprised to hear it. "All right. If I don't find him, I'll stop back by and take you home myself. No going off on your own, hear? It's not safe."

"No, sir."

I wished Gibbs had worked up his courage to go along with the constable. I was quite badly shaken, and desperate to speak more with Mrs. Moyle about Mr. Roscoe and his tea leaves. To make matters worse, Gibbs became a chatterpie after two cups of tea. You'd never know he'd just been out fumbling around on the heath in the dark looking for a dead man's personal effects.

Mrs. Moyle's worried gaze landed on me several times, and she did her best to hold his attention so I wouldn't have to pretend to be interested in his conversation. After about half an hour of this, Jack appeared. He had not met with Mr. Hilliard but had come on his own, sullen about his supper, after finding our cottage empty.

Mrs. Moyle brought Jack tea and bread with jam while I told him what had happened. He and Gibbs knew each other from work—Gibbs was a clerk at the mine office—which may have kept Jack from being as sharp as he would have liked.

Jack had not always been ill-tempered. It was just that he wasn't cut out for mine work, and he'd never had a choice. Da had mined tin on Goss Moor when he was a boy, like his own father, and then gone to work in the clay pits when they came along. Jack, too, was only a boy when Da first took him to Wheal Enys.

Growing up, my twin brother had been gentle and happy. He'd loved making up pretend games involving the fairies, and Robin Hood, and especially King Arthur, who'd lived in a castle in nearby Tintagel and hunted on Goss Moor. But after the mine, Jack grew less gentle and less happy every day.

When lung disease took Da one harsh winter, and Mum so wore herself out caring for him that winter fever took *her*, only Jack was left to provide for the two of us. That was when he took to drinking. Seeing what it was doing to him, I meant to go to the mines, too. Girls could get work turning clay in the drying buildings or hammering ore in the copper mines. Jack wouldn't hear of it, though. Said it wouldn't mean he'd have to work any less, and I had enough of a job in keeping house for us. He hadn't wanted me to go to The Magpie, either, but when I told him I'd let go of the idea if he stopped spending every night at The Wolf's Head, he quit arguing about it.

"You'll have to give it up now, Mina," said Jack as we set out for home by the meager light of his tin lantern.

His words were softer now that the tea and toast had sobered him and taken the edge off his hunger. Still, they frightened me more than the shadows the sputtering candle had set dancing.

"The Magpie?" I said, unable to steady the tremor in my voice.

"Hilliard's a windbag, but he had the right of it. You can't be out on the road with some rabid animal loose."

"No, Jack," I pleaded. "Mrs. Moyle needs me."

"She'll find someone else easily enough."

"No," I repeated with more force. "I'll make sure to be home well before dark from now on."

Thick, dark-red brows lifted over eyes the same pale shade of green as my own. "The light of day didn't come between *this* fella and a bad end, did it?"

We were just passing the spot where the body had lain, though the constable's men had removed it by now. I *was* scared of whatever had killed Mr. Roscoe, but not as scared as I was of leaving my job. I didn't know what would become of me if I had to go back to the way things were before. The silence of our empty cottage—the remembrances of what we'd lost there—might crush the life out of me.

"What if I wait there for you every night?" I said. "Mrs. Moyle won't mind. I can read her books until you get there. Then you can walk me home."

Jack scowled. "Both of us have better things to do than—"

"Better things?" I snapped, glaring at him. "Like drinking at The Wolf's Head?"

"Now, I work *hard*, Mina, I shouldn't have to tell you that. And I didn't choose it, any more than you chose to take on the things our mother used to do. I'm the eldest, and she would want you—"

"Eldest?" I let out a bark of laughter. Jack had emerged first from our mother's womb, and he never let me forget it.

"Mum and Da would want you to do as I say! Now you find yourself a husband, and then you can—"

"Do what *he* says instead?" Loneliness had turned my thoughts to it *many* a time. But any man who would marry me would likely be a miner, too, and he might not want me at The Magpie any more than Jack did. It wasn't as if I'd been turning down offers, anyway. There were plenty of girls in the parish with dark hair, or flaxen, and faces not covered in freckles. With easy smiles, soft eyes, and blunter tongues.

"I'm tired, Mina," Jack said, hard and flat. "And I want my supper. I'll say no more about it."

We were home too late for me to do more than cobble together a meal. I made pasties every morning for the tearoom and for Jack to take to work, but I always held one out for when I returned from work. Tonight I halved my pasty and served it with slices of apple from the tree out back and cheese from the market, along with the last of the hevva cake from the night before.

As we ate, I thought of a new argument to try. It occurred to me that Jack might need reminding that we were probably the only mining family in the parish no longer cooking over a hearth fire, thanks to Mrs. Moyle. She'd given me the cookstove she'd replaced after opening the tearoom.

But Jack finished quick and went straight to his bed—the one that had belonged to our mother and father, behind a folding screen downstairs. I left the washing for the morning and went up to the loft and my own bed.

Tucked under the covers, I prayed for sleep. Instead, I felt tears gather under my eyelids and squeeze onto my cheeks. I kept seeing Mr. Roscoe's face in my mind—in the shop with his newspaper and tea, then on the heath with his staring eyes and blood-smeared cheek. The way his head had been turned, and with the twist of collar and coat at his neck, I hadn't seen the wound. I was grateful for that now, though my imagination was doing plenty on its own.

Had it truly been an animal? What animal was big enough to take down a full-grown man like that? As far as I knew, the only wolves to be found in Cornwall were the ones in stories, and no fox could ever manage such a thing. I supposed it must have been a large dog.

Shuddering, I turned my thoughts to The Magpie, and Jack's decision. In a way, I dreaded going back there. I wished to see no more auguries. I could always empty the teapots without looking into them, of course, but would I really be able to? What if I missed something that could help someone? Yet what help had I been to Mr. Roscoe? I recalled Mum and her tea guests and wondered—had she been able to help *them*?

Weariness gradually slowed my thoughts, unraveling them until they no longer made any kind of sense. Still, as I was dropping off, there was a moment when a final clear thought did come to me: Though I had failed to make Jack understand about The Magpie—in losing our parents, we'd also lost the sympathy of feeling we'd shared all our lives—it was impossible for me to do what he wanted.

I fell asleep wondering what the consequences would be.

CHORUS

Like any other day, I woke to the peal of morning church bells and rose to make the pasties, boiling the onions, potatoes, swedes, and beef before filling the shortcrust, crimping the edges, and popping the pasties into the oven.

Jack always rose as the aroma began to fill the cottage. He dressed, washed his face, and broke his fast with tea and bread with milk. It was my habit to wrap a pasty from the first batch and hand it to him as he walked out the door. I thought he might ask about the number of them I was making this morning, now that he expected me to give up my job. But Jack was usually too tired from work and foggy from the previous night's drink to pay much attention to what I did—so long as meals appeared at the expected times—and today was no different.

He never said much in the mornings, and today he kept silent, avoiding my gaze until I was putting the still-warm pasty into his hand.

"You'll be all right today?" he asked.

"Yes," I said, lifting my chin.

A tiny, tired smile tugged at his lips. "There's my girl," he said, and this glimpse of the old Jack wrenched my heart. Never mind that the whites of his eyes were veined with red, and he looked like he'd hardly slept. "Nothing's going to bother you if you stay close to the cottage," he cautioned gently.

I gave him a short nod, though my face grew hot.

"I'm sorry things can't be different."

He might have been referring to a hundred things, but I knew what he meant: *Sorry about The Magpie*. His words seemed to make plain what I had already feared—that he had no idea of letting me go back, even once the dog, or whatever it was, had been caught.

Truth was, the attack on Mr. Roscoe had given him a reason for doing something he'd wanted to for a long time. I always figured Jack grumbled about The Magpie because it made me happier, and *he* couldn't be happy. Maybe also because of how it had changed me. I felt like I understood the world a little better from being around people who were different. And certainly from reading Mrs. Moyle's books.

Jack couldn't escape the life he'd been born to. I guessed he didn't want me to, either.

He turned and started for Wheal Enys, kicking a lone dandelion stalk that sprouted from the hardpacked road and setting the feathery seeds adrift like souls of the dead.

Recalling that he'd likely be walking home alone from the tavern, as usual, despite his cautioning *me*, I shouted after him, "You be careful, Jack! Be home before dark!"

He raised a hand without turning and then faded into the morning mist.

Sighing, I closed the door against the chill and went back to finish the baking. I tried not to think about what would happen when Jack learned I'd defied him. If I took care to get home before he did, he might not discover it right away. And if I could stave that off until the danger had passed, he wouldn't be able to use the same argument against me.

I pulled a pan from the oven and slid the last one in. Mrs. Moyle always said our customers came as much for the pasties as they did for her scones. "Oggies," Da had called them, and I made them the way Mum had taught me, though sometimes I changed up the fillings. In the spring I put in leeks and a few crumbles of yarg cheese, and those were a particular favorite at the shop. But the truth was Mrs. Moyle's scones and jams were known all over the parish.

She'd added pasties to the menu as the ladies who were regulars began bringing their husbands and children with them. My employer couldn't do all the baking herself, so besides giving me the old stove, she paid me enough to cover the ingredients and my extra efforts. This had allowed me to put better food on our own table, too—a fact that seemed to have escaped Jack's notice.

Once the pasties had cooled enough, I packed them into a basket and covered them with a cloth. But as I was leaving the cottage, I hesitated, then went back for my paring knife and slipped it in with the pasties. Maybe it wasn't much of a weapon, but I kept it sharp, which would count for something in a desperate moment.

Though I didn't regret my decision, I still felt guilty as I set out for work. I had never defied Jack outright before. But then he had never given me reason to.

The day was bright, and as I walked, the golden autumn sunshine and brisk air gentled my troubled thoughts. People were going about their business; a few strangers rode past me toward the village, and two farm carts full of apples rolled toward Carbis.

But as I drew near the place where I'd found Mr. Roscoe, uneasiness crept over me. I noticed where the weeds had been pressed down by his body and shivered. Like the victim, most of the scones that had spilled onto the heath were gone. A crow pecked violently at the last one, sending crumbs flying into the air. With a loud caw, a second crow lit beside the first, joining the feast. Mrs. Moyle's basket lay on its side nearby. I left it there, thinking I might find the courage to pick it up on my way home.

With less than half a mile of road between me and the tearoom, I hurried along and soon found myself safe inside the warm kitchen. I set the pasties on the long wooden worktable, where rows and rows of scones were cooling.

"How are you this morning, Mina?" asked Mrs. Moyle, coming down the cramped staircase from her room above. Like every morning, she was neat as a pin, her apron crisp and her magpie hair—black streaked with white—neatly pulled back and coiled. She looked tired this morning, though—as, I was sure, did I.

"I am well, Mrs. Moyle."

She eyed me doubtfully. "You know, you needn't have come today. You'd certainly be missed, but I could have managed. You've had quite a shock."

I gave her a gentle shrug. "I guess I feel like it's better to keep on with things."

She pressed her lips together and nodded. She crossed to the stove, picked up a towel, and opened the oven door, hinges protesting with a noise that was part creak, part groan. Removing a pan of scones from the oven, she said, "Mr. Hilliard came back again after you left last night."

"Oh?" A tremor lifted my voice. "Any news?"

She set the pan down and met my gaze. "Mr. Roscoe was, indeed, Mr. Tregarrick's solicitor. Down from Bodmin to see his client."

"I see." Did he have a wife? Children? I couldn't bring myself to ask.

"He said Mr. Tregarrick was very distressed at the news, which of course he would be. Though, despite having lived here most of my life, I've never met nor even seen the man."

"Did the constable say anything else about how . . . how it happened?"

Mrs. Moyle frowned, setting her towel on the worktable. "Both Mr. Hilliard and Mr. Perry seem to believe it was an animal attack. His body wasn't much damaged, but it seems the neck wound was fatal. Only . . ."

I waited, but she looked unsure whether she wanted to say more. "Only?" I prompted.

"Well, the exact cause of death is believed to be a loss of blood, but the gentlemen are puzzled by the fact there wasn't much blood where you found his body. Forgive me if that was more than you wanted to know."

"No, I wish to understand," I replied, though my stomach was souring. "I suppose Mr. Roscoe couldn't have been moved there from somewhere else?"

"That's exactly what I asked, but Mr. Hilliard said if an animal had . . ." She closed her eyes, shuddering visibly. "If an animal had *dragged* him, they would have seen some sign of it."

"What do they think, then?"

Shaking her head, she said, "I don't know, but with facts not quite adding up, I daresay there will be a coroner's inquest." She took a deep breath, eyes moving over the fruits of her morning labor. "What *I'd* be wondering, were I a member of the constabulary, is whether the poor man had been moved by some*body*."

This sent a chill through me. "Though it's awful enough, I think I'd rather it was only an animal."

"I have to agree." More reassuringly, she said, "And I expect that's what they'll conclude."

Mrs. Moyle began moving scones from the cooling racks to a large platter, and I put on my apron and helped her. Soon I felt her studying me.

"I'm going to guess you've done some fretting about what you told me yesterday, before all this started."

"I have," I admitted faintly.

"There was nothing you could have done, Mina. No way you could have known."

"I've told myself that, yet I wonder—what's the point of it, then?"

She nodded in sympathy. "That may come to you in time."

We heard the rattle of the front door, and Mrs. Moyle looked at the watch pinned to her apron and muttered, "Heavens." She covered my hand with hers for a moment, and I managed a weak smile. Then she went to open the shop.

I had hoped for a quiet day, but the tearoom filled quickly, everyone curious what their neighbors knew about the night before. At first I feared they'd stare at or even question me, but it soon became clear that Mr. Hilliard must have kept me out of the public account of the death. Likely it would come out at some point, but I still felt shaken and was grateful to be left in peace for a while.

As much peace as could be had in a busy tearoom. Mrs. Moyle insisted on working the front room, leaving me in back making tea, arranging scones and pasties on pretty, mismatched china plates, and filling small bowls with clotted cream and jam.

From the kitchen, I could still hear snatches of conversation, and some customers did seem to know that Mrs. Moyle was the one who'd sent for the constable. When they questioned her, she told them she'd been asked "not to share any information regarding the stranger's death until the investigation was concluded."

Before long, my employer began falling behind. On most days, I served customers while she kept to the kitchen, as her aching joints protested all the trips back and forth. A tray with tea service for one had been sitting on the counter long enough that the spout had nearly stopped steaming, so I called up my courage and carried it out to the dining room, trying to both keep my head down and look for someone sitting alone.

My breath caught as I noticed a man sitting at the same window table where Mr. Roscoe had sat, reading a book. My hands began to tremble, causing the teapot lid to clink.

Steadying myself, I moved toward him. Though the dining room was busy and buzzing, it was almost as if I moved through a kind of tunnel with him at the end of it. A strange calm had stolen over me, yet something at the back of my mind warned me to beware of this feeling. As if danger were everywhere, and only the fools around me couldn't see it.

It's the shock from yesterday. I drew a slow breath as I reached the table.

The man looked up from his book—not a novel like those that lined Mrs. Moyle's shelves, but a thick tome one would need both hands to carry. He wore spectacles with round, smoke-tinted lenses, and I wondered how he could see through them well enough to read.

"Good day, sir," I said. "Are you waiting for tea?"

He tilted his head forward, eyeing me over the top of his spectacles, and my heart flopped strangely. Often, customers took so little notice of me that I thought they probably wouldn't recognize me were they to pass me in the street. This man's eyes were awake and keen. And their color . . . a dusty dark blue that reminded me of a prune plum. His hair was wavy and ashen brown, gathered and bound at the back of his neck. A few strands had worked free and hung alongside his sharp cheekbones. The angle of his jaw swept in strongly from his cheek, gentling at last to the blunted tip of his chin. His lips were very dark, like the stain of a blackberry. Or a bruise. They made a strong contrast against his skin, even-toned and pale.

I realized then that I was staring at this stranger, and he was staring even harder *back*.

"F-forgive me for disturbing you," I stammered, dropping my gaze to the tray. "I thought this might be—"

"Indeed, it is. You may set it down." His bruised lips formed a tight, dry smile. Though I would have guessed he was near my own age, something in his manner made me think otherwise. There was a stillness to him. And watchfulness, too. He also sounded like a man well used to people following his orders.

"Yes, sir." Quickly I transferred teapot, cup, strainer, and milk pitcher to the table, noting that I'd brewed his tea in a pot patterned with clumps of blackberry fruit, leaves, and flowers.

As I lifted the pot and poured, I frowned at the dark color and lack of steam. "I fear your tea has sat for too long, sir. It'll be bitter and tepid. I'll fetch you a fresh pot."

"It's not necessary." His voice was low and smooth, but I had no trouble hearing him, even with the din in the tearoom. I still had the feeling of being in a tunnel with him.

"I'm afraid we're not up to Mrs. Moyle's usual standards today," I said in a fluster. "I hope you'll give us another chance. We're *that* busy, what with everybody wondering about the . . ."

"About the death."

"Aye, sir." Why on earth had I brought it up? Sometimes nervousness made my mouth move when it shouldn't.

I gave him a short curtsy and was turning to go when he said, "You're the one who found him, aren't you?"

I froze, hugging the tray to my chest. I glanced around the room, hoping no one had heard him. Moving close to the table, I said in a low voice, "Begging your pardon, sir, may I ask how you knew that?"

He lifted his teacup and sipped, hand trembling slightly. "Mr. Hilliard told me it was a young woman walking home from her job at The Magpie."

"Mr. Hilliard?" I echoed, surprised. As I studied the stranger, a thought startled me. "You're Mr. Tregarrick. Mr. Roscoe was your solicitor." He was not at all what I had imagined. Even if I *was* wrong about his age, he was still too young to have closed himself up in a medieval tower.

"I am indeed," he said.

"I'm so sorry, sir."

His lips curved down. "A tragedy, to be sure."

"Had he a family?"

The master of Roche Rock lifted a napkin from the table, touching it to his lips, though he'd taken only a sip of his tea. "I believe he did, though our relationship was strictly a business one."

I clucked and looked away. "The poor things. Everyone's saying it was an animal of some kind. It's so strange and awful."

"Yes. And very worrying. I wonder at your being out alone on the road again today, Miss . . . ?"

"Penrose," I said, heart skipping as I met his gaze. "Mina Penrose."

Again he frowned. "Well, Mina Penrose, don't you think it might be better if you kept close to home for a while? No one would want to see something like that happen to *you*. An out-of-town solicitor is one thing, but a young woman who must be familiar to many—"

"Begging your pardon, sir, but I don't see how my comings and goings are any of your concern." Tears stung my eyes, as I regretted my words almost before they'd finished coming out. But he'd sounded so like Jack for a moment, and I supposed I was still raw from our argument last night. Still raw from *all* of last night.

"No, of course not," he replied coolly, eyes lowering to his book. I had opened my mouth to offer an apology when he continued, "Thank you, Miss Penrose. That will be all."

I strode quickly back to the kitchen, cheeks burning. I found Mrs. Moyle there, hurriedly arranging scones and tea things on a tray.

"I'm so sorry," I said, moving to take over for her. "A tray was sitting here, and I took it out, meaning to help you, but got held up."

She laughed. "No need to apologize for getting held up by a young gentleman. I only wish we got more of them in here. He's an odd fellow, though, isn't he? I don't recognize him."

"Mrs. Moyle, it's Mr. Tregarrick!"

She raised her eyes from the laden tray. "Heavens! I'd thought him an old man."

"So did I, though I don't know why. I'm sure no one's ever told me anything about him."

Tipping milk into a pitcher, she said, "Did he mention his solicitor?"

"That's how I learned it was him. He asked if I was the one who found Mr. Roscoe."

Her brows lifted. "And did you tell him?"

"I didn't like to lie about it."

"What did he say?"

I let out a sigh and picked up the notebook of tea orders. "That I ought not to be walking around the village on my own."

"Well," my employer replied, lifting the tray, "he likely has a point. Frankly, I thought your brother would insist you stay home today."

"I'm too old for Jack—or Mr. Tregarrick—to be telling me what to do," I said shortly.

I felt Mrs. Moyle's eyes on me. "I'm not going to join the chorus, but if anything happened to you, Mina, I'd never get over it."

With that, she took the tray out to the dining room.

I was uneasy after that, and my thoughts kept drifting back to the master of Roche Rock and his oddness. There were things other than the ones I'd first noticed. Contradictions, you might call them. For example, though he was quite a handsome gentleman, as well as finely dressed, neither his face nor his clothing had looked very *lived in*. The wealthy could of course afford to take better care of themselves, but despite his paleness, Mr. Tregarrick looked fresh from the shop. Had he not been moldering away for years in that old tower?

There was something more that I struggled to put my finger on until almost closing time, when business had finally slowed. His address to me had been too familiar for a stranger.

I wonder at your being out alone on the road again today. How had he known I was alone? Something in his way of speaking had made me feel as if he were aware of my habits. It was true I walked alongside his estate going to The Magpie, but I'd never once seen him. I couldn't help wondering—had he been watching me?

Ridiculous. Why would he do such a thing?

By the time Mrs. Moyle locked the front door behind the last customers, we'd served every scone and pasty in the house. I heard the floor creaking as she made her way to the kitchen.

"You'd best start soon," she said as she joined me. "I want you home before sundown."

"I will, Mrs. Moyle. There's time for washing up."

I'd had to do some of the washing as we worked today so we could keep up with the orders. But there was a stack of dishes on the worktable I hadn't gotten to yet. As Mrs. Moyle heated water on the stove, I noticed the teapot decorated with blackberries—and went cold inside. My employer started chattering lightly about the day's business, but I heard not a word of it.

I've done it on purpose. Left his teapot until the end, without being fully aware of it.

I stepped to the worktable and picked it up.

"POETIC JUSTICE"

Harker

Pressing my trembling hands against the rough surface of my worktable, I surveyed my domain. A forest of gourd-shaped copper vessels and glass tubes. Iron implements of every sort. Crucibles, mortar, and bellows. Most critically, the small distillation furnace that transmuted an herb-infused Walachian wine into a lifesaving quintessence.

The chapel on the rock was built with the idea that a religious man would make his home here. It was a symbol of my ancestor's piety and devotion to the church. He had not designed it to accommodate a family. When my father was alive, the lower floor served as both dining and sitting room, while the upper floor was divided between sleeping chamber and his study. I now used the latter for my laboratory.

For many long years it had been my sanctuary, which perhaps was why I'd come directly here from The Magpie—and Mina Penrose. My venture into the village had shaken me to my core. I wanted the steadying influence of my work.

Though I had just completed a distillation, I began gathering the components of the apparatus to begin again. My movements were jerky, and a glass alembic slipped from my hand and shattered on the floor.

I squeezed my eyes shut and raked a hand through my hair.

Harker Tregarrick, you're a fool.

I had told myself it was right to go there, breaking my family vow never to step foot in the village except in direst need. Because shutting myself away here, though it had kept me safe for many decades, could now bring danger.

There would be rumors about Mr. Roscoe—*my* solicitor, found at the edge of *my* estate. Rumors that, if history was any guide, could so easily turn to shouting and calls for blood.

Poetic justice. In many ways, it would be easier to just let it happen.

In the year of our Lord 1854, people still feared Roche Rock. Most of them just couldn't remember why. Old stories of a wolf that prowled the estate, preying on solitary travelers who chanced to wander too close. The authorities would seek a more rational explanation, but all of it would still come back to *me*, and continuing to hide myself in Roche Chapel would only make things worse. I must allow them to see me as a man before they could make me into a monster (even if that's exactly what I was).

This was the story I'd told myself before donning my newest, most modern suit of clothes and stepping off the estate for the first time in many years. And I believed in my decision until the person I most feared on this earth—a tormentor I knew well, though only by her meadowsweet scent—appeared before me in a smocked blue blouse and faded plaid muslin skirt that had probably once been the same color as her hair.

How fitting that it was red.

Despite my alchemical elixir, my sluggish heart had *hammered.* The bloodlust had arced within me, and the slight rhythmic motion at her throat—I could hear, feel, and almost taste it. Had we met anywhere other than a crowded tearoom, she would never have survived.

I had not felt the thirst so powerfully since the earliest days of my change, when I'd been made prisoner in this tower for the protection of every beating heart in the parish. That time was shrouded in the red fog of my bloodlust, and to this day I was haunted by the not-remembering.

Mina Penrose was enough to chase me back to my tower, never again to emerge.

Yet that option was closed to me now.

SHAPES

I cradled the teapot in my hands, rubbing a thumb against the blackberry pattern and wondering whether others who read tea leaves saw shapes everywhere. I saw figures in the clouds and faces in tree bark. I saw them in the grain of a worktable, the surfaces of pools on the moor, and even the smoke coiling from a doused candle. Our father had said that Mum's stories turned both Jack and me fanciful, and I must have believed him. Because until recently, I'd never thought the shapes I saw were anything more than that.

But I'd always thought Jack more fanciful than I. Until he went to the mine, he was left more to himself, while I started taking on some of the household chores. My attention would occasionally drift to the window, where I could see him in the garden behind the house, carving arrows for the bow he'd made or trying to swordfight our goat with a stick.

Sometimes he'd catch my eye and salute me with a flourish of his weapon—like a knight to his lady—and I would have to stifle a giggle. The mine slowly crushed that out of him, though, and what the mine didn't crush, the drink finally drowned.

Our parents' passing had been different for me. In some ways, it had freed me; Mum would have laughed at the idea of me going to work at The Magpie when there was so much to do at home. I could never have worn her down about it the way I had Jack.

But then, if she'd lived, there wouldn't have been a need, and I'd have given anything to have both of them with us again. We'd all worked hard, and sometimes Da could be stern, but there was love in our home, and laughter, too.

We took our meals together and went to church on Sundays. Evenings when Da wasn't too tired, he would play his fiddle while Jack and I held hands and twirled around the room, or Mum would tell us fairy stories. Losing them both almost at once had somehow caused Jack and me to lose each other, too—and sent us off in different directions, looking to fill the emptiness. I only wished Jack could have found something besides the bottle.

Taking the teapot lid knob between my fingers, I thought again about Mum and her visitors. Instead of being afraid of what she saw in the leaves, she had used her gift to help our family. And sometimes there'd been little surprises, too. An especially fine pudding on a feast day, or a ribbon or sweetmeats on a birthday. Mum had even given us a picture book with children's stories for Christmas one year. When Da looked surprised at these miracles, she'd always say he was lucky he'd married a woman who knew how to make the most of her pennies.

These memories might have played a part in what I now saw in Mr. Tregarrick's teapot. Lifting the lid revealed a cluster of leaves that looked like nothing so much as the head of a wolf, nose raised and jaws open. The only wolf I'd ever seen—besides the one on the sign at the tavern—had been in that children's picture book, in the story of Little Red Riding Hood.

Letting my breath out in a whoosh, I plunked the pot on the table.

Mrs. Moyle turned, her eyes widening as they moved from the pot to my face. "Oh dear," she said.

I picked up the pot again and took it to her. "Tell me what *you* see, ma'am," I pleaded. "I don't trust myself."

She took the pot and squinted into it. After a moment or two, she shook her head. "I'm afraid I don't have the knack for it, Mina. All I see is a teapot that needs washing." She looked up. "What do you see?"

"A wolf. And I don't see how *that* can bode well after last night."

She looked again into the pot, frowning. "Now you mention it, that clump near the bottom does look like the head of a dog." She tipped the pot in her hands, studying the outside. "I don't recall who—"

"Mr. Tregarrick."

Her gaze came up, mouth forming an *Oh*.

I folded my arms across my chest, gnawing my lip.

Setting the pot beside the washbasin, she said, "I only exchanged a word or two with him. What was *your* impression?"

"Well"—I stared into the tub of cooling, soapy water—"by his dress and manner, he's a well-to-do gentleman, which he would be, born on that estate."

"Was he *well mannered*?"

"He was polite and courteous, though awfully serious. I did think it odd that he seemed to know I walk alone to the tearoom, when I've never seen him before in my life. And I'm wondering why he chose to come here for the first time today of all days."

"Maybe the same reason as the rest—hoping for information about the death. Mr. Hilliard may have told him that someone from The Magpie found his solicitor."

"Aye, he said as much."

"As for him knowing your habits"—she lifted an eyebrow—"you do pass by his estate most days, *twice*. Just because you haven't noticed *him* doesn't mean he hasn't noticed *you*."

Heat crept into my cheeks. "I suppose."

Mrs. Moyle emptied the leaves from the blackberry pot and dunked it first in the soapy water, then in the rinse water.

"What about the wolf?" I said. "What do you think it could mean?"

"I wish I could say. The obvious thing is that he, too, is in danger. Or maybe he is dangerous himself; we know nothing about him, after all. But it could simply be that Mr. Hilliard saying an animal attacked the solicitor—"

"Put an animal into my head."

She gave me a kindly nod. "It's something to consider. I'm sorry I haven't been much help. And I wish Jack didn't leave you alone so much. I think it's best you go on home now and stay there until tomorrow. Maybe consider staying there until there's some resolution to all this."

"I'm sure I'll be all right. There are always other people coming and going during the day."

"Well, you keep your door bolted when you get there."

"Yes, ma'am." I picked up my basket, checking under the cloth to make sure the knife was still there.

The day had turned dark, with low, leaden clouds and patches of fog drifting like ghosts over the heath, and my thoughts took a morbid turn. Though talking to Mrs. Moyle had helped, I couldn't stop thinking about shapes in teapots. How the magpie and dagger had seemed to warn me of Mr. Roscoe's death, yet I'd been helpless to prevent it. What if Mrs. Moyle was right that the wolf in Mr. Tregarrick's pot might mean he, too, was in danger? The killing had happened on his estate, or as good as. What if I said nothing, and he was the next one they found on the heath?

But what if the wolf means he *is the danger?*

I pictured him again in my mind. The dark lips and eyes, the smoky spectacles and ash-brown hair. Mrs. Moyle didn't seem to find it very surprising that he'd come to The Magpie today. And, indeed, it wasn't every day someone was killed in the village of Roche. It had *everyone* stirred up. But I couldn't help thinking that if he had questions about the killing, he might easily have sent again for Mr. Hilliard rather than visit a busy tearoom after so many years hidden away on his estate.

All of it made me uneasy. "Raised my hackles," as Jack would say.

"Miss Penrose?" I had been so much in my thoughts that I hadn't seen Mr. Hilliard himself approaching, on horseback, from the direction of my cottage. And now I noticed two riders crossing the heath below Roche Rock.

I recalled that the constable was one of the chorus of people who wished me not to walk alone on the road. "Good day to you, sir," I said sheepishly. "I'm just on my way home."

He nodded. "I think you're safe enough. The danger seems to have passed."

I knit my brows. "Have you found something?"

"The opposite, in fact. We've had men combing the countryside and the moor since early morning and found nothing. The animal that attacked the solicitor appears to have moved on. Or it may well have died. A dog, most likely—and most likely a sick one. Mr. Roscoe, rest his soul, found himself in the wrong place at the wrong time, I'll warrant."

My heart thumped as I recalled how easily it could have been me. "You're certain it was a dog, then?"

He shrugged. "Though a few things still don't add up, there's really nothing else it could have been, considering the wound. That's according to the surgeon *and* the coroner, who rode over from Bodmin this morning. Those gentlemen are far more qualified than I to make such a determination."

I hesitated, then asked, "I don't suppose we have any *wolves* in Cornwall?"

Frowning, he replied, "None in *England*, nowadays, I should think. Though if we did, I imagine a wolf is what we'd be looking for."

Jack was always complaining about the bosses at the mine—said they were unfair, and they pushed the men too hard. That may well have been, but I knew my question had probably sounded childish to Mr. Hilliard, and he'd answered plainly and politely. He'd been respectful with his questions the day before, too.

He raised his eyes, looking out over the heath. "I don't think we'll have any more trouble, Miss Penrose. But you keep alert when you're out walking, just in case, and get home before dark, you hear?"

"Yes, sir, I will."

He touched his hat brim, clucked to his horse, and moved on.

I wanted to feel relieved. I could see that Mr. Hilliard did. But I couldn't let go of the wolf. I found myself hoping the master of Roche Rock would return to the tearoom the next day so I could at least see he was unharmed. If some accident *did* befall him on his estate, I wasn't sure anyone would be the wiser—though he must have had others working for him besides the solicitor from Bodmin.

And if I did see Mr. Tregarrick again, I might get a better sense of him.

As if I'd recognize a man for a killer.

As if a few soggy tea leaves are more to be trusted than the constable and two medical men.

Sighing, I walked on to our cottage, where I exchanged my basket for a bucket. A few paces from our door was a pump that we shared with the other miners' cottages. The inn just beyond had a well of its own.

As I got to the pump, Mrs. Budge—our nearest neighbor down, who had a son at Wheal Enys—was just leaving it. We exchanged a pleasant greeting, though her face was etched with the same worry I'd seen on the faces of The Magpie's customers. I still shrank from the idea of my neighbors knowing I'd been the one to find Mr. Roscoe, and I hoped she wouldn't stop to gossip. I let out a breath as she moved away, full bucket sloshing.

When I got back with my own bucket, I washed up from the morning's baking. As I was putting away the dishes, I caught a golden glint through the window. A crooked seam had opened in the belly of cloud, and a beautiful light streamed across the downs that sloped away from the cottage. Out beyond our garden was Tregarrick land. The wall here was no more than a low line of rubble, but enough to mark the boundary.

I grabbed a bowl and went out to the garden to feel sun on my face while I picked more of the rosy apples, which I thought to cook up with onions and a mutton chop meant for last night's supper in a dish Mum had called squab pie (though there was nary a squab inside it). It was Jack's favorite, and I was keen to stay on his good side as long as possible.

Because eventually he was going to find out from someone—Mr. Hilliard, most likely—that I was still working at The Magpie. I felt guilty about my dishonesty, but I wasn't going to give up my job for Jack or anyone. Finding Mr. Roscoe like that—and realizing how easily it could have been me—had left me with a feeling that life was too uncertain to spend our days alone and unhappy.

But I didn't end up having to face Jack that night, because he came home so late I left out his supper and went to bed. Not that I actually slept. Jack was often late coming home in the evenings, but from The Wolf's Head, he had to walk the same road I did. So in spite of what Mr. Hilliard had told me, I lay awake worrying until I heard Jack come in, stumbling and muttering oaths. Shortly after that, everything went quiet, and I knew he'd fallen straight into bed.

No, I wouldn't be giving up The Magpie, because The Magpie was all I had left.

Jack rose late the next morning, bleary eyed and cross. He gobbled down the cold supper I'd left out for him and took his lunch from my hand without more than a mumbled goodbye.

I finished my baking, packed my basket, and started for work, rain drumming steadily against my bonnet. As I walked along the hedgerow, I couldn't help eyeing the tangle of thorny growth, looking for a hole someone might peep through. *Had* Mr. Tregarrick noticed me on the road? It gave me a strange feeling, knowing he might have been aware of me long before I'd been aware of him.

Mrs. Moyle was her cheerful self this morning, and I let myself get caught up in her stream of chatter. She had her days of low spirits like anyone else, but they were few and far between, and never lasted long. With her company, I was able to forget, for a while, the dark clouds that gathered heavy over my cottage.

The tearoom was much quieter today, and I thought it wouldn't be long before the village had forgotten about poor Mr. Roscoe—though *I* was likely to remember him for the rest of my days. I couldn't help wondering whether Mr. Tregarrick was truly touched by his death, or whether it had merely been an inconvenience.

Throughout the day, every time the front door opened, I looked up, wondering whether Mr. Tregarrick would again appear. It didn't seem very likely he would, and he didn't. Thinking again over the previous day's visit, it struck me that he hadn't asked me a single question about Mr. Roscoe once he knew I was the one who'd found him. At closing, I mentioned this to Mrs. Moyle.

"Did it occur to you," she said, "that he might have been curious about *you*? And might have been truly concerned about you?"

I frowned. "No."

She chuckled and went back to the washing, and my cheeks flamed. Mrs. Moyle liked to remind me from time to time that I was "very pretty." I thought I looked well enough when my dress was clean and my hair wasn't a weedy tangle, but neither I nor anyone else had ever used the word "pretty" in connection with *me*. Mum's curls had been dark, her skin smooth and flawless even as the creases in her face had deepened. My red hair and freckles—as well as Jack's—had come from Nanna, Mum's Irish mother.

As soon as the kitchen was put back in order, I started home, Mrs. Moyle urging me to be careful a little longer in case the lawmen had gotten it wrong. Another change in the weather had come, great, woolly white clouds moving in the breeze like ships across a sky-blue sea. As I drew near the place where Mr. Roscoe had fallen, I found my footsteps slowing, and then I was drifting off the road toward it, a weight like one of the dark granite blocks pressing on my chest.

The weeds had begun to spring back, and you could no longer see that a body had lain there. With the rain and cooler weather, the grass was greening again, and water droplets beaded the blades, sparkling like jewels in the sunlight. A few spikes of faded goldenrod nodded heavily against the stone wall in the breeze. I had noticed this morning that Mrs. Moyle's basket was gone, maybe taken by the wind. Or by someone unaware of why it had been abandoned there.

I glanced up the hill toward Roche Rock, studying the chapel's gap-toothed battlements and the upper floor's arched window, sunlight winking in the stained glass. Might he have seen me from there? It was too far, I should have thought, for him to see me very *well.* I wouldn't have been able to make out *his* features at this distance.

Now I turned my gaze south, letting it skim over the rocky heath and across the surface of a dark pool, finally landing on a thick cluster of silver birch on the other side. I caught the glint of something in the trees, and I squinted, trying to make it out. Likely just sunlight bouncing off water droplets, but I had met poachers in that wood. I believed the boys were at it regularly, and I thought if anyone had ever seen the master of the estate before yesterday, it would've been them.

Squinting again over the ground that sloped toward the black outcrop, I considered. The afternoon was still bright, with a couple of hours remaining before the sun set. Did I dare? Especially knowing now that Mr. Tregarrick might be watching me?

Let him. Let him come out and speak to me—shoo me off his land, even—instead of hiding up in those rocks like some great spider.

I glanced down at my basket, which contained the day's uneaten scones, and thought of leaving it behind until my return; the kitchen towel over the top would keep the birds out. Then I recalled the paring knife resting underneath and changed my mind. The blade was small enough for a pocket but would likely work mischief there.

After picking my way over a tumbledown section of wall, I stepped onto a deer path. The day had turned very fine, and it lifted my spirits. Less than a month ago, this ground had been covered with heather flowers—tiny and bell shaped, in white, pink, and purple—mixed in with bracken and sunny yellow furze. Some of the furze bushes still bloomed, and a few butter-yellow spearwort flowers nodded in the breeze around the edges of the pool.

The path I now trod ran beyond the heath and all the way down to Coldvreath, where Mum and I used to visit the holy well on days when we hadn't many chores to do. It was a secret between us, for Da never would have agreed to us crossing Tregarrick's heath. The road would have taken us there, too, but the walk was longer and not as pleasant, especially when the carts were kicking up either dust or mud.

I paused when I reached the birch trees, which looked like a thicket of long, white matchsticks with flaming-yellow tips under the October sunshine. I noticed the trickle of water that ran from the wood down to the pool. The sun glinted brightly on the water where it flowed over some smooth stones—which was probably what I'd seen from the road.

As I stepped slowly between the slender trunks on either side of the path, I caught the murmuring of voices and stopped.

"Who's there?" I called softly, and the murmuring ceased.

A twig snapped and a breeze rattled the dry leaves, but no reply came.

My heart thumped, and I wondered whether it might be better to turn back. The boys were harmless enough, but it could be someone else. *Someone rougher.*

Finally, a mop of straw-colored hair popped out of the trees a few yards ahead. "Passing through, miss?"

My breath moved freely again as I recognized the lad.

"I thought I saw something from the road and came to see what it was," I replied. "I'm not here to give you any trouble, though."

The boy stepped fully out of the trees. In one hand he held a snare with a brown hare in it. "Seen you before, miss," he said.

"I remember. Jeremy, is it?"

His head dipped. Another boy peeped out of the trees farther along the path, but he kept back.

"I've worried about you boys in here poaching in the full light of day. Aren't you afraid you'll get caught?"

"Nah," Jeremy replied with a grin. Jerking his head toward the chapel, he said, "The master hardly comes out."

"You've seen him, though?"

He shrugged. "Now and then from a distance. We always scurry off quick."

"So you've never spoken to him."

The boy shook his head.

"Well," I said with a glance over my shoulder, "you know a man was killed near here a couple days ago."

One corner of his lips twisted down. "They say a mad dog got hold of him. But they never caught it."

"No, so you boys should be careful."

"Always are, miss. And same to *you*, miss."

I couldn't help smiling. Eyeing his snare, I said, "If you ever have more than you need, I'm in that first white cottage on the right side of the road to Carbis. Come around to the back, and I'll give you threepence."

The lad grinned. "*Six*pence."

I scoffed. "Those old hares are mostly hide and bones! Now, if you had a nice, fat rabbit . . ."

He ducked his head. "I'll bring you one, miss."

I bade him good day and turned toward home. On a whim, I took a fork in the path that ran alongside the stream to the pool. There was a wide, flat stone next to it that Mum and I had sat on to eat our lunch sometimes on days like this. I raised my skirt and stepped up onto it.

The slab was pleasantly warm, and the breeze fresh. I reached into my basket for a scone to nibble. I thought about what Jack would say if he could see me now—or Mrs. Moyle, for that matter—and I did feel a pang of guilt. But this spot was a secret I had shared with Mum, and it was my first time coming here since she died. She would have called it a sad shame to remain indoors on an afternoon like this. For soon enough we'd have rain every day.

With this thought, the light dimmed, and I glanced up and saw masses of darker clouds moving to crowd out the woolly ones. The air was already cooling, and I even heard a rumble of distant thunder. Across the surface of the pool, which wasn't much wider than our cottage, I saw little circles forming before I ever felt a droplet on my skin. It was a gentle rain, without the bite of winter yet. I took off my bonnet.

As the first raindrops kissed my forehead, I realized I was crying. It had come on me quietly, one slow tear at a time. Next thing I knew, I was sobbing.

I think I'd been too scared to cry before then. Scared of whatever had come for Mr. Roscoe. Scared Jack would finally manage to take Mrs. Moyle and The Magpie away from me. Scared of what was becoming of my twin and me without our parents. Was it that the tearoom—with its books and newspapers and people from other places—had shown me how small my life was, and that it didn't have to be that way? Would I have been better off without that lesson?

It should have been me. I realized this dark thought had been lurking ever since that night on the road. Death should have come for *me*, not a man with a family and some kind of purpose in life.

But here I was being morbid again, and foolish, too. I had no idea what that man's life was like. And I had no real wish to die. Especially not in autumn, when there were fiery leaves and tart red apples. When slanting golden light visited the downs at the end of the day. When mist drifted in off the moor at twilight.

I heard the whisper of wings and turned my head. A magpie fluttered down near the edge of the stone slab. It pecked at a bit of silvery-green lichen, occasionally tilting its head to eye me. I broke off a piece of my scone and slowly held it out toward the visitor.

"Good day to you," I murmured. "I've got something I think you'll like better."

The magpie danced closer and eyed me again. I held very still as it stretched toward the crumb, finally nipping it out of my hand.

Laughing, I said, "I thought so."

The bird suddenly let out a stream of coarse chatter, startling me, and flitted away.

"Heavens," I said. "You're welcome."

I rose to my feet, careful not to slip on the wet granite. As I bent for my basket and bonnet, I heard a noise behind me—a rustling in the heather around the base of the slab. I turned, but before I could look closer, someone shouted my name.

I glanced up toward the sound and discovered fog was rising quickly. Roche Rock was no more than a deep shadow in the distance. The birchwood had disappeared altogether.

Who had called for me? It was a man's voice, so not my poaching friends. I hoped they'd moved on, because it might very well be that "the master" was somewhere on the heath.

"Hello?" I called back.

Then something struck me from behind.

"LEAVE HER FOR *DEATH*"

Harker

My eyes first picked out the red bonnet resting at the edge of the pool, one of its ribbons floating on the surface. Then the mist shifted and I saw her.

She lay on her side, facing me. I could smell the warm copper of her blood.

My head throbbed with the roar of an angry sea bashing the shore. *I* had done this. I knew that no rabid dog had taken the life of my solicitor, and I'd chosen to say nothing. To protect *myself*.

A movement caught my eye, and I froze—a slight rise of her chest. Training all my senses in the stillness, I could hear the breath passing between her lips. I could hear the throb of her heart and feel the pulsing of her honeyed blood.

Relief flooded me, and I stepped closer.

I. Can't. Do. This.

Yet what was the alternative? Leave her for dead?

Leave her for death. Because I knew in my dry husk of a heart that was exactly what would come for her if I left her where she lay.

And won't she suffer the same fate if I dare to touch her? Being so close to her—a woman whose blood I especially craved—was a test I hadn't set myself since discovering the formula for my vital essence. Truly, it was a test I had hoped to *never* set myself.

Even unconscious, she was flooding my senses, driving me to desperation. There was no separating my bloodlust from the base arousal worked by the sweet, ripe lines of her lips, the rise and fall of her breasts with her shallow breathing, and the dip of her waist against the curve of her hip.

"Mother of God, *help* me."

To my knowledge, no prayer uttered by me or my forefathers had ever been heeded.

Steel yourself. You are out of options.

I couldn't leave her. But what *was* I to do with her? Take her to her cottage? Now wasn't the time for a man hardly anyone would recognize as their neighbor to be spotted carrying an unconscious woman across the heath. And by the blood scenting the air, she likely had a wound that needed tending.

That I certainly cannot do.

Yet since visiting The Magpie, I had made it my business to learn what I could about Mina Penrose, and I knew there was a very real risk the brother she lived with wouldn't come home for hours yet. Even if he did, he might be stupid with drink.

If only she would open her eyes. *Silvered green, like garden sage.* I remembered how wide they'd gone in the tearoom when she realized who I was. And how they'd flashed when I'd advised her to stay at home. Small wonder she'd disregarded the warning.

I took another step toward her. The rich warmth of the blood that soaked into her hair terrified me. The scent clawed its way into my throat, choking me. My heart rattled as I bent over her, and my breaths—normally deep but few—came fast and light. With trembling fingers, I reached out and touched her chin—*soft as rose petals*. Gently

I tilted her head back, searching the flesh of her neck—*dear God, that maddening pulse*.

But no unholy marks. And no ragged hole, like they'd found on Mr. Roscoe. Instead I glimpsed a blood-smeared cut above one temple, a knot rising behind it, where her head had likely struck the stone.

I might have concluded from this that she had simply slipped, had I not seen with my own eyes the shadow that sprang at her from the fog. I could not have described it other than to say it was some spindling creature, tall and lethally quick. A creature like me, I knew it in my very bones. One that would have drunk his fill and left her cold had I not frightened him away.

In all my years of suffering the Tregarrick taint, I had never heard of another family with the same affliction. Not in Roche parish, nor anywhere in the medical and alchemical texts I'd pored over. Only in Eastern European mythology—and once in a ghastly tale penned by Lord Byron's physician—had I encountered other creatures that were anything like me.

So I'd thought that by breaking the Tregarrick line—by taking no wife and producing no heir—I had ensured the dreadful condition would fade away as I did.

I had no lofty idea of saving the villagers of Roche from the ancient evil I embodied, though the ancestors of these people had certainly been my family's responsibility. I had only wished to maintain my humanity—and my dignity—until I died quietly and alone on my family estate, be that a decade from now or a century.

Still, I would choose to save people like Mina, so bright and alive and so everything I wasn't.

Knowing now that my family was not uniquely afflicted, I'd come to the end of my privilege of hiding from the world.

Drawing a deep breath and holding it, I bent and worked an arm under her shoulders and another behind her knees. Slowly, carefully, I lifted her from the slab. I settled her body against my abdomen, feeling the warmth of her through her dress.

Her head had tipped back, long red hair slipping from its bonds, dark and flowing like a river of blood, the freckles across her nose and cheeks like spray from the violent surge.

My mind tortured me with images of what my body expected. Of what it *demanded.* Every ounce of my control was required not to bury my face in her neck, open her flesh with my teeth, and swallow until I was drunk on her.

Who was I to judge the thirst of Jack Penrose?

As I forced my eyes from her upthrust throat to the dark, mirrored surface of the pool, a fragment of memory breezed into my mind—one that had tormented me many times before.

Panic seizing me, I snapped my eyes shut, as if that could save me.

Her hair is dark satin threaded with silver. Her body is hot from the blood pulsing under her skin. She has been crying.

Her black eyes are wide with terror.

Clenching my jaw hard enough to crush bone, I stifled a howl of fury and anguish.

ROCHE ROCK

Drip, drip, drip.

The rain sounded like it was inside the house. Jack would have to climb up and repair the roof again. I burrowed deeper under the bedcover, hoping for just a few more minutes before facing the day.

A wave of confusion—and a dull, sickening throb on the side of my head—brought me fully awake.

Peeking out from the blanket, I discovered the light was all wrong. Across the room I saw an unfamiliar window, its casement partly open and a candle burning on the sill. A wine-colored velvet curtain hung heavily to one side, tied back with a gold cord. Rain fell against the window's outer sill (the reason for the dripping sound) as thunder rumbled over the downs. The smell of the place, too, was strange—spirits, herbs, and something that reminded me of church. *Cold stone and incense.*

Where am I?!

I sat up quickly, and the room spun. My head throbbed again, and I groaned.

Footsteps sounded on a creaking floor above me.

"Hello?" I called out hoarsely.

At one end of the room was a stone stairway that curved to an upper floor. A man was coming down, and my heart nearly jumped out of my throat.

"All is well, Miss Penrose."

Mr. Tregarrick! It came to me suddenly that I was inside the old chapel. *Inside Roche Rock.* The walls of this smallish, square room were mostly covered with paintings and tapestries, but I could see the black stone between them. How could this be?

Reaching to touch my left temple, I found a lump. The skin was sticky, and when I looked at my fingers, I saw a smear of blood.

My gaze darted back to Mr. Tregarrick, who was watching me closely from the foot of the stairs, where he'd stopped. He stood very still, as if afraid of frightening me away. *Like a fox watches a rabbit.*

"What—what has happened, sir?" I asked in a quavering voice.

His lips curved down. "I was hoping you could tell *me*."

I pushed back against the fear coiling around my brain, making it hard to think. *The pool. The slab. The startled magpie.* "I fell," I choked out. "I . . . No. Something knocked me down."

"And did you see it?"

I shook my head, causing another wave of dizziness.

In a voice low and calm, Mr. Tregarrick said, "I will tell you what I can, Miss Penrose. But first, there is water on the table for cleaning your wound. I've added quintessence of usnea—of old man's beard—to prevent putrefaction."

Following his gesture, I saw a washbasin and cloth on a tea table beside me. Though I was still bewildered, my heart slowed as I began to accept that there was no present danger.

The chair I rested in had a long seat, very much like one in the tearoom that Mrs. Moyle called a reading chair. The room around me was richly furnished, with white taper candles burning in each window and on every surface. A fire blazed away in the hearth, near my chair, and under the casement that I'd noticed on first waking was a small dining table. Two regular armchairs also rested near the hearth, covered in the same dark-red fabric as most of the room's other furnishings. I guessed that the chapel's upper floor, with its stained glass window facing east, must have served as the bedchamber.

My eyes moved again to Mr. Tregarrick, who still had not shifted an inch.

"How have I come to be here, sir?"

He let out a quiet sigh and seemed to steady himself before taking two steps toward me—and suddenly stopping. I noticed his dress was very different from the first time I'd seen him. This clothing, though just as neat and clean, seemed dated to my eye—fawn breeches, black boots, and a billowy white shirt with ruffles at the neck, like a character in one of Miss Austen's books might have worn. He wore no waistcoat or cravat, but the lawn of his shirt was soft looking and very fine. His wavy hair was gathered and bound, as before. The smoky spectacles were missing, and he looked younger without them.

Had I seen him passing in the village, my eyes would have followed.

Yet his gaze—gleaming and keenly focused on me—caused me to tremble.

"I found you unconscious by the pool and brought you home. You haven't been here long. Perhaps half an hour."

"*Brought* me?" Did that mean what I thought it did?

A few ticks of silence passed before he said, "Carried you. I thought it best."

My breath stopped, my brows knit, and my jaw fell half open. *He picked me up. Carried me across the heath in his arms.*

It was *a lot* to take in, and I sat quietly, trying. If something like that happened to a person, would they not feel it in some way afterward, even if they hadn't been awake? My eyes moved over his arms and chest, trying to imagine my body pressed against them. A fluttering heat filled my belly.

Swallowing thickly, I managed, "Did you see any . . . any *creature* nearby?"

One of his brows lifted. "I saw no more than a shadow, and by the time I reached you, it had fled."

I hugged my arms around my chest. "Do you think it might have been the same creature that . . . ?"

"That killed Mr. Roscoe?"

I nodded.

"According to the constable, my solicitor was killed by a rabid dog. I don't think that's what this was."

"But then . . ." I frowned, thinking. "It doesn't seem likely there are *two* creatures attacking people on the heath. Could Mr. Hilliard and the others be mistaken?"

The ghost of a smile visited Mr. Tregarrick's lips. "While I can't argue with your logic, I'm afraid I have no answers for you."

Yet I got the feeling there was more he *could* say but was choosing not to.

Unsettled by his keen, quiet manner, I glanced again around the room. I had seen no servants and began to think I might be here alone with him.

Clearing my throat, I said, "Well, it was very kind of you to rescue me, Mr. Tregarrick."

I shifted on the chair and lowered my feet to the floor. As I stood, a fresh wave of dizziness caused me to sway.

I felt cold fingers close around my upper arms and gasped. How quickly he'd reached me!

"Please sit, Miss Penrose." I found myself looking into his dusty plum eyes. "I insist. Clean your wound, so it doesn't fester. I'll bring you a cup of tea. Then I'll see you home, if you're feeling recovered enough."

Breathless at his sudden closeness, and still befuddled by the knock on the head, I managed only, "I thank you, sir."

Yet the urge to leave was strong. Were it known that I'd been here alone with him, it could start unpleasant talk. Jack and I had trouble enough between us. And though my host had been more than kind—and I was growing more curious about him by the second—there was also something about him that made me uneasy.

But Mr. Tregarrick, who everyone knew did not welcome visitors, had possibly saved my life by bringing me here. I wasn't willing to risk offending him by flying off against his wishes.

I watched him climb the stairs, his movements slow but not plodding. *Unhurried.* Yet a moment ago he'd been at my side in an instant. And the very idea that he'd had the strength to carry me across the heath to Roche Rock . . . up the steep stairway to the chapel . . . I doubted even hale and hearty Jack could have managed it! I had no birdlike figure. Mum had always called me heavy-boned, like her father, who'd brought his family to Cornwall from County Cork in Ireland so he could work in the copper mines.

I sank back down on the chair, picked up the cloth he'd left for me, and dipped it into the water, which smelled slightly of spirits. It stung as I pressed it to the lump, but the coolness was soothing. I took a deep breath and rested against the chairback. My uneasiness about Mr. Tregarrick seemed altogether unreasonable, considering how he'd put himself out to take care of me.

I could still hardly believe I was here. I'd never heard of anyone in the village coming to Roche Rock except Mr. Hilliard, the night I'd found Mr. Roscoe. At one time of my life, I would have barely been able to contain my excitement at the notion of bragging to Jack later.

He'll take to locking me in if he finds out about this.

The place was far more comfortable than you would expect from the outside. The fire easily heated this room, though I did wonder at the open casement, letting in the damp, chill air. While I was sure the black stone must have been cold to the touch, most of it was covered, and great rugs had been spread over the wooden floor planks.

A tapestry on the wall behind me showed ladies in filmy gowns dancing under great trees, and the many paintings were a mixture of fine scenery and old portraits. On the wall next to the stairway, a man wearing a dark cap with a white feather had a gaze that sent a chill through me.

I didn't know whether the chapel had ever been used for religious purposes. It was said the family had lived here all the long years since the manor burned. I found it strange, them remaining in such cramped quarters instead of simply building another house. Maybe hard times had come to them.

"I'm afraid I have nothing to offer you but tea," said my host as he came back down. He carried a tray to the dining table beneath the window. "I am unused to visitors."

I noticed for the first time that my basket and bonnet were resting on one of the dining chairs and said, "If my basket hasn't emptied onto the heath"—*again*—"I have Mrs. Moyle's scones to offer."

I stood up to join him, but again he protested, "I think you should be still, Miss Penrose. I can bring your cup to you."

"I'm feeling steadier, sir," I argued, "and I will have to walk soon enough. You can't carry me all the way home." Picturing this in my mind brought a flush of warmth.

"No," he admitted, looking down. "It probably wouldn't be advisable."

I noted he was saying that he shouldn't, not that he couldn't.

He reached for my basket and moved it from the chair to the table. He picked up my bonnet, too, and hung it over the chairback. For some reason, watching him handling my things raised another flutter in my belly.

He came toward me then, hand outstretched. "Allow me."

I studied his face. Though his expression was quiet and solemn, his eyes seemed to shine with something very different. *Fear?* Did my presence here make him that uncomfortable?

Slowly I reached out to take his hand, heart skipping as his fingers closed around mine. Again I noticed how cold he was, and again I wondered at the open window.

He led me to the table, and I sat down in the chair he'd emptied. My eyes followed him as he turned and walked to the hearth. When he came back, he held a glowing ember in a pincer tool. He set the coal in a small pot at the center of the table. Next to the pot was a jar of yellowish bits of rock. He opened the jar and took one out, broke it—not rocks after all—and set one half on top of the ember. A fragrant smoke began to rise, and I recognized the scent from feast day services at the parish church.

"What is that?" I asked.

His eyes touched mine briefly before he set down the pincers and lifted the teapot. "Frankincense resin. It's good for purifying the air."

Between the scent of herbs and the cool, rain-washed breeze drifting in through the window, the air in this room was probably the most *purified* I'd ever breathed. I noticed none of the common smells that went along with living. No cooking smells, nothing like unwashed linens or clothing, no pipe or cigar smoke.

My host filled a teacup and slid it toward me. "I have neither milk nor sugar," he said. "But you may find this doesn't need it."

Like my mother, I drank my tea strong with plenty of milk. But I was grateful for it regardless—especially since he'd made and poured it *himself.* I wondered again about servants, as well as whether there was a kitchen on the upper floor. I couldn't imagine it, yet there must be one *some*where.

I picked up the cup and breathed in the vapor, surprised by the smoky aroma. Taking a sip, I discovered he was right. The tea had a very smooth flavor. I had learned a little about tea since Mrs. Moyle took me on—Ceylon, Darjeeling, Assam—but I'd never tasted anything like this. Then I realized it did remind me of something. My employer had offered me a dram of Scotch whisky once at the New Year—said it had been the last of her husband's bottles. The tea had a similar smokiness, though the whisky had burned my throat and made my eyes water.

Mr. Tregarrick filled his own cup and sat in the chair opposite me—after sliding it about a foot back from the table. *Like he doesn't want to get too close.* I glanced down at my cup, hiding my embarrassment. He was the finely dressed master of an estate; I was a miner's daughter wearing a tea-stained dress with a muddy hem. In the course of today's adventure, my hair had come unpinned and now hung almost to my waist. I was bruised and bloodied and probably looked like some poor creature who'd just stumbled out of a fairy ring.

Fidgeting in my seat, I finally broke the silence. "May I ask what kind of tea this is, Mr. Tregarrick?"

He watched the steam rise from his cup. "It's called Caravan. Traders used to drink it on routes between Europe and the East."

"It smells like a woodfire."

His quiet smile opened a chink in the somber mood. "It's a blend that includes Lapsang souchong—tea leaves that are smoked. I find it warming." Without thinking, I glanced at the open casement—and he noticed. "I suppose I enjoy the fresh air. Are you chilled, Miss Penrose?"

"Maybe a little," I admitted, and he stood and closed it most of the way, causing the candle to gutter. Raindrops streamed down the panes both inside and out.

Sitting down again, he said politely, "I'm sorry if you don't like the tea. You needn't drink it."

"I do like it," I said. "I'm wondering whether it's something The Magpie should serve. I mean, people tend to like what they like, but Mrs. Moyle likes trying new things."

At last he sipped from his cup, eyeing me over the rim. "How about you, Miss Penrose?"

A flame flickered in my belly. "Me?"

"Do you like what you like, or do you like trying new things?"

I let out a nervous laugh. His gaze remained fixed on me, and I realized he wasn't teasing.

Straightening, I replied, "Both, I guess. Sometimes new things make me feel afraid at first. Like my job at The Magpie."

He nodded. "I think that's true for us all." Studying me a moment, he continued, "You're reflective for someone so young."

Guessing what he really meant was for someone so *simple*, I narrowed my eyes. "And what are you, sir? One hundred?"

His gaze dropped to the table, and in my head I muttered a curse. "That was rude, Mr. Tregarrick, I'm sorry."

"No indeed, it was well deserved. I do often feel like I'm ancient."

Glancing around the room, I said, "I can see how living in this old place with no one but ghosts for company might cause that."

When he didn't answer, I thought maybe I *had* offended him this time. But then I noticed that he seemed to be squelching another smile. *I amuse him.* I wasn't sure how to feel about that.

Cheeks flaming, I reached for the basket. "Will you have a scone, sir?"

He shook his head. "Thank you, no. But you should eat."

I slipped my hand under the cloth, forgetting what was there besides scones. I muttered a curse—out loud this time—and drew back my hand. Blood dribbled down my finger, and my host sucked in a breath, his chair digging hard against the wood floor as he slid farther back from the table.

"It's not deep," I said quickly, grabbing the cloth and pressing it against the cut. "I forgot I'd put a knife in the basket."

"Do you need the surgeon, Miss Penrose?"

Hearing strain in his voice, I looked up. He'd gone very pale.

"Is it the blood?" I asked. "I know it bothers some people."

For a moment he looked shocked to his core; the intensity of it frightened me. But just as quickly his features loosened. "Yes, the blood," he said. "I'm sorry I cannot assist you."

Things began to make more sense now. The way he'd kept his distance until I'd cleaned the wound on my head. How he'd sat back from the table. I was relieved to learn it hadn't been something about *me*.

"Heavens," I said, moving my injured hand beneath the table. "I must be your worst nightmare."

His dry laugh caught me by surprise. Slowly he moved to his chair, scooting it back to the table. "You're very considerate. I'm all right now."

Near the window, a vase containing a bouquet of goldenrod rested on the table, and he reached to adjust it slightly. "The knife is a wise precaution," he said. "Though still I wonder at your going out on the heath alone after what happened. You're either very brave . . ."

"Or very foolish. Yes." I waited until he met my gaze and continued, "I know I had no right to be on your land, Mr. Tregarrick. I've caused a great deal of bother, and I'm truly sorry."

"It's not the first time." My stomach twisted, but then I caught a glint of mischief in his eyes. "That you've been on the estate."

"No, sir, it's not. But I promise not to do it again." The idea of giving up the heath caused a pang, but trespassing on the estate now that I knew him and had been a guest in his home, now that I'd gotten in over my head and needed rescuing . . . it was no longer possible.

"Under normal circumstances," he replied, "I don't mind you on the estate any more than I mind the boys who snare rabbits in the birchwood." Smiling, he added, "Yes, I know about them," and I thought I must have looked alarmed. "They might as well eat them, since I don't."

"That's very kind of you, sir."

He reached for the pot and filled our cups again. Rain continued tapping against the sill, and cool air ribboned through the narrow opening. He seemed to have gotten over his uneasiness about the blood, though I wouldn't have gone so far as to say he looked comfortable.

I couldn't help wondering what his story was. Something awful in his past, maybe, that had left him alone and unwilling to seek out the company of his fellow creatures. It made me sad for him, and grateful for Jack and Mrs. Moyle. Jack and I had hit a rough patch of road, but we'd been together all our lives. If I lost him, I'd never be the same.

Sipping the smoky tea for courage, I said, "Do you truly live here all alone, Mr. Tregarrick?"

His eyes lifting to mine brought a rush of warmth. "I do," he said.

"How do you manage with no servants?"

"Very likely the same way *you* manage with no servants."

I frowned. "Forgive me for saying so, sir, but I don't think it *is* the same. I wasn't born on an estate such as this. My brother and I were raised to do everything for ourselves because there was never going to be anyone else to do it for us."

He gave a slow nod. "You make a fair point. Yet what I said was no more than the truth."

Still struggling to believe him, I said, "You do all your own cooking?"

"I have simple tastes."

Simple. Glancing around the room again, I thought about what very different worlds we'd been born into.

"Until yesterday," I said, "I'd never seen you in the village or the market. Where do you shop?"

"Ah, you have me there. I've an agent in the village who sees to things that need seeing to, and I suppose that's a kind of servant. He buys supplies as I need them and handles things like my correspondences. And of course I have—*had*—a solicitor for estate matters."

My heart gave a heavy thump. "Poor Mr. Roscoe," I said softly.

"Poor Mr. Roscoe," he agreed, glancing down. He fiddled with his empty cup. "You're nearly alone now yourself, since your parents died, are you not?"

I stared, wondering how he knew. I supposed he would have information from his "agent" when he wanted it, though I couldn't imagine why he would interest himself in *me*. I recalled what Mrs. Moyle had said. *Did it occur to you that he might have been curious about you?*

"That's right," I replied. "It's just Jack and me."

"That must have made your life much harder."

"In some ways. But we were nearly grown when they died. Mostly I just miss them." Feeling a familiar ache in my throat, I drained the last of my tea.

"You have no other family in Roche?"

I shook my head. "My mother's family are all in Ireland. Her parents lived here since before I was born, but they're both gone now. Da's parents and two brothers went up north to the cotton mills. They wanted us to go, too, and they quarreled with Da over it. We haven't heard from them in years."

I noticed his features had softened as he said, "But you and Jack manage on your own well enough?"

This wasn't an easy question to answer, and I somehow got the sense he knew that. "I'm grateful for Jack," I said. "We're twins, and we've always been close. But both of us have changed since our parents died. We don't always agree about things."

"I don't imagine he would like you being *here*."

I laughed wearily. "He doesn't really like me being anywhere except home." Although this was true, I had a feeling that Jack would, in fact, go up in flames of rage if he knew where I was.

"Perhaps Jack's afraid of losing you, too."

I met my host's gaze, still focused softly on my face, and felt a stab of guilt. It was possible I'd been somewhat blinded by my anger and hurt feelings.

"You could be right," I said. "The world feels somehow bigger since I started working at The Magpie. All Jack has is what he's always had—the mine." *And the bottle.* "I've assumed he holds that against me. Maybe it's not as simple as that."

"I think things rarely are."

Offering a careful smile, I said, "I suppose being a hundred years old has made you wise."

I only meant to tease him, but his gaze dropped, and though my head still hurt and I shrank from the idea of going out in the rain, I felt like I was wearing my welcome thin.

"I thank you for the tea, Mr. Tregarrick," I said, stirring in my chair. "I'm feeling much better, and I should probably get home."

Now his gaze lifted, seeming to pin me in place as a rumble of thunder charged the air. "Forgive me if I seem cold or inhospitable, Miss Penrose. I fear I've lived alone so long my manners have suffered."

Some of my worry seeped away as I laughed. "I deal with 'ill-mannered' enough to know it when I see it. You have some of the finest manners I've ever seen."

His smile was doubtful.

"You seem to know all about me, Mr. Tregarrick," I ventured, "and I confess I've always been curious about *you*."

The doubtful smile lingered. "Indeed?"

"Well, our cottage is on the edge of your estate. Jack once told me an old sorcerer lived up here."

My host's smile broadened. "Perhaps he's right."

"Well, supposing he is, what does an old sorcerer *do* up here all alone, day in and day out?"

"The truth is that 'old sorcerer' is not far off. I'm an alchemist."

I frowned, not recognizing the word. "What does an alchemist do, then?"

"The aim of alchemy is transmutation. Performing a series of actions on a substance with the hope of changing it into a different substance."

"I don't think I follow," I said meekly, ashamed of my ignorance.

"But you do. You've done it yourself, I'm certain. Combine flour, water, and yeast, mix and knead them, apply heat, and you end up with something very different from what you started with."

My brows dipped. "Bread."

"It's true. Bread doesn't occur in nature. Creating it involves art and science, and something of magic, too, I'd argue. I'm not a baker, but what I do is not all that different."

"What kinds of things do you make?"

He took a breath, gathering his thoughts. "Alchemy is most known for its pursuit of chrysopoeia—the creation of gold from lesser metals. I have dabbled in that pursuit, but my focus is medical alchemy, which concerns itself with bodily imbalances. I work mostly in the distillation of herbal quintessences."

The meaning of all this remained murky to me, but he was more animated than I'd seen him yet, and I wanted him to go on.

"Like what you put in the water for cleaning my wound."

He looked pleased. "Precisely, Miss Penrose. You're a quick study."

The praise warmed my skin. "Are they medicines for yourself?"

I watched the heaviness settle over him again. I could have sworn I saw secrets scurry behind his eyes like hens fleeing a fox. "Mostly, yes."

I waited for him to go on, but he didn't. He looked out the window.

Before I could get out another of my questions, he rose from the table, saying, "If you're feeling up to it, we should get you home before your brother misses you."

The dark clouds made it impossible to say whether the sun had set, but likely it had. There was still enough light to make it home without a lamp. Jack likely wouldn't be there for a while yet, but I had his supper to make.

"Yes," I agreed, rising. "But you needn't go with me. You've been very kind already, and—"

The look he gave me stopped my words *and* my breath. "Miss Penrose, leaving aside the fact a head injury rendered you *unconscious* not more than an hour ago, it is obvious the danger in Roche has not yet passed. I shall by no means leave you to find your own way home."

I swallowed, shaken by the change in his manner. He went from soft to hard as suddenly as he did from slow to quick.

But he was right. And as the excitement over my visit to Roche Rock wound down, the facts began to sink in as they hadn't before. Though I had no real memory of it, I'd been attacked on the heath just like Mr. Roscoe.

"Thank you, Mr. Tregarrick," I said, a tremor in my voice.

Carefully I put on my bonnet, picked up my basket, and followed him to the heavy, iron-studded door, where he donned a hat and greatcoat that hung on a tree there. He slipped his spectacles from a pocket and put them on.

As we stepped outside, lightning stabbed across the sky, followed by a closer thunderclap.

I jumped, and his fingers came briefly to my waist to steady me; there was no real landing at the top of the steps, and barely enough room for two people to stand. He was close enough that I could feel how cold he was even through my clothing. *It's not just his hands.* Yet his nearness caused another flush.

"I don't like setting out in this," he said, "but I don't see it letting up before dark."

"No," I agreed. "At least it's not far."

"You must take my hand for support."

I wasn't sure there'd be any surviving a fall down the steep, wet stairway, so I reached with my uninjured hand to grasp his. The steps weren't wide enough for us to stand abreast; he went down in a sideways fashion, one step ahead of me. It made for slow progress, but I was grateful.

Halfway down, the rain changed to pea-size hail. I hunched my shoulders and ducked my head, but this only led to ice sliding down my collar in back. The weather had been so fine when I left The Magpie that I'd forgotten my shawl, and my blouse was wet through.

When at last we reached the bottom, we exchanged a glance. "Are you all right?" he asked.

He, too, was hunched against the hail, now mercifully giving way to rain again. His hat didn't provide as much protection as my bonnet—which was a very fine one, with a wide brim, that Mrs. Moyle had given me last Christmas—and droplets slid over his cheekbones.

Despite my best efforts to contain it, I let out a bark of nervous laughter. "Do you think we've done something to anger the heavens, Mr. Tregarrick?"

He grinned, and for a moment I saw the boy he must have been once. "I think perhaps we have. Let us keep going."

We followed the path that led around the oak wood to the gap in the hedgerow—the same one I passed every day. I had never expected to find myself on this side of the hedge and wished I could take everything in. Instead I kept my head tucked against the rain.

After a few minutes we reached the road—deserted in the violent weather—and started for Carbis. When finally we arrived at our cottage door, it felt wrong not asking Mr. Tregarrick to step inside out of the weather. But of course I couldn't, and he was already taking his leave anyway.

"You feel well enough to remain here on your own until your brother comes home?"

"Yes, I'm much recovered, and I must thank you again, sir. I believe you may have saved my life."

"I believe I may have, too. I know I have no right to ask you to do anything, but please—for my sake if not for your own—take more care, Mina Penrose."

The chill brought on by my wet clothing fled as he spoke my name.

He was turning to go, but then he stopped and said, "Might you have a cross you can wear?"

A *cross*? I frowned. "My mother wore one that I still have, though I've never worn it myself. You don't mean for . . . for *protection*?"

"I know it may sound strange, and I confess I don't think of myself as a religious man, despite the fact I live in a chapel. But would you . . . would you wear it for *me*?"

For him! My heart skittered to a stop. The request so surprised me that my wits fled, and I didn't ask what I really should have—what did he know about the creature that had killed Mr. Roscoe that made him think it might be bothered by a cross?

Instead, I replied, "If you like." Then, on impulse: "May I know *your* name, sir?"

"That's just what *I'd* like to know."

I gasped at the sound of Jack's voice. He stood a few yards behind Mr. Tregarrick, on the road in front of the cottage.

STORIES

Mr. Tregarrick turned as Jack approached. How I hoped he wouldn't notice Jack's slight sway—but he didn't seem to miss much.

"Mr. Penrose," he said politely, "I am Harker Tregarrick."

Jack's eyes widened. "Tregarrick!" He looked our neighbor up and down. "Not the Tregarrick of Roche Rock?"

"The very one. Your sister had a fall out on the heath. She hit her head, and I walked her home to make sure she got here safely."

I wondered at him not mentioning the attack, though I was in enough trouble as it was and certainly hadn't intended to tell Jack myself. Thankfully he had also left out the detail of my brief stay under his roof.

My chest tightened as Jack's head swiveled in my direction. "On the *heath*, you say? I think you must be mistaken, sir, since I told her she was to stay near the house."

"I . . ." began Mr. Tregarrick, eyes moving from Jack to me.

"Thank you for seeing me home, sir," I said, trying to hurry him along before Jack could cause trouble. "I'll be all right now."

Taking the hint, he tipped his hat and said, "Good evening, Miss Penrose. Mr. Penrose."

Jack glared after him as he turned for home. The gentleman's figure dissolved quickly in the twilight, rain, and fog.

My heart thumped against my ribs as I turned and went inside the cottage. I took a match from the box by the cookstove and lit the oil lamp and candles.

"Mina," said Jack in a cold, hard voice.

Waving the match out, I closed my eyes and mouthed an oath before facing him. "You're home early, Jack. Is The Wolf's Head still standing?"

Though I hated fighting with my brother, I had never been afraid of him. But until now I'd never seen him so angry he couldn't form words. His watery, bloodshot eyes seemed to bulge from holding it all in.

Best to have it out and over with.

"Well?" I goaded.

In the same steely tone, he said, "Today in the pit, some of the Irish boys were talking about the 'pretty red-haired lass that works for old widow Moyle.'"

Oh Lord. "Well, that's nice of them," I said, a bored note in my voice. "I best get to fixing your supper, hadn't I?"

"Be still, Mina."

My hands trembled as I planted them on my hips. The lump on my head began to throb.

"One of those boys had to leave his shift early yesterday and saw you walking home from work. *After* I told you that you were finished at The Magpie."

I shrugged, as if my heart weren't hammering away. "I spoke to Mr. Hilliard, and he told me there's no more danger. Whatever got that solicitor has moved on now. Most likely a rabid dog." I was twisting the truth pretty far, but I'd take the sin if it could save my job. Even after what had happened today.

His eyes narrowed. "You *know* that I meant you were finished for good, Mina."

"Why do you think it's you who gets to decide that?"

His cold tone finally flared hot as he replied, "Do we have to do this *again*? Because Da is gone and I have to speak for him. I know he'd say the same, and so do you. Now, I won't have you defying me! Aren't you ashamed those boys were speaking about you like you were some bit of—"

"Jack Penrose, don't you dare!"

I'd shouted so loud he took a step back. *Good.*

Bringing my tone down a notch, I said, "I know you think you're taking care of me, Jack. But I don't care what some strangers said about me, and you shouldn't, either. It doesn't sound to me like they meant any disrespect, anyway. I don't so much mind being called a 'pretty lass' by *somebody*. But if you don't want them talking like that, next time just tell them you're my brother and you won't have it, instead of coming home and shouting at *me*."

"And a good thing I did come home," Jack muttered hotly. "Tregarrick, of all men! What were you thinking?"

I shook my head, annoyed that once I'd won my point he'd simply moved on to his next complaint. "What are you on about *now*?"

"Don't you know half the village thinks he had something to do with the murder?"

I stared, speechless for a second. "Why on earth would they think that?"

"There's something not right about that old place. Not right about *him*. Everyone in Roche knows that, and you should, too. They found that solicitor almost—"

"Me," I gritted out. "*I* found him." Tears stung my eyes, and I knotted my fists in my skirt, fighting to hold them back.

Jack noticed, and the lines around his eyes softened. Even his voice was softer as he said, "Point is, didn't you wonder why his body was just outside the wall, while his bag was *inside*? And the fact that there was no *blood* there at all? Somebody moved him off the estate, Mina."

I stared at Jack with my mouth hanging open, trying to take all this in. Though I couldn't believe he had come up with it on his own, there was sense in it. For a few seconds my chest was too tight to breathe.

Finally I said, "Mr. Roscoe died from an animal bite, Jack. You shouldn't pay so much attention to talk at The Wolf's Head." But even Mr. Tregarrick had seemed to question this, and I had to ask myself why I was hiding so much from my brother.

"Next time you see widow Moyle, you ask her if she knows any of the old stories."

"*What* stories?"

"Stories about the Wolf of Roche Rock."

My heart began to thump as I remembered the wolf in Mr. Tregarrick's cup. But he had saved my life! Granted, I only had his word for that, but the idea of *him* attacking me made no sense at all. Yet I knew there *were* old stories of a wolf on the estate.

By the light in Jack's bloodshot eyes, I could see he thought he was winning, and I wasn't about to go along with the notion that Mr. Tregarrick might be guilty of murder.

"That's nonsense, Jack," I snapped. "This comes of too much drink, and cheap talk with others who've had too much drink."

At first, he looked like he'd been slapped. Then his expression hardened, and he stepped closer to me.

"You're not to set foot out of this door without my leave. I know you think you're smarter than me now, but I'm still the head of this house."

He turned and walked out, slamming the door behind him.

I shook with frustration. I picked up the nearest thing to hand—the small milk pitcher we used for tea—and flung it at the door. It shattered, painted ceramic bits showering the floor.

I took a deep breath and let it out hard before going for the broom.

I wrapped a strip of linen around my cut finger and made Jack's supper anyway. Exhausted, I went to bed with a headache and didn't hear him come in. Next morning he again ate his cold supper for breakfast and left without a word.

Things were getting bad between us, and they were likely to get worse. Jack and I had once known each other so well we could complete each other's thoughts. When we were children, Mum had joked about us talking in half sentences. I knew that Jack was as shaken up by the murder as I was; it knocked another hole in a foundation already unsteady after our parents' deaths. And I knew he saw my questioning and defiance as dangerous and ungrateful.

Yet I couldn't go against my own nature, simply taking his word for everything while remaining safe and quiet at home. We were twins; why couldn't he understand that such a life would be the death of me?

Which was why as soon as he left, despite my fear of whatever lurked on the heath, I made pasties and packed my basket. I was about to set out for The Magpie when I remembered Mr. Tregarrick's request. I climbed back up to the loft and opened a small wooden box that had belonged to my grandmother. Inside were a few precious things I had collected over the years, including Nanna's wedding ring, hair ribbons Mum had given me on my birthday, and her necklace with the silver cross.

Tears stung my eyes as I lifted the necklace, watching the cross swing on the delicate chain. After Mum died I'd been too sad to wear it, but more time had passed now, and I'd made a promise. *Wear it for* me.

I recalled Mr. Tregarrick's expression as he made the request. He'd looked fearful, I thought, and maybe a little sad, too. Like it had cost him something to ask.

I fastened the chain around my neck and went back down.

Though I felt tired today, the lump on my head had gone down, and the cut—quite small for the amount of blood that had seeped into my hair—had scabbed over. My head still ached, which was just one more reason I probably should have stayed at home. But there were many things I wanted to talk over with Mrs. Moyle.

As I walked, I couldn't help looking out for Mr. Tregarrick. I thought about what Jack had said of the talk in the village. I knew, of course, that people had always whispered about the old place and its master, but folk would whisper about *anything* strange. It was the season for such stories, too. Hallowe'en was only a few weeks away, and Mum had believed it was a time of spirits and fairies.

Mum and Jack and I had always carved faces in fat, hollowed-out turnips and lit them with candle stubs, hanging them outside the cottage so any evil spirits would pass us by. Now that I thought of it, Da had insisted we hang one in the apple tree in the garden to frighten off the "Wolf of Roche Rock." He'd wink and we'd laugh—we liked when Da joined in the fun—but he had always been leery of the old estate.

I glanced through the gap in the hedge as I passed, rubbing Mum's cross between my fingers. The grove of Cornish oaks, with their gilded autumn leaves, made a papery whispering sound as the breeze rattled through them. But all else on the estate was quiet.

I arrived at work later than usual and found that Mrs. Moyle had finished all the opening tasks and was boiling water for tea.

"I'm so sorry, Mrs. Moyle!" I said as I stepped into the warm kitchen. "I'm moving slow this morning."

She laughed. "It's the first time you've been late in two years, Mina. I think we can overlook it."

She turned as I was removing my bonnet, and her sharp eyes went right to my bump. "Heavens, what has happened to you?"

I winced. "Is it *that* noticeable?"

"Well, perhaps only to me, but are you well, dear?"

Nodding, I took a deep breath. "I have so much to tell you—and ask you—that I don't know how I'll ever get through it before we open. I think I'll have to go in order of importance and leave some for later."

She folded her hands and said, "All right, I'm listening. Only, be kind to an old woman and start with what happened to your head."

"I had a fall on the heath," I said, taking my neatly folded apron from the worktable, "but I'm all right. There's much more to the story, which I will try to get to in a moment. But first I thought you should know that Jack and I have been arguing about my working here. He says he doesn't want me leaving the cottage because of Mr. Roscoe's death, but I don't think he means for it to be temporary."

"Oh, Mina," said Mrs. Moyle, frowning deeply. "As much as it saddens me to hear that, I can't say I'm surprised. You've hinted before that Jack doesn't like you working here. And I'm sure he truly is worried about you."

"That may be, but I have no intention of giving up The Magpie, and it's not his business to force me to." I let out a sigh. "With that said, he's not himself these days, and I'm not sure he won't try. If he ever shows up here, I'll go home with him quietly, before he can make trouble."

She reached for my basket and began moving the pasties to a platter. "I'm glad you've told me. I think we should talk more about this, but go ahead with the rest."

"Well, I met with Mr. Tregarrick again yesterday."

Looking more curious than surprised, she said, "Oh, indeed?"

"He happened by when I fell, and he helped me—there's much more about that, but it will have to wait. He walked me home, and Jack came home at the same time."

Her brow lifted. "And how did that go?"

Frowning, I replied, "About as well as you might imagine. But something came up that I wanted to ask you about. Jack said you might know some old stories about the Tregarricks? About some kind of evil on the estate? I know people are scared of the place, and my da sometimes mentioned the 'Wolf of Roche Rock.'"

Mrs. Moyle let out a sigh and sank onto a stool next to the worktable.

"Gracious, child. There are a hundred questions I might ask, but to answer yours, yes, there *are* old stories. And I believe they did grow out of a *very* old belief that a wolf lived on the estate. But that's all they are—stories. At least, that's my view of it."

"I guess it's no wonder people are gossiping, what with the constable saying it was a dog that killed Mr. Roscoe. I asked Mr. Hilliard about wolves, but he said there aren't any in England."

"I would imagine he's right about that. I've never known anyone to have seen one, aside from the one on the sign at the tavern—which may have taken its name from the stories. If a real creature *did* inspire that tale, it has long since gone to its rest. But to me it sounds like the kind of story the lord of a manor might circulate to frighten off poachers."

It did indeed, maybe one of Mr. Tregarrick's ancestors. And mightn't the wolf in his cup have simply been a warning about the talk in the village? I thought about the weathered wooden sign hanging above the tavern door—a wolf's head painted against a background of heather. I had never connected it with the wolf Da had spoken of.

"So *you* don't think there's anything to this idea that Harker Tregarrick somehow had to do with his solicitor's death?"

Something glimmered in my employer's eyes. "'Harker,' is it? First time I've heard his Christian name."

"That's how he introduced himself to Jack," I said, needlessly smoothing the front of my apron.

"Well, what I think is that people are frightened because of the death, and probably shut inside too much now that the weather's changing, and it gives them something to talk about. It doesn't help matters that the constable and his men couldn't find the animal responsible."

I looked at her. "Jack's got the idea that Mr. Tregarrick moved the body, and that's why there was no blood where I found it."

Her brow knit as she went to the stove and moved the steaming kettle from the fire. "I can't see any sense in that. Why would he kill his own solicitor? And how could he make it look like an animal attack well enough to convince both the surgeon and the coroner?"

"It really only makes sense if he's some kind of monster," I said faintly.

"I daresay you've exchanged more words with the man than anyone in the village. Is that what *you* think?"

I hesitated, unsure how much to tell her. But Mrs. Moyle was my friend as well as my employer. Who else could I talk to, now that Jack and I no longer saw eye to eye?

"I was alone with him," I confessed. "For quite a while. He could have killed *me* if he wanted to. Instead he carried me to Roche Rock and gave me medicine for tending my wound. The man is *afraid* of blood. I saw it with my own eyes."

I could see that I'd finally managed to surprise her with these details, yet all she said was, "Well, there it is, then." She raised a finger. "But you *take care*, Mina. I'm not worried about wolves or monsters, but there may still be some diseased creature lurking about. And just as worrisome is people in the village getting too worked up about all this. You don't want to get caught in the middle of it."

I nodded. "I'll be careful, Mrs. Moyle."

She turned and started toward the front room. "We'll talk more about all this after closing."

We didn't get the chance, though. Business wasn't exactly brisk that morning, yet still I only made it until the noon hour before I had to sit down in the kitchen and rest.

"Drink a cup of tea, and then I want you to go on home," said Mrs. Moyle, smoothing her hair so she could take my place in the front room. "And I want you to stay home tomorrow, too. You need to rest and make peace with your brother."

"But how will you manage, ma'am?" I protested.

"The same way I managed before you came to work for me—poorly. But you're not of much use to me right now, anyway."

My employer said this with kindness, yet it was just the bit of honesty I needed to convince me. She came to the door as I was going and touched a hand to my back. "I must say I envy you your youthful adventures, and I expect details about Roche Rock when you come back."

I smiled, though I knew her tone would have been very different had I told her the whole story of how I'd been injured.

"And try not to worry yourself over the events of the last few days," she continued. "These dark clouds will pass over, you'll see. Even the trouble between you and Jack."

How I hoped she was right.

Once on the road, with the fresh air cool against my skin, I began to feel better. At the gap in the hedge, I paused, thinking I might glimpse

Mr. Tregarrick and speak a word of warning to him about what Jack had told me. *I owe him that much.* But I saw no more sign of him than I ever did on these walks.

"Mr. Tregarrick?" I called, in case he might be on the grounds within hearing.

No answer.

The estate was clear of fog today, and I knew now that it would only take a few minutes to walk to the chapel from here. But the path edged the woods, and if ever there was a place for a creature to hide . . .

For my sake if not for your own—take more care, Mina Penrose.

It was hard to believe the master of Roche Rock had ever said such a thing to me.

Even if he hadn't, I wasn't fool enough to take the risk.

I walked on home, and by the time I got there, my head hurt from both the lump and too much thinking. I went straight up to my bed.

On waking, I was confused about the time of day. But I felt well enough, and I tossed back the coverlet and climbed down the ladder.

I slipped out the back door of the cottage for some fresh air and to reset my clock, and Jenny, our old nanny goat, bleated a greeting. The hens came running, expecting scraps.

"Don't come to *me*," I scolded them. "Get to work on those apples on the ground, so they don't go to waste. Might even get a worm or two in the bargain."

I felt guilty I hadn't pickled more of them this year, but my job didn't leave me enough time to do all the things Mum used to do. I'd put by enough for Jack and me for the winter, though. It occurred to me that I should pick a basket for Mr. Tregarrick. Despite him using bread baking to explain alchemy, I got the impression he didn't eat very well.

Peckish myself after my nap, I plucked an apple from the tree. The fruits were big this year—dark red, tart, and crisp—and I ate only half of it before holding the rest out for Jenny. We no longer got any milk out of the sweet old thing, and we could afford cow's milk since I'd been working for Mrs. Moyle. Jack was always after me to boil Jenny for stew, saying there was no point in feeding such a useless animal, but mean as Jack could be these days, I knew he wasn't serious. Mum had loved Jenny. And she was no trouble. There was so much bramble and sweetbriar for her to eat around the house—not to mention the apples—that the only time we had to feed her was in the bleakest weeks of winter.

Rubbing between her curved horns while she grunted, I looked out and tried to guess the time by the light. Cloudy again today, but I thought it was around the time The Magpie usually closed. Three, most days. Four if the afternoon business was brisk.

Though Mrs. Moyle had asked me to spend the day at home, I felt restlessness coming on. I wasn't used to being idle. I remembered the milk pitcher and got the idea to go back to town and buy a new one. Then Jack wouldn't have to ask me where it was, and I wouldn't have to tell him I'd smashed it in a fit of temper, and just maybe he wouldn't notice the difference. Especially if I could find a pattern that was similar.

It won't hurt me to walk a little. If I did start feeling poorly, I could turn back.

I donned my bonnet and shawl and set out. It was warmer today and, though overcast, less dreary. A breeze moved through the weeping boughs of the old willow next to the road, halfway between our cottage and The Magpie. The branches reached all the way to the ground, and their swaying made the tree look like a golden waterfall.

Those branches had been a favorite hiding place of mine and Jack's when we were children. We'd often pretended it was Camelot and we were Knights of the Round Table. One time Billy Budge—our neighbors' son, who was close to the same age as Jack and me—burst in on us and tried to take over our game. He said he would play Lancelot and that I must play Guinevere because girls couldn't be knights. Jack took one look at me trying not to cry and knocked Billy to the ground.

As The Magpie was on the outer edge of the village, I had to pass it on the way to the other shops. I knew Mrs. Moyle wouldn't like my being out after she'd sent me home to rest. I told myself that if she saw me, I could blame it on the broken pitcher and my fear of Jack's temper. (*Who* did the smashing?) But I knew she'd only offer me one of The Magpie's pitchers, and then I'd have no excuse to do the thing I'd really come to town for—might as well be honest, at least with myself.

I held my breath as I passed in front of St. Gomonda, the parish church, which was directly across from The Magpie. Looking through the tearoom's windows, I could see that it was empty.

I continued up Fore Street, passing Teague's Sundries Shop—where I was most likely to find the pitcher I needed—and stopped outside the business next door, The Wolf's Head. A low-slung building of rough, grayish brick—blotched here and there with whitewash that had all but faded away—the tavern might just be the oldest in the parish. The sign above the door creaked as it swung in the stiffening breeze.

I studied the sign more closely in light of my conversation with Mrs. Moyle, and I noticed something I hadn't before—a dark blob among the heather in the background.

Roche Rock.

Gaze lowering to the door, I took a deep breath. A clump of Michaelmas daisies had sprung up from the hard earth beside the entrance, pale-purple heads bobbing on thin stalks.

Am I really doing this?

This was the place Jack had spent most evenings since Mum died. It looked quiet now, too early for the mine workers. Maybe not even open yet. Holding my breath, I reached for the door handle.

THE WOLF'S HEAD

The door swung open and I stepped inside, hesitating as my eyes adjusted to the low light.

Wood paneling completely covered the tavern's walls and ceiling, and a couple of oil lamps gave off a dim yellow glow. Two heavy wooden chandeliers hung from the ceiling, but none of their candles had been lit.

A potbellied coal stove put out heat at one end of the room, and at the other end was a large, open hearth, looking as though it hadn't been used in some time. Tables were scattered around the floor, and a bar with a snug at one end lined the back wall. A couple of men too old for the mines sat on barstools with pints in front of them, but otherwise the place was empty. A gangly, sandy-gray wolfhound had flopped down on the flagstone floor near the stove. The dog's eyes noted my presence before its tail gave one heavy thwack and then stilled.

"What can I do for you, miss?" The publican had stepped from behind the bar and approached me.

"Good day, sir," I said, trying to sound more confident than I felt. "Maybe you'll think this strange, but I have a curiosity about this old tavern, and if you have a moment, I wondered whether I might ask you a few questions."

He frowned, grizzled brows angling down toward his bulb nose. "We're not in the business of answering questions at The Wolf's Head, miss. Nor are we in the business of serving unaccompanied young ladies."

His refusal disappointed but did not surprise me. "Beg your pardon, sir."

But as I was turning to go, he said, "Aren't you the lass that works at The Magpie? Jack Penrose's sister?"

"I am."

Scratching at the stubble on his jaw, he continued, "Sure as the moon, your brother will appear before the evening's out, so I suppose it wouldn't be too much of a stretch to call *him* your escort." I could only imagine what Jack would have to say about that. "If you'll sit down and order a glass of sherry—and if you don't intend to harangue me about your brother's habits—I might be persuaded to answer a question or two."

"That's very kind of you, Mister . . ."

"Couch."

"Thank you, Mr. Couch."

I sat at a small table near the door. Though the publican knew who I was, I kept my bonnet on, hoping no one who came in would recognize me. The two men at the bar had turned as I'd entered, but they'd soon gone back to their ale.

Mr. Couch went behind the bar, poured amber liquid into a small wineglass, and returned to my table. Placing the glass before me, he said, "What is it you want to ask me, Miss Penrose? I'll warn you again—if it has to do with your brother, I don't discuss my customers' business."

"No, sir. Mrs. Moyle, the lady I work for—she was telling me she thought this tavern might be named for a story that used to be told about a wolf people had seen on the heath."

His brows lifted. "So it was, but that was many long years ago. The Wolf's Head—used to be an inn as well as a tavern—has stood here for about three centuries. That brute Richard Grenville, who fought for the king during the Civil War—he once stayed here, at least according to my granfer. It's not as old as the black chapel, but old enough."

"The black chapel. You mean the Tregarrick place?"

"Mmm." He tilted his head to one side, studying me. "Maybe you don't know, but there's a mineral in that granite called tourmaline that gives it its color."

"No, I didn't know." I sipped my sherry. It tasted sweet and burned in my throat, though not nearly as much as Mr. Moyle's whisky. "Do you know if there was ever a *real* wolf, or was it just stories?"

The publican's lips—and the mustache above them—turned down, his eyes narrowing. But he looked like he might be trying not to smile. "I know I must look pretty old to you, but I'm not *nearly* old enough to answer that question."

"No, sir," I said, smiling.

It had been worth a try. I reached into my pocket for money to pay him.

"Now if you ask my *opinion* . . ."

I looked up.

"I've always assumed those stories were really just about folks being scared of the old place and jumping at shadows. Now, with the constable saying a dog killed that solicitor . . . I'm not sure what to think."

I swallowed. "Do people think it has something to do with Mr. Tregarrick?"

"It's almost all my customers are talking about. Doesn't help matters that no one has ever laid eyes on the man. Leaves the imagination a little too free."

So Jack had been telling the truth. "I've met Mr. Tregarrick."

His eyes widened. "You don't say?"

"He came into The Magpie a few days ago."

"The Magpie? For what?"

I shrugged. "For tea."

"Hmph. What did you think of him?"

I rested my fingertips on the stem of my glass. "He was quiet and polite. Seemed a fine gentleman to me." *Let him chew on that.* "What do *you* think, Mr. Couch? You don't really believe Mr. Roscoe's death had anything to do with Mr. Tregarrick, do you?"

"Well," he said slowly, "I couldn't say, Miss Penrose. But you won't catch me going anywhere near the place."

I let out a quiet sigh, and I dug a few coins from my pocket. "What do I owe you, sir?"

He waved my money away. "On the house this time. Your brother must be spending half his pay in here."

With an inward groan, I replied, "Thank you. For the sherry, and for answering my questions."

He folded his arms, eyeing me shrewdly. "Can I ask *you* one?"

Wary, I answered, "All right."

"Why come in here asking about wolves in old stories? And don't try telling me again you're *curious*. People like us who have to work to put food on the table don't have time for idle curiosity."

Why, indeed. My reasons were complicated, to be sure, having been the one to find Mr. Roscoe, as well as being possibly the only one in town who knew Mr. Tregarrick. And *more* than just knowing him, owing a debt to him.

I decided to give Mr. Couch the reason he'd best understand—and find least concerning. "We practically live on the heath, sir. I walk by Roche Rock every day on my way to work, and Jack comes home by himself, after dark and in his cups most nights. I just wanted to know what people were saying. If I should be worried."

He nodded, seeming to accept this. "Well, I know Hilliard thinks the danger's past, but I think you can't be too careful right now." He pulled a towel from his shoulder and wiped at something I couldn't see on the tabletop. "Now, you sit there as long as you like, Miss Penrose. Our rowdier customers won't be in for some time yet."

He was going, and I said, "If you wouldn't mind, Mr. Couch, I'd rather Jack not know I came here today."

He winked at me. "Like I said, I don't discuss my customers' business." Then he went back to the bar.

I didn't really want the sherry, but neither did I want Mr. Couch to think me ungrateful. So I sat and sipped it, thinking about the things he'd said. It seemed to me that until Mr. Roscoe's death, the publican didn't believe in the Wolf of Roche Rock any more than Mrs. Moyle did. Yet like most everyone else, he was wary of the place.

When I'd finally emptied my glass, I left The Wolf's Head and went into the sundries shop. Mrs. Teague had a few ceramic pitchers to choose from, and I bought one with a pattern of pink roses, similar to the one I'd smashed.

The sherry had made me feel sleepy, and the headache was coming on again, so I walked home after that. Back at the cottage, I made Jack's supper and left it out for him, ate my own, and went to bed early. Before I'd had time for any reflections on my day beyond a growing uneasiness, sleep came.

I'm walking home from The Magpie at dusk.

I hear the call of an owl, and dogs barking in the distance. As I reach the dip in the grass where the hedge meets the old wall, I see a man. Drawing closer, I discover it's two men—one lying on the grass and another bent over him. Hearing my step, the bending man straightens and turns.

Mr. Tregarrick. *Blood dribbles down his chin. I try to scream but can't make a sound.*

I look to the road for someone to help me, and from the direction of the village, I see people marching toward us. Many *people, as if everyone in the village has turned out. Their voices are angry, and some of them stab rifle barrels or pitchforks into the air. Out in front—leading them—is Jack.*

When I look again at Mr. Tregarrick, his face is clean. No blood stains his fine white shirt. His eyes are gentle and sad, like when we talked in the chapel.

He starts walking toward the angry crowd, and I try to cry a warning, but still no sound comes out of me.

Casting a glance over his shoulder, he says, "It's for the best, Mina."

I woke suddenly, the warning that I had been trying to shout finally sounding—though no more than a muffled squeak. By the light in the room, I knew it was morning.

How yesterday's conversations had preyed on my slumbering mind!

Only a dream, but I couldn't let go of the feeling that I must *do* something. Yet what was it in my power to do?

Get up and get on with the chores. If nothing else, it might help to order my thoughts.

Things were still cool between Jack and me, and I thought—hoped, even—we'd not speak before he left. But it wasn't to be.

As I was handing him his lunch on the way out the door, he said, "I won't hear of you walking to The Magpie this morning, will I?"

Grateful that there'd been no more talk about me at the mine and that Mr. Couch had kept his promise, I said dully, "No, Jack."

The plain relief in his haggard face caused a twinge of regret. I had blamed his recent outbursts on resentment and the bottle, but I remembered what Mr. Tregarrick had said. *Perhaps Jack's afraid of losing you, too.* I harangued him about his drinking for the same reason.

When he was gone, I did something I rarely had time for—sat down to drink a cup of tea by myself in the quiet cottage. As I was about to pour, I thought about my mother and her visitors, and I removed the strainer from my cup.

I took a deep breath. "Show me, Mum."

I sloshed the tea around in the pot to lift the leaves from the bottom before filling my cup. Heart beating faster, I began to sip the bitter brew, which had been steeping long enough that it really needed milk to be drinkable.

I tried to imagine what would've happened next when Mum had done this. People would have had some reason for coming to her. Perhaps they'd ask a question.

"What am I to do about Mr. Tregarrick?" I murmured. Then I swallowed the last of the tea and tilted the cup to catch some light from the window.

The leaves had all clumped on one side. I carefully rolled the cup until I could see more clearly—and my breath caught.

There under the handle was a copy of what I'd seen in Mr. Tregarrick's teapot.

Another wolf's head.

I let the air fill my chest, trying to slow my racing heart.

I had been thinking about wolves all of yesterday. Maybe the leaves could be affected by that. Or it might have to do with my visit to the tavern. Or the gossip in the village.

It could be another warning that he's dangerous.

I let out a frustrated sigh. How was this ever of any use to anyone?

Maybe don't expect to be an expert the first time.

I rose from the table and cleared the dishes. After that I paced from one end of the room to the other. Mr. Tregarrick was all I could think of. His many kindnesses, and how he'd sacrificed in all he'd done for me—confronting his fear of blood, allowing a stranger to invade his private sanctuary, exposing himself to Jack's anger.

Though I wasn't going to work today, I'd made a smaller batch of pasties for Jack and me. I wrapped up two in a cloth and put them, along with my knife, into my basket. I went out behind the house and picked half a dozen tart, rosy apples and added those, too.

I stood a minute under the tree, listening to the reddening leaves rattle in the breeze, giving Jenny a scratch, and feeling the sun on my skin. Today's sky was clear and the color of cornflowers, and the air had a crispness you could smell. I thought October might be the best month of them all. I had always loved her golden days and moody mists in equal measure.

"Wish me luck, Jenny."

She looked up at me with her strange eyes, black rectangles surrounded by a color like light shining through honey.

I picked up my basket, walked around to the front of the cottage, and started down the road. This time when I reached the gap in the hedge, I took the knife from my basket and hurried straight through before my courage could fail me, or guilt over disregarding the advice of those who cared about me could turn me back.

I followed the path around the oak wood, knife in hand, peering into the deep shadows beneath the branches. I wondered whether Mr. Hilliard had searched there, too. Half expecting to find a pair of eyes glowing in the rusty bracken, I walked faster.

As I neared the chapel, I wove around slabs and big blocks of *tourmaline*-laced granite, strewn about as if by a giant at play. Some of the larger pieces looked like standing stones. Faded heather clumped around their bases, along with a furze bush here and there. Much of the scrub that covered the uneven, sloping ground had dried to gold or bronze in the final hot weeks of summer. Though with the recent cooler, damper days, some things were greening again. The few remaining wildflowers looked timid and fragile, as if they knew they belonged to the previous season. Dewy spiderwebs sparkled in the grass.

At last I reached the foot of the roughly hewn stone stairway, and my gaze followed the tower's stark lines. I saw that the casement on the lower floor was open, as before.

"Mr. Tregarrick?" I called, thinking it best to give him some warning of my arrival.

I waited a few moments, but no face appeared, and no answer came. He might have been on the upper floor, or somewhere on the grounds.

Or he might not wish to see me.

I placed the knife back in my basket, then took a deep breath, raised my skirts so I wouldn't trip, and started up.

"WHY AREN'T YOU AFRAID?"

HARKER

She is coming.

Not passing on the road. Not crossing the heath. She was coming to my very door. I knew it as sure as if I'd spotted her from the battlements.

This is my own doing. I never should have brought her here.

Drawing an unsteady breath, I checked the furnace beneath the copper cucurbit that I used for distilling my vital essence. The vapor was collecting nicely in the alembic and had already begun traveling down the pipe to the receiver. It could be left unmonitored for a while.

"Mr. Tregarrick!"

I jumped at the sound of her voice. I took slow steps to the top of the stairs and stopped, jaw clenching. The last thing I could afford to do was admit this woman into my home again. *Ever.*

I must be your worst nightmare.

Indeed, the last time had very nearly resulted in tragedy. Despite carrying her injured from the heath, I had been in no way prepared for that sudden flow of fresh, hot blood—even if just a trickle—when the knife opened her finger. That metallic, red stain was to me as opium to those in its thrall. *Far* more to me than the vital essence that merely kept me alive. How I had bargained with myself in that moment. *The smallest taste will be enough. Just this once, and I'll forget her.*

I fought something very like addiction in not admitting her now. I fought my own nature. And God help me, I fought a burgeoning curiosity that likely would never have swollen fully to life had I not brought her here the first time.

A series of thuds landed against the chapel door. I closed my eyes.

"Mr. Tregarrick?"

I crossed to the chapel window, a stained glass depiction of Christ healing a leper. From here I could watch her go. Make sure she made it safely back to the road.

She'll only come back. Little as I knew her, I suspected a stubborn streak. Again she pounded on the door, punctuating my thought.

"Why aren't you afraid of me?" I muttered, though there was no one but Christ and the leper to hear.

Because you're not trying hard enough, fool.

I would have to try harder, or one of the monsters on my estate was going to end up killing her. And I'd sooner die myself.

THE ALCHEMIST

I was going when the door swung suddenly inward, causing my breath to catch.

"Come in, Miss Penrose," Mr. Tregarrick greeted me stiffly, turning and moving away from the door. "Leave it open," he said as I crossed the threshold.

"It's a lovely day," I said brightly, though I was clearly unwelcome. Best to keep this visit short. "I'm sorry to disturb you, sir. I've brought you some lunch in thanks for your recent kindness, but mainly I wanted to—"

"Please sit down."

I hesitated near the door, studying him. His dress was the same as last time I saw him—fine, but old-fashioned. I noticed the top button of his shirt was loosed and the ruffled collar lay open, revealing the small hollow at the base of his throat. Something red had blotted the white fabric just below that. I hoped after what he'd told me that it wasn't blood.

His hair hung loose in waves to just past his chin, and his face was drawn and very serious. He gestured to one of the dining chairs, which was turned out to face the room.

I don't belong here. I should go.

My heart lost its rhythm as I walked to the chair.

"I can see that I'm intruding," I said quietly, unable to fully hide my hurt at his manner. "There are some rumors in the village having to do with you and your solicitor. I thought you should know, so I've come to tell you. After that, I'll go."

"There is something I must tell *you*, Miss Penrose."

I stared at him, confused by how changed he was from the day he'd brought me here. Wary, I said, "All right, sir."

"You must not come here again."

I nodded, feeling small now, as well as hurt.

"Of course," I said, voice trembling slightly. "I'm sorry if I've said or done something to offend you, Mr. Tregarrick. It's the last thing I—"

"Miss Penrose," he said, huffing in disbelief, "this estate is *dangerous*. I would think you of all people would understand this by now. You risk your life in even setting foot on it."

My chest loosened and I let out a breath, finding this easier to stomach than the idea I had made him angry with me. "It was out of concern, sir." I held back from saying *for you*. I'd overstepped enough. "You took considerable trouble in helping *me*, and I thought it only right—"

"You thought *wrong*." His look was almost baleful, the color of his eyes deeper than I remembered, making me think of the pool on his estate. His cheekbones looked higher and sharper. He stepped closer, stopping my breath. "Understand me, Miss Penrose, it's not just the estate. *I* am dangerous."

I stared at him, heart thumping like a rabbit's foot. I remembered last night's dream, and the wolf in my cup this morning. A voice inside me screamed *Go*.

He saved my life. I set my jaw. "I don't believe you."

My heart nearly bounded from my chest at the cold fury in his eyes. "You think I would say such a thing in jest?"

"I don't know *why* you would say such a thing," I said, growing exasperated. "What I do know is that I was injured on your estate, and you brought me here, into your home—which I know must have been uncomfortable for you—and *cared for me*."

"'Dangerous' is what I said I am. Not 'callous.'"

I sat up straighter and set my basket on the floor beside the chair. "I'm sorry, sir, but that makes no sense to me. And you should be careful saying such things, because it's what people in the village already think. It's what I came here to warn you about. Some of them believe that you had something to do with Mr. Roscoe's death."

His chest sank as he released a breath. In a slightly less frigid tone, he said, "I am grateful for your concern, but it was only a matter of time."

I rubbed my lips together before venturing, "Because of the old stories, you mean."

His gaze sharpened on my face, and I shifted uncomfortably. "What makes you think they're wrong, these people in the village?" he said. "The fact that I helped *you* doesn't prove I didn't kill Mr. Roscoe."

My hands clasped tightly in my lap. "While I don't know you *well*, I know you better than they do."

His expression flattened. "You don't know me at all, Miss Penrose."

For a long moment we simply stared at each other. The cold of the place seeped into my bones. I heard a sound like dripping coming from the upper floor, but otherwise the silence was complete. We were locked in a kind of dance that I didn't understand. But I did, at last, begin to feel there was something dangerous about it. Ice crystals seemed to form along the back of my neck.

Finally I found the courage to ask the loudest question in my head. "Are you saying you *did* kill Mr. Roscoe?"

His reply was low, but with something sharp behind it. "What I'm saying is I easily could have."

He seemed to be trying to convince me that he was in fact some kind of monster. But *why*? Frightened—but also frustrated and confused—I slowly shook my head.

Suddenly he stepped forward and took hold of my hand. I let out a squeal as he pulled me up from the chair.

"Let go!" I cried, trying to free myself.

But it was all I could do to stay on my feet as I hurried to keep up with his long strides. We reached the stone stairway and started up. I had the idea to allow myself to stumble with the hope of bringing him out of this strange fit, but what if he just continued to drag me? As we neared the upper floor, a dozen nightmares came to life inside my head.

In a voice breaking with fear, I said, "Mr. Tregarrick, *please*."

At the top he released me abruptly. I fisted my hands at my sides, tears stinging my eyes. *Only a fool ignores* so *many warnings.*

"Look around you, Miss Penrose."

Taking a shuddering breath, I met his gaze. I was struck afresh by his eyes. Not only their color, but the expression in them—part angry, part sad, but more than half *wild.*

"What kind of creature are you?" I whispered.

He winced, as if my words had traveled on a dart. In a softer tone, he said, "Now you're asking the right questions. Look around you, please."

I did this time, and it was not at all what I had imagined. I had assumed his bedchamber must be up here because it was the only place it *could* be. But this space was mostly taken up by a long table covered with copper and glass vessels, iron instruments like tongs and pokers, and towers of books. One large copper vessel sat atop a kind of brick oven resting almost in the hearth. I could see a fire burning through its arched opening, and the heat released soft hisses and bubbling sounds.

Taking in the rest of the room, I saw there was indeed a narrow bed against one wall—beneath the stained glass window that faced the heath. In the pointed tip of the window was a rose design, and below that a scene from the Bible. Shelves against the back wall contained more books, clay jars, and at least a dozen bottles of wine, all with the same label, which had a kind of lettering I didn't recognize. On one shelf my gaze paused on the neck of a fiddle; the rest of the instrument seemed to be resting in pieces beside it, broken strings poking out like strands of grizzled hair. Bunches of herbs had been hung to dry in the corners farthest from the hearth.

Next to the hearth a few pots and pans were stacked, and a teakettle hung from a hook over the fire. I understood why his meals were simple—*this* was his kitchen. Of course, I had cooked on a hearth fire for most of my life, but I wasn't the master of an estate.

My gaze returned to the table with its collection of instruments. "These are for alchemy?"

"That's right."

"Are alchemists dangerous?"

"As a rule, no."

I looked at him. "Then what is it you wish me to be afraid of, Mr. Tregarrick?"

He took a deep breath, and his gaze drifted. "This is my laboratory. It's where I formulated something I call my vital essence."

"Is that like a quintessence?"

His eyes came back to my face. Mrs. Moyle had suggested he might be curious about me, and I had begun to believe it. I felt it almost every time he looked at me. Sometimes he seemed to be angry or confused, but often he looked like he was trying very hard to understand exactly what I was. Like *I* was the one the village told stories about.

"You have a good memory, Miss Penrose," he said. "It *is* a kind of quintessence. Distilled wine infused with herbs, distilled again to increase potency. A process I've refined over the course of . . . many years."

"And is it one of your medicines?"

"Yes."

My eyes moved over his face, shoulders, and chest. The old-fashioned shirt draped softly over the lines of his body. Though his skin lacked luster, and the bones of his face were sharp and angled, his form didn't appear wasted. I could make out the curve of muscle just below the tips of his shoulders, and above the crease of his elbow.

"It's not something you can see," he said, and my cheeks warmed.

"Then what?"

"A type of inherited disorder. My father had it, and his father."

His voice had dipped low. He almost seemed not to be breathing. Again I noticed the fullness of his dark, berry lips, and my heart began to thump.

"Do you know what a vampire is?"

Vampire? The word was familiar, and I tried to think why.

When I didn't answer right away, he continued, "Maybe you've heard stories of a creature that rises from the grave at night to drink the blood of the living."

Now it came to me. Jack was still a boy when he'd started at the mine, and one time a German man he worked with told him a story like this. Jack told it to *me*, and it scared me so badly I had nightmares. The next Sunday I even refused to enter the churchyard because of the graves. Father Kelly, the parish priest, came to see what was the matter. Though I'd all but forgotten about vampires until now, I remembered him saying, "I don't claim to know everything, Mina, and there *are* some very strange things in this world, but I can assure you that the souls in this churchyard sleep peacefully."

Mr. Tregarrick had watched me working through these thoughts, and now I gave him a hard stare. "What are you saying, sir?"

"It's what I am," he said simply. "A vampire."

My blood froze, and my heart stilled. "Are you telling me that you're dead?" How ashen he was. And how cold. *No. It's not possible.*

"I have never died," he said, and I thought it a strange way to answer the question. "But I do crave the blood of the living. My ancestors have always drunk it to survive. As I said, it is a family affliction."

Can he be mad? Though I was shaking, I took a step toward him. I could see the vein in his neck pulsing. *How slow it is.*

"It's only another old story," I said, voice unsteady. "Like the Wolf of Roche Rock."

"Most old stories have some basis in truth."

I remembered my dream. *Blood dribbles down his chin.*

His arms had gone rigid at his sides, hands clenched. "Come closer."

My heart bounced, and I swallowed dryly. *This can't be.* I took two more steps, until my head had to tilt back to meet his gaze.

I smelled herbs and brandy. His lips parted slightly, and my breaths grew short and quick. Then I saw them. The very white, very sharp points of two teeth resting against his full bottom lip.

I staggered backward with a gasp. Head half turning toward the stairs, I tried to think how many seconds it would take me to reach the front door.

Too many.

"Mr. Roscoe," I choked out.

His gaze felt heavy. So heavy I wondered whether I would be able to move again if I tried.

"That wasn't me," he said. "But I believe it was another vampire. The same as attacked you on the heath."

I remembered his words from earlier. *What I'm saying is I easily could have.*

"The rumors are true, then?" Fear lifted the pitch of my voice. "You *are* a killer." *And Jack tried to warn me.*

His eyes drifted to the window. "You're not wrong, but it's a little more complicated than that."

"*How* is it more complicated?"

My tone—half anger, half terror—drew his gaze. I was shaking—*hard.* The cold air in the tower bit into me, and I wrapped my arms around my chest.

He clasped his hands behind his back. "Your instinct, once you believed me, was the correct one. Flee, Miss Penrose. You've heard enough to understand why you must stay away from me."

Free to go. One message of warning delivered and another received. Yet I hesitated, studying him. *Hermit. Alchemist. Vampire.* He didn't look dangerous anymore; he just looked tired. And deeply sad.

He's more lonely than I am.

"*You* chose to tell me this," I said finally, "and to make me believe it. A man has died, and I'm not going to leave here with half an understanding."

He closed his eyes, letting out a breath.

My gaze moved again to the gourd-shaped copper vessel near the hearth. Steam and droplets collected in the vessel's glass cover, and I heard a trickle of liquid traveling through a thin pipe into a second vessel.

"The medicine you make here," I said, "does it somehow keep you from . . . ?"

His brows lifted. "That is excellent detective work, Miss Penrose." While I wasn't sure I knew what "detective work" was, I understood him to mean that I'd guessed right, and I breathed somewhat easier. He continued, "My vital essence is a replacement for the blood that I otherwise must drink to survive."

"It doesn't have blood in it?"

"No. I can explain if you like. It's rather technical."

"Please."

He folded his arms, brow knitting as he gathered his thoughts. "The Greek philosopher Aristotle wrote about the four elements that make up all matter—fire, air, water, and earth. These elements manifest the qualities of hot and dry, hot and wet, cold and wet, and cold and dry. In the human body, ideally these elements are in balance, but in reality, they often are not. Such imbalances are at the root of illness. Do you follow me?"

Though only just barely, I nodded.

"A vampire is an excess of earth—cold and dry. Blood is hot and wet, and drinking it helps make up for this imbalance. My vital essence is formulated to do this without blood. It is a distillate of Walachian wine. Early alchemists dubbed distilled wine 'aqua vitae,' but essentially it's brandy. Between distillations, I infuse the wine with fenugreek, *Angelica sinensis*, elderflower, foxglove, and the dark berries of *Atropa belladonna*—nightshade. Also dew of lady's mantle, which purifies and potentiates the elixir."

I followed his gaze to the shelves, where there were rows of bottles. The wine bottles with the labels I couldn't read, but also bottles with amber glass containing dark liquid, or clear glass filled with clear fluid and herbs. Other shelves held jars of dried leaves and flowers, and a few jars contained shiny, dark berries. *Isn't belladonna a poison?*

"I've included herbs with warming and moistening qualities," he continued, "and *Angelica sinensis* is also a blood tonic, as is elder. Foxglove helps my heart cope with the sluggishness of my blood, and the nightshade berry somewhat dulls my heightened senses. It also gives the essence an unusual side effect"—he raised the tips of his fingers to his bottom lip—"but the medicine is not as effective without it."

"The bruised color," I said. "And your eyes—is that why you sometimes wear dark spectacles? So people don't notice the color?"

"Partly. But mostly because nightshade causes mydriasis." I frowned, and he explained, "My pupils are always dilated, and daylight hurts my eyes."

He crossed to the furnace and fed it some small pieces of wood, rousing the flames inside. I didn't have his learning, and I didn't fully understand some of the things he'd told me, but one thing seemed clear enough.

"It sounds to me like you are no longer a danger to anyone, Mr. Tregarrick."

He turned, and his glower stopped my breath. "Let me be clearer, Miss Penrose. The vital essence gives me a fighting chance against a deadly craving. That is all."

A deadly craving.

"It's not the same, you mean," I said quietly.

"Not even close."

My gaze moved again around the room. "That's why you hide away here." I remembered the day he brought me to the chapel. How it must have tested him! To have carried me, bloodied, from the heath, and then . . .

"When I cut myself with the knife—the blood bothered you, but not for the reason I thought."

"No indeed."

"And now?" I asked uneasily, brow furrowing. "Is it uncomfortable for you that I'm here?"

His dark lips curved down. "If not for my essence, you would already be dead."

A hard shudder ran through me. My heart knocked against my ribs.

He took a few slow steps toward me. "Are you afraid of me *now*?"

ENTRANCED

"Yes," I admitted, and I could see the relief in his eyes.

Again I felt myself on the edge of flight, and I believed that was what he wanted. But something kept me rooted where I stood. He had cracked my world open in a way I still struggled to understand—far more than even Mrs. Moyle's books had. Like I was falling, without knowing how far the bottom was.

What of the wonders Mum had spoken of? I'd never seen gentle folk or spirits, but if vampires were real, might they, too, be more than children's stories?

And the Wolf of Roche Rock? If the Tregarricks were killers, might they have inspired *those* stories?

Most old stories have some basis in truth.

Did I not have a strange truth of my own? The prophecies I read in tea leaves?

I took another long, shaky breath and met his gaze. "Have you always been like this?"

He ran a hand through his ashy-brown waves, which resettled around his face. His head turned, and I followed his gaze to an old painting that hung between shelves on the back wall. It was a gloomy prospect, due to both age and some damage, but its subject appeared to be a manor house.

"It's always been in me," said Mr. Tregarrick, "ever since I was born. But the craving didn't begin until I came of age. It was the same for my father. And his father. All the way back to the son born to the Tregarrick who built this chapel at the beginning of the fifteenth century."

My eyes moved over the lines of his face. "When I first met you in The Magpie, I thought we were close in age. But since then, I haven't been sure. The clothes you wear, and the way you talk sometimes . . . Earlier you said you had been working on your vital essence for many years. Forgive me, but how old *are* you, Mr. Tregarrick?"

His gaze drifted to the narrow bed beneath the window. Mine followed, and I noticed a long line of short gouges in the stone just above it. There were scores of them.

"I was born a vampire when I was one and twenty," he said, "and one and twenty I have remained for nearly sixty years."

"Sixty years!" I stared. "But why haven't you aged?"

His eyes came back to my face. "I don't have an answer for that, other than to say the affliction seems to slow everything. My breathing. My heartbeat. My appetite. Everything but my mind and the horrible thirst. I live here in unnatural stasis."

I added the figures. *He's at least eighty years old.* "No one would ever know," I said, aghast. "I can hardly believe it."

He nodded. "The truth is neither can I. I can't feel the years at all, even when I try. I feel the same as I did the day I changed, and all the years since then are like a long, unhappy dream. My father told me it was the same for him."

"How old was your father when he died?"

Shrugging, he said, "I can only guess at that. He was nineteen when he became a vampire. Nineteen he remained for a century, maybe more. But after my change, he began to age again. Quickly. For much of my life up to then, he'd felt more like my brother than my father."

"And your mother?"

His eyes lifted to mine, and again I glimpsed the depth of his sadness. "I never knew her. She died the day I was born."

He returned then to the hearth and opened the teakettle that hung there, filling it from a pitcher of water that rested on a nearby table.

The fire had burned low, and he tossed in what looked like bricks of turf, which sometimes made their way to Roche from Bodmin Moor.

"It was the same with my grandmother," he continued. "It seems they couldn't survive the birth of a monster."

His voice sounded flattened by a lifetime of grief pressing down on him. Monster or no, I pitied him. He hadn't chosen to be what he was.

He came away from the hearth again, but he kept a careful distance now that he had nothing to prove to me.

He craves my blood. Yet here I still stood. As if entranced by him, like the powdery, gray moths that slipped inside and fluttered around our lamp.

"How is it they were able to . . . to marry?" I asked, heat creeping into my cheeks. "You're uncomfortable with me even in your house." There was living together, which would have been hard enough. But there was also the seeding of children.

He stared at the floor between us, again clasping his hands behind his back, shoulders tipping forward under the weight he carried. "They learned to manage their thirst in other ways," he said. "We're still human for the most part. There is still love, and the drive to reproduce. To continue a family line, even if it's a cursed one. There is still frailness. And hope. Always hope that the next generation will be free of the curse."

I felt a tug in my throat at the tragedy of it. *Yet they are killers.*

"What do you mean by 'other ways'?" I asked. "Did the ones who came before you have their own vital essences?"

He looked up. "No."

I folded my arms over my chest against the chill in the air, waiting for him to say more. But *he* seemed to be waiting for me to come up with the answer on my own. After a moment, I did, and my heart lurched.

"They drank other people's blood instead."

He slowly nodded. "I won't lie to you, Miss Penrose. There would certainly have been lovers and wives killed, even with the best intentions. Probably *many* of them over the centuries, because it was always a risk. An unacceptable one, in my view. When you . . . when you *want* someone, the temptation is even stronger." His eyes flitted to mine, and a fire flickered in my belly. "It's a very cruel trick of the disease."

It was a horrible, heartbreaking family history . . . and made my squabbles with Jack seem childish and small. Yet I knew the pain of loss and loneliness, and in that moment I hurt for him more than I feared him.

"Thomas Tregarrick, the first of us to be afflicted, was a hunter," he continued. "But toward the end of his long life, he did try to assert some control over his thirst, and this carried through to future generations. All of us gain more control as we age—or as we accumulate years. But also my family's ancient wealth, with careful management, only increased over the centuries, which opened the door to various alternatives."

"Ways to avoid killing, you mean?"

"Yes. Agreements were struck with surgeons and physicians, for example, who in the process of treating patients sometimes acquire blood that would otherwise be discarded. Or a trusted family physician might harvest blood from willing donors." He frowned. "Feeding the old way was still preferred, and there were always people poor enough to risk just about anything."

Unsettling as this was, it seemed to suggest at least the possibility they could feed on people without taking their lives.

"Now, Miss Penrose," he said as his gaze came back to me, "you will want to ask me a question."

I swallowed, feeling pricks along the back of my neck. "Have you ever killed anyone?"

I watched his chest rise slowly. The kettle over the fire began to whistle, and he started toward it, muttering, "Possibly."

My heart raced as he tipped the water into a teapot, and I thought about the madness of being served tea by a blood-drinking monster. The smoky smell of "Caravan" drifted through the room.

I find it warming. To balance his cold, dry earth.

"You've taken a chill," he said, placing the teapot on a tray. "Go downstairs and I'll bring you a cup of tea. After that you're going home, where you will have a decision to make."

Though I wasn't sure what he meant, I did as he asked, and his boots sounded softly on the steps behind me.

He set the tray down on the dining table before closing the front door and going for an ember from the hearth. Then he began the same ritual with the frankincense. Suddenly I realized it wasn't about purifying the air, or at least it wasn't only about that.

In a tone of surprise, I said, "You can smell my blood."

One of his eyebrows lifted as he glanced at me. Then he returned to his task. *No reply necessary.* The flame that flickered again in my belly also took me by surprise. His awareness of me—the way I affected him—caused my heart to jump in a way that was more excitement than fear. Which confused me, and made me wonder if maybe I really was as careless of my own safety as Jack seemed to think.

To cover these emotions—and also because it felt upside down for him to serve me—I took the cups from the tray and filled them. He reached for his, but instead of joining me at the table, he remained standing behind the chair.

"Knowing how uncomfortable you are around me," I said, "I'm even more grateful for what you did for me on the heath."

He shook his head. "That was a simple calculation."

I met his gaze, but he looked down.

"Much of what you say is hard for me to understand," I admitted, "but I think you must mean that you believed the monster"—*the other monster*—"was more likely to kill me than you were."

"You understand me perfectly, Miss Penrose."

"Well, it is the fact you *cared* that I am grateful for, sir. That was no calculation."

He smiled thinly into his tea. "As I said before, for the most part, I am still human."

There is still love . . . There is still frailness. And hope. The mixture of sweetness and sadness in him caused my chest to ache.

"But this other vampire perhaps is not?" I said.

His smile vanished like the steam from our cups. "As to that, my calculations have thus far proved useless. Because the blood was drained, the most likely explanation is that it is someone who suffers the same affliction. But I've never met with another family like ours, nor even read of one in a medical text. And as the constable has said, Mr. Roscoe's wound was like something made by an animal."

I couldn't bring myself to ask what kind of wound he himself might leave. Instead, I asked, "Have you looked for this other?"

Setting his empty cup down, he replied, "I have, but I've never caught more than the shadow I saw on the day you were attacked. Tonight the moon is full, a time when our thirst has always been stronger, and I will seek again."

"What will you do if you find him?"

He glanced at the casement; the heath below us was awash in autumn sunshine. Enough light came in that I could see what he meant about his eyes. It wasn't just the color that made them unusual; the black center circles were very large.

"He may be a hunter like my ancestor," he said. "Or it may be that he has only recently become a vampire. We are more dangerous—and less careful—at that time. In either case there may not be a possibility of reasoning with him, but I hope he will at least respect a request from one of his own kind to leave the area."

"Do you think he would hurt *you*?"

"Perhaps if he feels threatened."

"Then you must take care, Mr. Tregarrick."

He eyed me with disbelief. "*I* must." Laughing dryly, he said, "You are a wonder, Miss Penrose."

This caused a flare of temper. "Don't laugh at me, sir. I'm sure I must seem simple to you, and maybe those *less* simple are quick to forget a kindness. I don't find that admirable."

He sobered. "I assure you the last thing I find you is simple. Please forgive me. As a monster who's lived far too many years alone in a tower, I'm not used to anyone caring what happens to me."

"I find *that* sad, Mr. Tregarrick."

"So do I."

Drawing a breath to cool my heat, I lifted the teapot and refilled both our cups, his eyes following my every movement. In a more reasonable tone, I said, "Was it loneliness that made you come into The Magpie this week?"

He shook his head. "I came to terms with that long ago."

"What, then?"

Bending to lift his cup, he said, "As you might imagine after what you've heard today, this is not the first time a death has occurred on or near the estate. But many years have passed since anything happened to revive the old stories, and in these times, people are more uneasy about the estate than they are fearful of it. I worried Mr. Roscoe's death could change that."

"Well, it seems you were right to. But I still don't understand what that has to do with The Magpie."

"I went there to be seen. I thought it might stave off the whispers if people could see that I was no different from them."

I stared. "Do you have a looking glass?"

One corner of his lips lifted. "It was a failed experiment for many reasons, but mainly because I found it was too much for me. You, in particular, were too much for me."

My heart skipped. "Me!"

"Mr. Hilliard had told me that the woman who found my solicitor worked at The Magpie, but I didn't realize she was someone I knew. Though until you appeared at my table that day, I'd only known you by . . ." He trailed off, and I saw the muscles of his jaw tighten.

"By what, sir?" I asked, both curious and uneasy.

"By your smell."

I stared at him, truly horrified. My gaze dropped to my dress, and I tried to remember the last time I'd properly cleaned it. But then I remembered the frankincense. "You mean my blood."

"Not precisely. I can smell things most people cannot. I've known you for some time not by your name, but by the way you smell to me as you pass near my home. Part of that is indeed the maddening, warm, copper-and-salt smell of your blood. But the rest is . . . honey and almonds, like meadowsweet blossoms. I recognized it the moment I walked into the tearoom, and when you came out with my tea, I was flooded with it. I nearly choked on it."

My tongue had stuck to the roof of my mouth. Finally, I managed, "Not an *unpleasant* smell." Even then it was not lost on me that he'd made it clear how badly he thirsted for my blood, and I was somehow more worried that something about me might have disgusted him.

His brows lifted. "No, Miss Penrose."

My ears throbbed with the heavy thumping of my heart. My feelings were in such a jumble I could hardly sort them, like after a cat's been in the yarn basket. Some of what I felt was fear, but there was also the strange new excitement—part wonder, part anticipation. Which didn't seem the right kind of feeling to be having.

So I thought about Mr. Roscoe, and I reminded myself of what Mr. Tregarrick was.

Straightening in the chair, I said, "Who was it that you 'possibly' killed, Mr. Tregarrick?"

His lips pursed and his gaze lowered. I noticed his eyelashes were thick, and darker than his hair and brows.

"I believe I mentioned that our earliest days as vampires are the most dangerous," he said. "My father knew this, and when I came of age, I was confined in the chapel, and my thirst was managed in ways that risked no one's life."

His eyes came to my face, and I merely nodded, afraid if I interrupted him he might not go on.

"My memories of that time are fevered and fragmented. I couldn't even say for sure which are true recollections and which are memories of dreams. In my memory, I hunted. I let the bloodlust take me. The thrill of it was terrifying."

My breathing shallowed and my heart raced as I waited for more. But his attention seemed to have drifted inward. A tremor in my voice, I replied, "But you said you were confined to the chapel. They *must* have been dreams."

"I'm inclined to agree, but there is uncertainty on one point in particular." The blue-black of his eyes deepened even as the whites brightened. I held my breath. "For a decade of my life, my father paid a woman to teach me violin. I grew attached to her, I suppose because I never had a mother or sister. But she was also very beautiful, and when I was older, I fancied myself in love with her."

Warmth flooded my belly even as dread gnawed my heart.

"From the time of my change," he continued, "I never saw her again. When the feverish state finally left me, I asked my father about her, and he said that he'd released her from our employment for her own safety. But one of the dreams I had during that time—one I still have to this day—is a dream of . . ."

He turned his face from me to the fireplace. I remembered the smashed fiddle I'd seen upstairs.

Steadying my hands against my lap, I said, "You think you may have killed her."

His eyes closed, and his throat worked as he swallowed. "The dream feels *very* real."

His story had indeed given me the shock I'd hoped for. A shock strong enough that it *should* have jerked me out of my chair and sent me back home where I belonged.

"Even if . . ." I took a deep breath. "Even if it is as you fear, if all you've told me is true, you're not the same man now that you would have been back then. One who could be overtaken by such a savage urge."

His brow furrowed as he frowned. "I've never truly been tested since then. I've never been willing to take the risk."

"Until two days ago on the heath, when you were overtaken by a very different kind of urge."

He blinked. "Yes."

I couldn't hate him. I could barely *fear* him. Monster though he might be, he was also a man. One who had saved my life. One who had told me his dangerous secrets. And in this moment he seemed a softer, kinder man than my own brother.

But I wasn't likely to see him again, and I still wished to offer him what small help I could for what he'd done for me. *Even if he laughs at me.*

"What are you thinking about, Miss Penrose?" asked the vampire, his hand going to the back of the chair in front of him. For a moment I thought he might sit, but he didn't.

"About the things I see in tea leaves." He waited, puzzled but attentive, which gave me the courage to go on. Had he not told me *his* unlikely truth? "Sometimes what I see is the future."

"You practice tasseography."

The same word Mrs. Moyle had used. "I suppose I do, though I'd never done it purposely until recently. It just comes to me."

"What have you seen?"

"The day Mr. Roscoe died—was killed—I saw a dagger and a magpie in the leaves in his teapot. I was worried about it. Even mentioned it to Mrs. Moyle. But I didn't know what it meant. Then I found him on the road."

While he considered this, I watched his face for signs of disbelief. "It sounds as if you have a gift."

I gave a small shrug. "I think my mother may have secretly read tea leaves for people, for extra money. The day you came to The Magpie, I saw something in *your* teapot as I was emptying it." Which suggested that I hadn't looked on purpose, when in fact I had.

"What was it?"

"A wolf's head." His expression tightened. "Then, this morning, I saw the same in my own cup."

He looked truly grim now, and his voice was deeper as he said, "Your gift seems to be trying, without much success, to warn you about me."

"Or maybe to warn us both about this other vampire." His eyes narrowed, but I continued, "The stories about the Wolf of Roche Rock may have started because of your ancestors, but the people in the village are wrong to connect it with *you.*"

"While thus far I've found all your *reasoning* sound, I begin to worry about your judgment."

I folded my hands on the table. "Mr. Tregarrick, from what you've told me, both you and your father have always taken great pains to avoid harming anyone."

His thumb rubbed the chairback, his expression going cold as he replied, "You seem to have glossed over critical points in my story."

In my memory, I hunted. I let the bloodlust take me. The thrill of it was terrifying.

Shifting in my seat, I said, "I understand what you are. At least, as well as I may. But do you want to know what *I* think?"

His nostrils made a tiny movement—a slight flexing. "By all means, Miss Penrose."

I took a breath to steady my courage. "I think that you're a lonely man with a good heart who's living with an awful secret. A man who decided he didn't want to prey on his fellow creatures and found another way. You also risked everything you've worked for your whole life to save a woman who is nothing to you." I leaned forward. "And she's not about to forget it. I'm not strong or especially clever, Mr. Tregarrick, but now that I know your secret, it may be that I can help you."

He leaned forward, too, bracing himself against the chairback—and pinning me with his gaze. "What happened to you being afraid of me?"

Though my heart raced, I didn't allow myself to shrink from him. "That's what you wanted, isn't it? To frighten me so that I'd stay away. I'm not fool enough not to fear you, sir, but you didn't abandon me when *you* were afraid."

I could *see* his fear now, darkening his eyes and hollowing his cheeks. Both hands gripped the chairback, so hard his knuckles went white. With a sudden loud crack, the chairback snapped, and I scooted quickly away from the table, upsetting my own chair as I jumped to my feet.

"Go home, Mina," he growled, then strode toward the stairs.

Dismayed that I'd angered him—and by his sudden departure—I did something foolish. I reached out as he was passing and caught his sleeve.

He stopped cold, sucking in a hissing breath. I saw the tips of his wolf teeth against his bottom lip. I let go of him and drew back, not daring to breathe.

His head turned, his eyes meeting mine, and for a long moment, he just stared deep into me while my heart galloped. I fancied even my thoughts couldn't hide from him.

In a blur of movement, his hand came suddenly to close over my arm, and he dragged me against him. I let out a cry of panic as his other arm came around my waist. I tried to free myself by shoving at his chest, but he might as well have been a carved slab of marble.

His fingers dug into the hair at my neck, and I heard pins falling to the floor as he tugged my head back. He bent over me, and I whimpered as his breath puffed cold and dry against my throat. Then he drew a long breath through his nose, and I felt a shiver run down the length of his body, hard against mine.

Before my lips could form a plea for mercy, I felt those glittering white points against my throat like the prick of needles. My limbs and belly went warm, liquid, and pooling. My heartbeat slowed, and my body began filling with the most delicious heat and light. My hands melted limply to my sides. I drew in a long, shuddering breath and let it out again.

I had already closed my eyes and wanted nothing more than to sleep, yet a small part of me fought this surrender.

Wake, Mina!

"CRAWL IF YOU HAVE TO!"

Harker

I am lost.

I drifted in an ecstasy made up completely of her. A current of terrifying strength that pulled the both of us toward a dark fate.

Drink. Take her in. Make her yours.

I had tried the unripe seed of the poppy flower in an early formulation for my vital essence—another failed experiment, as it only increased my craving. But it was the only formulation that had brought me even close to feeling *this*.

Knees weakening in this languid bliss, I stumbled toward the table. Cups and saucers shattered on the floor as I swept her onto it. She might have escaped me in this state, but she had ceased to struggle. Even as I rode the gentle swells of satiation, a sob welled up inside me.

My downfall was only ever going to be *her*. The woman who had tormented me for two years now—the longest of my life. Coming to know her these past few days, watching her closely and listening to her voice, learning the lines of her face with my eyes, and of her body with *my* body as I carried her to the chapel . . . A part of me had hoped that putting an end to the mystery of her would break the spell.

You fool.

I felt a rustle of movement then. *She lives. It's not too late.* These thoughts wormed their way through my bloodlust, but for the life of me—*for the life of her*—I couldn't let go.

Her hand fumbled between us, soft and fragile as a moth's wing. Suddenly a searing pain tore through me.

I staggered back, hand going to my neck. I could smell my own charred flesh.

A sob heaved out of her as she sat up on the table edge, a gleaming curtain of red hair concealing the punctures in the silken flesh of her throat. She held something high in her fingers—a tiny silver cross with a delicate chain dangling from it.

"Bless you, Mina," I choked out, tears streaming down my cheeks.

When was the last time I'd had enough moisture to weep? When I buried the wasted husk of my father?

She stood on trembling limbs, managing a single step toward the door before falling to her knees.

"Get out!" I barked. "Crawl if you have to!"

I dug the heels of my palms into my eyes so I wouldn't see her moving along the floor like wounded prey. *Exactly what she is.*

I tried to ignore the whispers of her skirt and creak of the door.

I pushed back against every instinct that screamed I could have her again in half the space of a heartbeat.

DEADLY CLOSENESS

Two days later

I couldn't feel my body. Wasn't sure I even *had* a body. As if I'd stretched out on the ground, been covered over by soil and weeds, and not moved for a century.

Is this what it feels like to be dead?

I drew a breath, and slowly sensation worked its way out from my expanding chest to my arms and legs, fingers and toes tingling as they woke. I shifted slightly, and a deep muscle and bone ache loosed a quiet moan from my lips.

"Thank *heaven*."

My eyes fluttered open at the sound of the familiar voice. Mrs. Moyle sat in a chair beside the bed—my parents' bed. Jack's bed, now.

"Wh—" The breathy sound was all I got out before I started to cough.

Mrs. Moyle reached for a cloth on the bedside table, dipping it into a bowl before bringing it to my lips. I had never tasted anything better than those precious drops of cool water, even with the flavor of kitchen towel.

"Don't exert yourself, dear," said Mrs. Moyle. "Do you want more?"

I nodded, and she brought the cloth to my lips again.

"When you feel strong enough to sit up, we can try a glass."

"What happened?" I finally managed.

Her brow furrowed. "I want you to rest for now. We can talk about it when you've recovered a little. I'll put some broth on the stove for you."

As she was rising, I heard movement in the room beyond the folding screen, and my head turned—causing a stinging at my neck. Something pressed against my throat, and when I raised my fingers, I found a bandage had been wrapped around it.

My memory returned.

He attacked me. Held me close like a lover, then opened my throat and drank my blood. He had tried to warn me, but I wouldn't listen. I had struggled to imagine him as the fiend he'd described.

I don't need imagination now.

And yet somehow, I hadn't wanted him to stop. Even though I knew I would die. What he had done to me—it felt like drowning in pleasure. And delicious closeness.

Deadly closeness.

Only a tiny part of me had held on to life. Felt the cool silver of my mother's cross against my skin. The cross I'd worn because he'd asked me to.

Footsteps sounded, and Jack stepped around the screen, face lined from lack of sleep, eyes rimmed red from drink but open wide. He was my twin, and I could see both the worry and the relief in his expression.

"Why aren't you at the mine?" was the first question that bubbled up and out.

"Sunday, dear," Mrs. Moyle said quietly, coming back in.

"Was it *him*, Mina?" asked Jack in a low voice.

I tried clearing the gravel from my throat. "What?"

"Tregarrick. Was it him that attacked you?"

Jack *knew*? But how?

No. If he knew, he'd have said so. This was just more of the same nonsense from before. *Only it's no longer nonsense.*

I glanced at Mrs. Moyle, whose gaze moved warily between Jack and me.

I recalled how Mr. Tregarrick had said I'd have a decision to make once I was home. Now I understood what he meant. Would I reveal his secret? Everything had changed since then. But also, nothing had. He wasn't the one who'd killed Mr. Roscoe. He had almost killed *me*, but it wasn't the same.

How is it not the same?

"Mr. Tregarrick?" I said finally. "No, Jack. Of course not."

He frowned. "Then who was it?"

I moved to sit up, and Mrs. Moyle came and adjusted my pillow. "I don't know. I didn't see what attacked me."

I realized my mistake too late. His frown deepened. "You don't know it wasn't him, then."

"She's bound to be confused right now," said Mrs. Moyle, coming to my rescue. "Maybe if we let her rest—"

"He has to be stopped," snapped Jack, fixing flinty eyes on her. "Or are you happy for him to go after someone else?"

"I *am* feeling foggy," I said, trying to rescue *her* from the Penrose temper. "If you could tell me what happened—how I came to be here—it might help my memory." I'd told a pack of lies already. What was the difference?

Jack folded his arms over his chest. He was simmering, but at least he hadn't confronted me about leaving the cottage after he'd ordered me not to. *He's got his eyes on a bigger target.*

"You collapsed on the road in front of The Magpie, dear," replied Mrs. Moyle. I'd had wits enough to go to *her*, at least. Roche Rock was closer to town than it was to our cottage, and Jack would have been at the mine. "Father Kelly sent for Jack and the surgeon," she continued, "and we brought you home. Because of the wound in your neck, Mr. Hilliard was sent for, too."

"What did the surgeon say?" I asked, more worried for Mr. Tregarrick's sake than my own. How he must be hating himself now. Yet if I had just left him alone like he wanted, none of this would have happened.

"Mr. Perry doesn't quite know what to think, I'm afraid. Your wound, though in the same place, is very different from the solicitor's. It's neat and small. He doesn't believe it was made by an animal. Though there was no blood on your skin or clothing, the surgeon does believe you suffered blood loss as Mr. Roscoe did. The constable thinks you managed somehow to escape your attacker, else . . ."

"You'd be dead, too," said Jack, because Mrs. Moyle didn't seem up to it. "Probably he was just in less of a hurry this time."

I looked to Mrs. Moyle, hoping for a different answer, but she said, "The constable does seem to have the idea now that a man—one who is not well in his mind—may be responsible for both attacks."

I'd gone to Mr. Tregarrick to warn him about the gossip in the village, and instead of helping, I'd made things worse.

Grasping, I said, "Our mother used to talk about fairies on the heath, and she also used to say some fairies are vicious. I know we're not meant to believe in them these days, but—"

"Fairies!" Jack let out a snort, though as children he and I had both believed Mum's stories. If he'd been through what I had in the past week, he'd probably be less likely to scoff. "Might as well call it an actual wolf," he said, "like some of the dullards at the tavern. It's Tregarrick. Mark my words."

"But *why*, Jack? Why would he do such a thing?"

"You heard what Mrs. Moyle said. Because he's not right in the head! Probably runs in his family, and it's the reason for those old stories."

The fact that Jack was *so close* to right didn't keep me from wanting to have the last word about it. But before I could fire back, Mrs. Moyle, in a tone of motherly authority, said, "I don't think this is good for Mina right now. It's the Sabbath, Jack. Why don't you take your day of rest, and let me take care of your sister. We can talk of all this later."

He gave a dissatisfied grunt, but he went back around the screen without protest. I heard him clomping about for a minute or two, and then the front door opened and closed.

I sighed.

Mrs. Moyle gave me a smile tinged with worry, and then she excused herself to take the broth off the stove. I also heard her bolt the front door, a thing we rarely bothered to do.

Jack was going to be impossible now, and even kind Mrs. Moyle would forbid me from going to The Magpie until this mystery—though no mystery to *me*—was cleared up. I couldn't blame her for that, but I didn't know how I was going to just sit behind a bolted door while everyone was out trying to find someone to blame for the attacks. I was afraid of what would happen to Mr. Tregarrick.

Which means I'm *the one who's not right in the head.*

I also feared the attack might have left him more dangerous. He hadn't drunk blood in many years. Would his thirst be worse now? Or perhaps the blood might lessen his thirst; he'd made it clear his vital essence was a poor substitute.

Mrs. Moyle came back with a steaming cup, then set it on the bedside table before opening the window curtain partway to let in some daylight.

"I'm sorry about Jack," I said. "He wasn't always so . . ."

"Angry?"

"Mmm." My hand shook as I lifted the cup, but Mrs. Moyle had wisely filled it only halfway. The broth was salty and satisfying.

"I think people sometimes become angry when they feel powerless," she said. "First the two of you lost your parents, and two days ago he almost lost *you*. He has been worried sick about you, Mina."

"I suppose finding someone to blame makes him feel better." I couldn't help sounding bitter.

My employer eyed me keenly. "You can tell me the truth, you know."

Heart missing a beat, I met her gaze. She had been a trusted friend. In some ways, like a mother even. How I wished I *could* confide in her! But I feared *this* truth would be too much for her.

"There is more I could say," I replied carefully. "I've learned things in the past week that have shocked me, but they are very private and were shared only for my protection. One thing I'm sure of, though—Mr.

Tregarrick isn't going around attacking people on the heath any more than I am."

I held my breath as she continued to study me, then let it out as she nodded. "I believe you," she said. "But Mina, you almost died. And I can't help wondering now about your fall on the heath last week—there are things about *that* I know you've yet to tell me."

"Yes," I agreed, nodding sheepishly.

"Jack is right. This could happen to someone else."

"I know, and I believe Mr. Tregarrick himself has the best chance of preventing it."

Her brow furrowed. "Why would that be?"

What could I answer without exposing him, or terrifying *her*? I settled for, "He understands the creature that's doing it."

Eyes going wide, she said, "Why not tell the constable, then? Wouldn't it be better if they worked together?"

I sipped my broth and thought about that. "It likely would be, except I don't think Mr. Hilliard—or anyone else—would believe Mr. Tregarrick's story. And since they're already looking for a man who's not right in his mind, telling the constable would probably make matters worse. They might arrest him, and I don't know if they can find or stop the killer without him."

Mrs. Moyle rubbed her lips together, thinking. "I don't like the idea of them fixing on an innocent man, especially with the rumors already swirling about him." She looked at me. "You're sure of his story?"

"If he was the killer, I would be dead."

I thought about the ways he had convinced me of what he was. I hated to imagine what would happen to him if people in the village knew. I recalled the angry mob from my dream.

Mrs. Moyle shivered. "All right. I don't like this, but I know you've got a good head on your shoulders. It sounds as if Mr. Tregarrick has taken you into his confidence, and I don't believe confidences should be betrayed without very good reason. More than that, however—from the things you *have* told me, I've begun to suspect that he has been acting to protect you in recent days." She fixed her eyes on me. "But hear me, Mina. *You* are not the one to help him stop this killer."

"No," I agreed, because she was more right than she knew.

I slumped against the pillow, feeling warm and sleepy after the broth.

Mrs. Moyle came and took my cup. "Try to rest now, dear. There'll be a joint of beef for dinner to strengthen your blood."

When next I woke, it was to the aroma of fresh bread and boiled beef. Feeling lonely and confined, I made my way to sitting up and then swung my legs down. My heart labored after only this small movement.

When I stood, everything hurt, like I'd been walking for days without a rest. Flashes of memory came to me then—of a slow and creeping journey between the chapel and The Magpie. I could feel the bruises on my knees from the times I'd stumbled and fallen. For stretches of it, I had crawled. The short walk had taken *ages.* I remembered how I'd fixed on the idea of reaching The Magpie. *Only a little farther now. Soon you can sleep.* Driven by fear of the monsters of Roche Rock.

With a shaky breath, I smoothed my shift and wrapped up in my shawl before making my way slowly out to the kitchen.

Mrs. Moyle fussed to see me out of bed, and when I refused to go back, she made me sit down at the table and drink a small glass of brandy, which she'd brought from home—also "to strengthen my blood." I recalled brandy was somehow involved in Mr. Tregarrick's vital essence, so perhaps there was something to it. It did warm me.

When dinner was ready, the two of us ate without Jack. I tried to imagine where he'd gone. The Wolf's Head was closed on the Sabbath. The sun would set in an hour or so, and I worried about him walking home after dark. I worried that his suspicions about Mr. Tregarrick might have taken him onto the estate.

Though I felt stronger and steadier after the meal, Mrs. Moyle wouldn't let me help her clear up. After she'd finished, I tried to send her home.

"I can't leave you here alone, Mina," she protested.

"I'm much better," I told her, determined, "and you have a business to see to." I'd learned over dinner that she'd been taking care of me so Jack wouldn't have to miss work (that was her stated reason, though more likely she'd been unsure whether he was up to it). "Jack will be home soon, and his dinner's made, thanks to you. I promise I'll go back to bed."

She eyed me, unsure. "You must also promise you won't try to come to The Magpie tomorrow."

I agreed. Even if I felt up to it, I knew better than to test Jack's patience right now. If he could only look past his own stubbornness and pride, he'd see The Magpie was probably a safer place for me than anywhere else. Our cottage was right on the edge of the heath.

"All right," she said with a sigh. "But I'll come back in the morning before opening, just to make sure all is well."

"You haven't walked here alone, have you?"

She smiled. "Ghost escorted me."

Mrs. Moyle had a cart she used when she couldn't get purchases delivered. It was pulled by a dapple-gray gelding—a kind old gentleman called Ghost—that her husband had kept for her at the livery. She loved him like a pet, and he was still boarded there by the new owner.

"Well, go *now*, then," I said. "Before the sun sets. And ask the stable boy to see you home."

Reluctantly she went, and though I didn't usually like being alone in the cottage, this evening it was a relief to have time to think over everything without having to answer more questions. *Or tell more lies.*

The master of Roche Rock had not been out of my thoughts for a single moment since I'd woken. The attack should have made me afraid of him in a way his words had failed to, but instead, I continued to worry about him. Besides hating himself, he might be wondering whether I was alive or dead. And he might be wondering how long it would be before the lawmen came for him.

When I finally went back to bed as I'd promised, my busy mind wouldn't let me sleep. I kept remembering the attack, and what stayed with me was not a nightmare of blood and pain—there had *been* no pain beyond the second it took for his teeth to pierce my skin. What my mind chose to dwell on instead was his arms crushing me against him. His hand cradling the back of my head. His hair tickling my throat and, most of all, his lips against me. I had never felt so alive as when I was dying in his arms.

God help me.

In the moments that I did manage to push all of this from my mind, I went back to wondering what Jack was up to. Sundays he usually drank at home and slept. Sometimes he would take care of things around the cottage that I couldn't do for myself. I kept imagining him appearing at the chapel door to confront Mr. Tregarrick, and my stomach tied itself in knots. How would the master of Roche Rock respond to such a meeting? Again I worried that drinking my blood might have worsened the vampire's cravings.

At last, I got up and dressed. I was in no fit state to go searching for my twin, but I could at least have a look around outside before the light was gone. Sometimes he stood between our cottage and the Budges' place smoking a pipe and jawing with Billy. Or he might be working on something in the shed out back.

As I started for the door, someone knocked on it, and my heart skipped.

I laid a hand against the wood and bent close. "Who's there?"

"Roger Carew, miss. Agent for Mr. Tregarrick. I have a letter for you."

Now my heart leaped into my throat. I drew back the bolt and opened the door.

A smartly dressed gentleman stood outside, holding the reins of a sleek chestnut horse. His other hand gripped the basket I'd carried to Roche Rock. He held it out to me, and inside I saw a folded paper resting atop a book. The letter had flowing handwriting on the outside. Though I hadn't read a great deal of handwriting, Mrs. Moyle sometimes wrote out lists and instructions, and I was able to make out my name—*Miss Mina Penrose*.

"Thank you, sir," I said, taking the basket.

"I'm to read it to you, if it's needed," said Mr. Carew. I studied him, but his face wore no expression.

Lifting my chin slightly, I replied, "That won't be necessary."

He touched his hat brim and got on his horse.

"Mr. Carew," I called, and he looked down.

"You'll let him know I'm all right?"

The agent touched his hat again and then clucked to his horse.

Gripping the basket handle, palms damp and shaking, I stepped out the front door. It was all I could do not to take up the letter at once, but I looked up and down the road as I'd intended, if for no other reason than it wouldn't do for Jack to catch me reading it.

A cart full of carrots and swedes rattled by, a boy in the back lifting a hand to wave as it passed. Other than that, the road was as deserted as I might expect on Sunday evening just after dinnertime.

I wondered whether the whole village had heard about what happened to me. Mr. Hilliard had shown he wasn't one to spread tales, but Mrs. Moyle said I'd been found in front of the tearoom.

Most likely everyone knows. Afraid I might meet a neighbor, I quickly ducked back inside.

I set the basket next to the door, slipped the letter into my pocket, and went to boil water for tea. A cool head would serve me best.

Once I'd dosed a steaming cup with plenty of milk and sugar for courage, I stepped out the back door and called for Jack, in case he might be in the shed. No reply came, and I sat down on the old milking stool under the apple tree. The sun had set, but the sky behind Roche Rock was the color of a pearl. I had a little time yet.

I drank my tea and watched a hare cross the downs with its long, rolling lope. I chatted absently at Jenny and the hens while the fresh air soothed my nerves.

Finally, I took the letter from my pocket.

> Miss Penrose,
>
> Mr. Carew has been watching your cottage for a time when your brother and employer might both be away. He has assured me that you live, and that good Mrs. Moyle appears to be staying with you. I hope you will forgive me this trespass. I know you cannot forgive me for the other, nor would I wish you to. I will never forgive *myself.*
>
> I've instructed Mr. Carew to deliver this letter into your hands only, so if you are reading it, you are well enough to answer the door, and I thank heaven for it. Nay, I thank *you* for it. For granting my wish that you wear the cross, as well as for finding the strength to wield it against me. I ask that you grant me one last favor, though I have no right to. Please keep to your cottage, unless in the company of others, until I am able to secure the village of Roche against the present threat.
>
> Finally, though you don't need my permission, I will give it: You are free to share what you now know—about myself and about the other—with anyone you see fit, if indeed you have not done so already.
>
> When the present threat has been removed, if I am still master of Roche Rock, and you feel secure enough to walk again on the heath, know that I will sense your passing and will be remembering what time

we were given to become acquainted. Friends are a luxury my affliction has denied me.

I wish you good health and a long life with all my heart.

Sincerely,

HT

Was it some kind of spell he'd cast over me that, instead of feeling angry for what he'd done, my heart wrenched over the aching loneliness behind all his words?

No. I couldn't see how *anyone* who read such a letter could think him truly a monster.

I folded the paper and put it away. Before going inside, I cast a last glance out at the gentle landscape—and froze. The mist had risen thick as twilight came on, but I was certain there was something moving on the heath.

As if feeling my gaze, the thing halted—and seemed to watch me back.

IN THE LEAVES

"Mina?"

I jumped. Jack had come up behind me from around the side of the house. I had bolted the front door, and he'd probably been knocking.

"What are you doing out here?" he said.

"I . . ." I glanced back to the heath, straining to see as the mist drifted. The thing I'd glimpsed—or thought I'd glimpsed—hadn't seemed to be a person. It had moved in a low, rolling way, almost like a hare, though it had been much larger.

"Mina."

I turned to Jack, pressing a hand against the pocket where I'd tucked Mr. Tregarrick's letter. "Just—just getting some air. Where have you been? Mrs. Moyle made dinner, but I didn't know when you'd come back, so we ate already."

I was practiced at knowing how much he'd drunk by his eyes and his speech. He was more sober than I'd seen him in a while, if you didn't count mornings, when he was peaked and ill-tempered from the previous night's drinking.

"At church," he mumbled.

I stared, thinking he must be joking. But he looked troubled. "What were you doing at church?"

He frowned. "It's the Sabbath, an't it?"

Now I *knew* he wasn't serious. When our parents were alive, we went every Sunday. Since then, I'd made it to services only once or twice a month, and really only to visit our parents' graves. But Jack never went. He said he "could sleep through the morning at home and be more comfortable, too, thank you very much."

"Fine," I muttered, "don't tell me."

Opening the back door, he said, "You come on in. It's not safe for you to be out here alone."

His voice was gentle enough, but I felt the distance between us more keenly than ever.

I followed him inside—with one glance back to the heath—and then went to reheat his supper. As I set it before him, he took a bottle of gin from his coat pocket. I knew he was sober because he actually poured it into a glass.

After waking rested and stronger the next morning, I baked pasties for Jack's lunch and for Mrs. Moyle, since she had promised a visit. When she came, she drank a cup of tea and stayed long enough to look me over. Declaring me much improved ("The color is back in your freckles"), she returned to open The Magpie.

Once she'd left, I curled in a chair with the mending while my thoughts spun in circles. In bed last night, I had all but convinced myself the thing I'd seen on the heath had simply been a deer that the twilight, the fog, and my imagination had turned into something else. Yet this morning my mind kept returning to it. I'd read Mr. Tregarrick's letter again and again. *Until I am able to secure the village of Roche against the present threat,* he'd said. He was still searching for the other vampire. Might that be what I had seen?

With every passing moment, it became plainer that I wouldn't be able to tolerate sitting quietly inside all day, as Jack had admonished. I could see through the window that the weather was fine. I could rest outdoors as well as in. *And* I could keep an eye out for the creature from last night. If I saw it again, I would find a way to get word to Mr.

Tregarrick. Mrs. Moyle might know Roger Carew, and if she didn't, she might be able to ask around.

Just as I was putting away my sewing things, there came a knock at the door, and my heart bounced. Had Mr. Carew come back? I called through the door, but the voice that answered belonged to Mr. Hilliard.

My da once told me that only people who had something to hide were afraid of the constable. I supposed I was one of those people now, because I had to wipe sweat from my palms before I opened the door.

"Happy to see you so recovered, Miss Penrose," he said, removing his hat. His gaze lowered to the bandage around my neck. "May I come in?"

"Yes, sir," I replied, stepping back to admit him.

I invited him to sit at the table, and I put on the kettle for tea. Mainly to have something to do so he wouldn't notice how nervous I was.

"No need for that," he said. "Come and sit down. I just have a few questions for you."

I took off the kettle and joined him.

He set his diary on the table and took out a pencil. His brows lifted. "I hate that this has happened, lass. Especially when I told you I thought the danger had passed. I want to apologize for my mistake."

"You aren't to blame, sir. It's a strange case."

"That it is." He studied me more closely, and I swallowed. "Jack tells me that when you woke, you couldn't remember what happened to you. Have you remembered anything since then?"

My fingers knotted in my lap. This was the moment. I could choose to tell him the truth, or from this point on, I'd be heaping lie on top of lie. I shuddered to think someone else might die because I didn't speak when I had the chance. Yet unless I told the constable *all* of Mr. Tregarrick's story, he wouldn't understand. Even understanding, he wasn't likely to believe.

Flattening my palms on my skirt, I said, "No, sir. I'm sorry."

He sighed. "Are you able to tell me where you were when it happened? If not, the last place you do remember."

"Last I remember, I was walking to the village." As something I did often, this seemed the least likely to raise an eyebrow.

"On the road between Roche and Carbis, like Mr. Roscoe."

"Yes, sir."

"Did you see anyone else on the road?"

I shook my head. "Not that I recall."

He wrote in his diary, and I reached, absently, to touch the bandage at my neck.

His gaze darted up. "Does it pain you?"

"Hardly at all."

"The wound is very clean compared to Mr. Roscoe's. It's the damnedest thing." He frowned. "Begging your pardon."

I nodded and held my tongue. More talking could only get me into trouble at this point.

"We now think it most likely a *man* attacked both you and Mr. Roscoe."

"Yes, sir, Jack told me."

"What do *you* think, Miss Penrose?"

Steady, now. "I guess that makes sense, though I can't imagine why a man would do such a thing."

"Nor can I. I don't think any sane man *would*. I think we're looking for a man who's not well. Maybe even a medical man, by the efficiency with which he went about his business."

I shifted in my chair. "And Mr. Roscoe?"

The constable grunted. "That's the question. Maybe our killer was in more of a hurry the first time."

"I wish there was more I could tell you, Mr. Hilliard." That at least was not a lie, unlike almost everything else I'd said to him.

"There *is* another question you might be able to shed some light on." I nodded faintly, heart thumping. "I arrived here after you were brought home, while Mrs. Moyle and the surgeon were in with you. I tried to speak to Jack, but . . ." He hesitated. "Well, the truth of it is he smelled of gin and had his temper up. I had trouble following his reasoning, but he seemed to believe it was Mr. Tregarrick that attacked you. Do you know what would make him think that?"

Heat blooming in my cheeks, I replied, "I'm not sure reasoning has much to do with it, sir. Jack has been listening to gossip at the tavern. Since Mr. Roscoe, people have been telling the old stories about a Wolf of Roche Rock."

The constable's brow clouded. "I've heard some of that gossip myself. It's the opposite of helpful."

"Yes, sir."

I took a slow breath as he made a few more notes, thinking we must surely be coming to the end of the interview. I was unprepared when he looked up and said, "You don't seem very rattled, Miss Penrose."

"Rattled, sir?" I knew what he meant, but I gained a moment to think by pretending that I didn't.

"Someone tried to kill you. Aren't you frightened?"

"Yes, sir. I certainly am." And that was no more or less than the truth. I was afraid of this other vampire, and I was afraid of Mr. Tregarrick being blamed for his crimes.

"I also wonder about your coming and going as usual after finding a man murdered next to the road. Though I know it was likely due, in part, to my faulty counsel, I won't lie to you—I find it surprising."

I sat a moment, considering my words. There were reasons that I *could* share with the constable.

"Well, sir, I have a job, just as you do. Jack has been after me to give it up, but the cottage is lonely with my parents gone. And ever since the night I found Mr. Roscoe, unwelcome thoughts come into my head when I'm alone."

Mr. Hilliard's features softened, and he nodded. "All right, Miss Penrose. One last question and I'll let you rest."

He set down his pencil, reached into his waistcoat pocket, and drew out something that glittered in his fingers. *Mum's cross!*

Placing it on the table, he said, "You were holding this when they found you. The surgeon had to pry it from your fingers. Do you know where it came from?"

"Aye, sir. It was my mother's."

"I see." He looked disappointed, if not surprised, and it occurred to me he might have hoped it belonged to my attacker. "I didn't notice you wearing it the last two times we spoke."

My heart skipped. "I took to wearing it after . . . after Mr. Roscoe."

His brows knit. "For protection?"

I began to feel Mr. Hilliard was rather good at his job, saving his trickiest questions until he was about to take his leave.

"You'll think me foolish."

"I think no such thing, Miss Penrose. It seems that it worked. The clasp is broken, as if you yanked at the chain. Do you remember doing that?"

"I don't, sir."

I recalled how Mr. Tregarrick had suddenly let me go, bounding back, hand flying to his neck where the cross had touched him. Did it mean a vampire was a kind of demon?

Does a demon tell you his weakness and then thank you for using it?

Whatever else he was, I didn't believe for a moment Mr. Tregarrick was evil.

Mr. Hilliard now closed his diary and slipped it back into his coat pocket. "I'll leave you now. I thank you for your time."

I walked him to the door, and as he was going, he said, "I can't help feeling there are things you aren't telling me, Miss Penrose. I know Jack can be hotheaded, and maybe that's the reason for your reticence. But if you do think of anything that might help us catch this killer, for everyone's sake, I hope you will send for me. Jack needn't know."

My hands were trembling, and I clasped them together. "I will, sir, thank you."

He studied me a moment longer, maybe hoping I'd say more. Then he put on his hat and went out to his waiting horse and gig.

I closed the door and fell against it.

I am completely useless. I couldn't help Mr. Tregarrick. I couldn't help Mr. Hilliard. I couldn't go to my job. All I could do was sit here and wait, hoping no one else would be attacked.

I might go mad.

Breathing a heavy sigh, I straightened, then noticed my basket resting beside the door—with the book inside! Mr. Tregarrick's letter had so taken up my notice that I had completely forgotten about it.

In the Leaves: A Primer on Tasseography, by Jane Rochester.

I snatched up the book and went to the stove to put the kettle on again. Flipping through the pages while I waited for the boil, I saw the book had many sketches of sample readings. *Dear Mr. Tregarrick!*

I placed book, pot, and cup on a tray, carried them out back, and set them on the milking stool, shooing away the curious animals. After dragging over a rickety chair that Jack hadn't gotten around to mending, I sat down in a sunny spot.

While my tea steeped, I continued paging through the book. The author turned out to be the woman Mrs. Moyle had mentioned—the one who ran the school for young ladies in Yorkshire. Mrs. Rochester wrote that no special steps were required for reading tea leaves, but that "simple spells can amplify your efforts, focus your intention, and yield more accurate results." I was sure Mum hadn't learned from a book, but without her here, this was the next best thing.

I poured tea into my cup without straining it, and following Mrs. Rochester's instructions, I took hold of the handle and spun the cup three times, chanting, "Leaves of tea, reveal to me whatever I most need to see."

Then I drank almost to the bottom before flipping the cup over onto the saucer to drain out the remaining liquid. Holding my breath, I righted the cup.

No shapes jumped out at me this time. The author had mentioned that people should only read their own leaves if they had no one else to do it. It was hard to be clearheaded about your own cup. I desperately hoped not to find more wolves, and I figured this was exactly what Mrs. Rochester meant, so I tried to pretend I was reading someone else's cup.

Turning it this way and that, I picked out two clumps that held promise. One was so clearly a cross that I couldn't believe I hadn't seen it right away. The other looked like a candle.

At the back of the book was a list of symbols with their meanings. They came with this advice at the top: *Correspondences are malleable. One cup's death warning is another cup's promise of a fresh start. Be guided by your intuition.*

According to Mrs. Rochester's list, a candle meant hope, or finding your way in the dark. Finally something encouraging! But then the cross . . . there was no happy way to read that. Trouble on its way, or suffering, or even death. Or it might mean a sacrifice would need to be made.

I looked at my farmyard family. Jenny was nosing a half-rotten apple while the hens searched out insects among the fallen leaves. "But it doesn't tell me what to *do*," I complained to them.

The red hen, Rosie, let out a series of clucks that were easy enough to read: *If you are going to idle about in the garden, you could at least bring stale breadcrumbs or table scraps.*

Aware that it was silly to expect so much from a quick skimming of the text, I sank back and paged to the book's beginning. The important thing was that, thanks to Mr. Tregarrick, I had a place to start. And I didn't feel so alone.

Though my seat was both hard and unsteady, I somehow managed to doze off before I'd read more than a page or two. I suppose I hadn't fully recovered from my ordeal yet. I woke to the sound of anxious clucking, my neck sore and my chin dipping toward my chest. The book had slipped to the ground and Jenny now nibbled at one corner, but she raised her head suddenly and let out a bleat. I followed her gaze beyond the garden.

A patch of fog had risen no more than five or six yards away. Inside it, something was *moving*. I could only make out what looked like antlers. Or more like tree branches. Long and twiggy, spreading like a fan from the head of a tall shadow. Too tall for beast *or* man. Too tall for the creature I'd seen yesterday—yet I couldn't help feeling I was seeing that creature again.

My skin went cold and clammy, and I jumped up. The hens began squawking, down feathers flying loose as their wings beat the air. Rosie fled back toward the coop, the others flapping after her. Jenny, too, gave another fearful bleat and ran around one corner of the cottage.

Then I noticed two small rounds of fiery light.

My courage fled. I snatched up my book and ran inside, bolting the back door.

ST. GOMONDA

From the cottage window I looked for the creature, holding my breath as my heart pounded in my ears. But the branch-antlers were gone, the fog already thinning.

I remembered the night I'd found Mr. Roscoe, and the movement I'd noticed beyond the wall. Then, too, I thought I'd seen antlers. Might this creature have had something to do with Mr. Roscoe's death? Mr. Tregarrick thought another vampire had done it, but what if he was wrong?

He needs to know about this.

I would write to him. If Mrs. Moyle came again to check on me, I would put a letter in her hands for Mr. Carew. If she didn't know him, she might ask around at the tearoom.

This decided, I sat down at the dining table with one of Mrs. Moyle's notebooks and a stub of pencil, which she'd given me to practice my letters. Yet it wasn't long before I was sighing in frustration. Reading was one thing, but writing—I could put simple things to paper, but a letter like the one Mr. Tregarrick had written was beyond me. At last I settled for:

I saw a creature on the heath. There is more to tell.
Send your man to me and I will tell him.
M

I folded the note, put it in my pocket, and started on supper.

Just as I was pulling bacon-and-egg pie from the oven, the front door rattled. Next someone pounded on the door.

"It's me, Mina," called Jack.

I hurried over and opened it, eyeing him as he came inside. Though he smelled of ale, he was steady enough on his feet. I was relieved to see him home earlier than usual. Thus far he'd heeded my plea to come home before dark about as well as I'd heeded his to stay indoors.

"Supper's ready," I said in an easy voice. "Still hot, too."

"All right." His tone was even, but his brows knit.

I cut two thick wedges of pie and set them on the table. As I took my seat across from him, he said, "They found another one today."

My eyes darted to his face, belly going cold. "Another *what*?"

"Another body. This one down near Coldvreath."

"Oh, Jack. Who?"

He shook his head, cutting into the pie with his fork. "Don't know yet. No one the constable could identify right away."

I waited for him to answer the question burning in my mind, but it seemed he was going to make me ask. "Was it—were they . . ."

"Same kind of attack as the first one. But they say it happened before the solicitor, by the state of the body."

"Who found it?" I asked thinly, feeling sick.

"A fella from Coldvreath. Friend of old Couch's—mushroom hunter, I guess. His dog dug it up in some leaves and loose soil on the edge of Tregarrick's property."

I took an unsteady breath. "What did Mr. Hilliard say?"

Jack's expression was grim. "That he'd asked the Police Watch Committee to send more men to look for the killer. Which is a waste of time, since we all know who it was."

"Jack, you can't still think—"

I broke off as his gaze landed hard on mine. "I don't know what it is with you and him, Mina, but you need to start facing facts."

"'Facts,' Jack? That people around here are too simple to do anything but suspect a man who's minded his own business for years, all because of some old stories?"

His eyes flashed. "You calling me 'simple' now? You're better than us, smarter than us, now you've read a few books and met the lord of the manor, is that it?"

"Maybe that's *exactly* it!" I snapped, my bloody temper getting the better of me again. It mattered not at all that his "detective work" wasn't too far wrong. I took a deep breath, simmering down, while he scowled at his plate. I could see that his anger was masking real hurt over my words.

Softening, I said, "I didn't mean that, Jack. I just don't see the point in making up our minds about anything—dragging a man's name through the dirt—until Mr. Hilliard has had a chance to do his job."

He glared at me. "By the time Hilliard does his job, somebody else will be dead."

I sighed. Again, he wasn't necessarily wrong. "I just don't understand what makes you think you know more than the police."

"This isn't London, Mina. *The police* around here are no different from the rest of us, and there is no reason at all why their opinions should count for more."

"How about the opinions of the only people who've actually had a conversation with Mr. Tregarrick, then? Me—who, I'll remind you, he was kind enough to walk home after an accident on the heath—and the constable—who, if he thought Mr. Tregarrick a murderer, would have him in jail already."

Shaking his head, Jack grumbled, "We're talking in circles." He gave his plate a shove, got up from the table, and started for the door.

"Where are you going?" He yanked open the door without answering, and I panicked. "Jack, don't! It's not—" *Safe.* The door closed on the end of my sentence.

I got up and started stacking the dishes, knocking them loudly together out of frustration—and fear. If I'd said that I believed a creature on the heath was responsible for the killings, would it have stopped him? Then I recalled that I'd suggested something very like that yesterday, and he'd laughed at me. *Fairies! Might as well call it an actual wolf, like some of the dullards at the tavern.* Maybe he'd even accuse me of making up a story to protect "the lord of the manor."

It occurred to me that Mr. Tregarrick and I were living in a world apart from regular folk. One Mum would likely have believed in. Jack and I had scoured our corner of the parish looking for fairies without success, and we'd grown out of believing in her stories. Then I'd started seeing warnings in teapots. Then I'd met a vampire.

After clearing away supper, I went up to the loft with a candle and *In the Leaves*. But I was too plagued by worries to follow it. I reached under my pillow, where I'd tucked Mr. Tregarrick's letter and the note I'd written him. It began to feel even more urgent that I get word to him. None of us would be safe until the killer was stopped. And though I had been fussed over and warned to take care since Mr. Roscoe's death, Jack was likely more at risk.

It was late when he pounded on the door to be let in. After he'd finally fallen into bed, I went back up and slept.

In the morning, once Jack had left, I took up Mum's cross and removed the broken chain; I threaded a thin purple ribbon through in its place and tied it round my neck. I went then for the paring knife, still in my basket, and tied a handkerchief around the blade before slipping it in my pocket with the note for Mr. Tregarrick. Finally, I put on my shawl.

I thought I might meet Mrs. Moyle on her way to our cottage, and if not, I'd go on to The Magpie and speak to her about Mr. Carew.

As I opened the door, I found Mr. Hilliard climbing down from his gig, and my stomach lurched.

"Miss Penrose," he called. "You aren't going out, are you?"

"Only for some air, sir," I answered, wary. How many interviews with him would it take for me to get crossways with one of my own lies?

He joined me at the door, and I said, "Jack told me someone else has been found."

He nodded, and I could see how tired he was. "May I come inside a moment?"

I stepped back in and held the door open for him.

"I won't keep you," he said, "but Jack spoke to me at the mine. He said he met Mr. Tregarrick recently, right here at your door."

Oh, Jack. "That's true, sir."

"Can you tell me about that?"

Though faint, I could hear accusation in his voice. "Jack seems to think Mr. Tregarrick is going around murdering people. I think that idea was inspired by old stories, and it seems pretty foolish to me."

The constable's eyebrow lifted. "That may be, Miss Penrose. But right now I want to hear about anything unusual, and Mr. Tregarrick leaving his estate and mixing in with the rest of us is exactly that. Why did the gentleman come to your cottage?"

I matched his raised brow with one of my own. "He walked me home because I fell on the heath and hit my head. He wanted to make certain I got here safely. A man with murder in his heart, to be sure."

"I'd ask that you dispense with the sarcasm, Miss Penrose."

My face warmed. *This isn't helping, Mina.* I took a deep breath. "I'm sorry, Mr. Hilliard. Jack and I have been arguing over it, is all."

"I understand. Just try to answer my questions as straightforwardly as you can. When you say 'on the heath,' do you mean on the Tregarrick estate?"

"Aye, sir. I cross it sometimes, same as other people."

"Whereabouts did you have your fall?"

"Near that pool with the big stone slab, between here and the chapel."

"Mmm." He scribbled in his diary. "That slab, and the piles of smaller stones right around there, are all that's left of Tregarrick manor."

I eyed him with interest. "I always wondered where the ruins of that old place were. And why they never built another one."

"As the story goes, the family was beset by hardship after that and didn't have the spirit for it. But it's so many years ago, it's hard to know for sure. Anyhow, what was it caused you to fall?"

Without thinking, I reached up and fiddled with Mum's cross, and the constable's gaze followed. I let it go and shrugged. "I got hung up in my skirts stepping down from the slab, and I bloodied my head." I touched the spot where the lump had been, still tender, and again his eyes followed. "Mr. Tregarrick happened to be nearby and came over to help."

"Did you have much conversation with him?"

"Only a little. But he seemed a kind man."

"Did you talk about Mr. Roscoe?"

I hesitated, considering my words. "I told him how sorry I was about what happened. I could see how it weighed on him."

He nodded and continued writing.

"Mr. Hilliard?" He looked up from his diary. "I'm worried about Mr. Tregarrick. From what Jack's told me, people are making up their minds about him. I worry about what might happen to him, but also about what might happen to *us* if everybody decides it was him and stops looking for the real killer."

He studied me closely. "You seem pretty convinced he's innocent."

"I know I'm nobody, but I don't believe he'd do such a thing."

He closed the book and put it away. "On the contrary. As a victim yourself, and as one of very few people who've ever actually spoken to the man, I take your thoughts on the matter quite seriously. I'll leave you now, but if you have any more encounters with Mr. Tregarrick, I want to know about it."

"Yes, sir." On impulse, I said, "Are you going the way of the village, by any chance, Mr. Hilliard?"

"I am, yes."

Did I really have the cheek to ask him to take me to The Magpie? What if Jack had told him I was barred from going there?

Instead, I found myself saying, "With all that's happened, I was thinking I might like to speak to Father Kelly. If you're not in too much of a rush . . ."

I trailed off as he nodded. "I'll take you. I saw him out on the grounds on my way here."

Father Kelly could quite often be seen among the gravestones at St. Gomonda. So often that Mum had believed he spoke to spirits.

The constable took his watch from his pocket. "I believe it's a while yet until the tearoom opens. Do you think Mrs. Moyle would be willing to run you home?"

"I'm sure she would, sir." I knew Mrs. Moyle would be glad to hear I'd spoken with the priest. And I'd have my chance to give her the note for Mr. Carew—which was of course the real reason I wished to go to the village.

My hand went to my hip, steadying the knife in my pocket as the constable helped me up to the gig. A few minutes later we rolled to a stop in front of St. Gomonda, and he bade me good day.

The parish church was pretty as a picture, built of weathered moorstone and surrounded by graves from as far back as 1700—likely older ones, too, whose stones you couldn't read. Mum and Da were buried here, and though I'd only used the church as an excuse for coming to town, I felt a sudden desire to visit them.

After passing the church entrance and bell tower, I made my way to the back of the yard, where the simpler folk were buried in the hazel grove. There were more yellow and orange leaves than green now, and nut husks littered the root-studded, rocky ground.

I soon found the plain wooden crosses marking their graves, low mounds covered over with grasses and leaves.

Tears welled, and my voice broke as I spoke to Mum, who had been so much in my thoughts over the last week. "I wish you were here to help me talk to Jack. And to teach me about the tea leaves."

A hazelnut dropped, landing in my hair. I glanced up to see a red squirrel, with its funny ear tufts and fluffy tail, skittering along a branch. Da once said there were hardly any red squirrels left, and it was lucky to see one. *Heaven knows I need it.*

Often when I came here, I found myself wondering whether I'd ever have anyone besides Jack in my life. Whether I'd ever marry. After a couple of years working at The Magpie, I wasn't sure where I belonged anymore. When I thought of the change from keeping house for my brother the clay miner to my husband the clay miner, it seemed like hardly any change at all.

Maybe it felt different when you were a wife. Was it possible to find a man suited to my station in life who wouldn't forbid me from working outside our home, or view my books as idleness? Even if it was, babes followed marriage, and they would leave no time for such things.

Hearing leaves rustling, I turned to find Father Kelly approaching in his black coat and shovel hat.

"Mina," he said, looking relieved, "how happy it makes me to see you recovered from your ordeal." He was a handsome man with crinkles about the eyes, his collar bright against dark-brown skin, and a neat beard that showed traces of white.

"Good day, Father," I said with a bow of my head. "I want to thank you for your help that day."

"I'm grateful I was nearby and able to give it." He smiled. "It's good to see you at church again."

My cheeks warmed. "I suppose it has been some weeks since I came to service."

"And more since your brother came. Yet just yesterday he, too, made an appearance. Our present troubles seem to be returning many in the parish to God."

Jack had been to church after all! "He told me he had been here," I said. "I confess I didn't believe him. I suppose he came to visit our parents, too?"

Father Kelly clasped his hands in front of him. "I found him in the nave praying for your recovery, and we had some conversation."

"He . . . ?" I stared. *Praying* for me? "Forgive me, Father, but that doesn't sound much like Jack."

The priest's expression was gentle. "He was very worried about you, Mina. But I imagine like most people right now, he also came for reassurances we don't have a devil among us."

This sounded more like it. "You told him we don't?"

By his look, I knew he thought that I, too, was hoping to be reassured. What I really hoped was that he'd talked some sense into Jack.

"It's hard to deny that a man who could do such things does seem a kind of devil," he said. "But I urged your brother to trust the constable and his men, and to pray for God to use them as his instruments."

This gave me some relief, though I had my doubts as to whether the priest's advice would be heeded. I imagined Jack had stopped believing in God granting prayers the first day Da had taken him to the mines. I thought I knew what he'd really come here about.

"I suppose he asked if you knew any old stories about Roche Rock." I couldn't bring myself to name Mr. Tregarrick.

"He did, in fact. And he asked some questions about the wall painting in the bell tower."

I frowned, trying to think what he meant.

"The one of St. Gomonda slaying the demon," he continued. "It was a good opportunity for a lesson about the stories of the saints, and how those stories have been preserved, in part, to remind us that righteousness and true devotion to God are the best armor that we can wear."

I recalled the painting now. Da had pointed it out to Jack and me once when we were children, though what was left of it was too high for us to see very well. I had no memory of anything he'd said about it. Most of my time in church was spent wishing to be anywhere *but* church. Though I did remember that Jack had gone up on Da's shoulders for a better look. A battle with a demon was just the kind of story he loved.

"Would you show me the painting, Father?"

"Of course," he replied, pleased.

Feeling guilty for deceiving a priest—because my interest in the painting had nothing to do with saints and everything to do with why *Jack* was interested—I followed him back across the graveyard and through the tower's arched doorway. Inside, the tower was empty but for a rough stone stairway that curved up toward the bell.

There wasn't enough light to see by, and Father Kelly bade me wait while he fetched a candle from the nave. When he returned, he raised the flame close to the only section of the painting that remained, above the doorway we'd entered through.

"That is St. Gomonda in the center," he said, pointing out a robed figure. "He is something of a mystery and not heard of outside Cornwall. We know next to nothing about his life. One ancient document—lost now, but described in church records—indicated he was an apothecary. Beyond that, all we know is what we see in this single section of a much larger painting, which likely survived the slow destruction of time simply because it's high enough on the wall to avoid being touched by every . . ."

I lost the thread of what the priest was saying as my gaze stuck on a different figure, opposite the saint. My breath caught, and for a moment I thought the flickering candlelight had played a trick on my eyes.

The figure had *tree branches* fanning out from its head.

"What is *that*?" I asked, heart thumping as I pointed at the figure. The creature was willowy and tall, but its face had been mostly worn away. All I could make out was a long jaw studded with pointed teeth—like a dog, *or a wolf*.

The priest cleared his throat—I had probably interrupted him. "I would guess a nature spirit of some kind."

"But didn't you say this was a painting of the saint slaying a demon?"

He nodded. "As far as the early church was concerned, there wasn't much difference. The ancient Romans went to war against the religion of the Britons, which was a kind of nature worship, and that war never really ended. Over the centuries, those old ways were all but stamped out."

It seemed to me that "nature spirit" might be another way of saying "fairy," and if so, the priest's explanation made it clear why my mother had told me never to talk about fairies in church. But what struck me most was the bit of the creature's face I could see. Could this be the Wolf of Roche Rock? With its branch-antlers, I thought it must be the same creature—or at least the same kind of creature—that I'd seen on the heath.

Continuing to study the painting, I saw that the figure of St. Gomonda held a bow nocked with a strange kind of arrow; it seemed to be sprouting *flowers*. Another flower arrow hung in the air above the scene, and a third stuck out from the creature's chest. Besides the two main figures, there was another robed man holding a large cross before him like a shield. People who had been slain were strewn over the ground. My breath caught again as I noticed a woman with a line of red running from her neck into a small pool of the same color.

In the backdrop of all this, high on the wall, was a steep, black outcrop.

"That's Roche Rock!" I said.

I realized the priest was watching me closely now. "So it is."

Rising on my toes to see better, I said, "There's no chapel, though."

He raised the candle higher, casting light farther up the wall. "The story of St. Gomonda is much older than both the chapel and this tower. They were both constructed in the fifteenth century, and the original church of St. Gomonda—elements of which can be found in the current structure—is centuries older than both."

Stomach knotting, I pointed out the bleeding woman. "And what do you make of that, Father?"

"Mina." His earnest tone drew my gaze. "I'll tell you the same thing I told your brother. This story has nothing to do with the killings in the parish. Or with your attacker. I think what we can take from it is that though we may face danger and even death, God is the shepherd who protects his faithful flock from . . ."

Again his voice faded as my thoughts grew loud. I wished for a chair or stool so I could go up and see everything closer, but Father Kelly clearly wanted to discourage both Jack and me from dwelling on any possible connection between Roche Rock and the murders. And that was just as well.

The priest had finished speaking, and I smiled and nodded as if I'd heard all he'd said. "Thank you very much for showing me, Father. I won't take up any more of your time."

His gaze, keen and searching before, began to soften. "Of course, Mina. Now you go on home and stay there until the constabulary sorts this out, all right? You've been through quite enough."

"Yes, Father. I will."

I glanced at the wall one last time—and noticed something I hadn't before. Along one side of the doorway arch, someone had used something sharp to scratch a word below the painting. The letters were small and crooked, but I could make them out: "Goosevar." The word meant nothing to me and might simply have been someone's name. But I repeated it to myself several times so that I would remember it.

I felt Father Kelly's eyes on my back as I walked around the front of the church to the road, turning toward home—though I was not going there. Nor was I going to The Magpie. There was no time for what I had planned this morning. To explain myself to Mrs. Moyle, or for her to find Mr. Carew.

I had Mum's cross, and my kitchen knife. I would carry my letter to Roche Rock and leave it at Mr. Tregarrick's door.

"AND YET I LIVE"

Harker

Though my acquaintance with Mina—which she had thankfully survived—would now come to an end, it hadn't stopped me from thinking of her.

That first hint of her honeyed scent on the breeze almost drove me from the battlements onto the rocks below. My feelings about her had become so entangled with the bloodlust that there was no separating them. I craved the sound of her voice. The fragrance of her skin and hair. The taste of her own sweet vital essence.

I could have none of these things, and if I tried, she would be lost forever to me and everyone who loved her. I felt a twinge of sympathy for my father and his father, whose marriages I'd viewed as no better than murders. Mina had shown me that staring down countless long decades with no companionship was a fate worse than death.

And yet I live.

The constable had entered my home yesterday evening for the second time, having come to notify me that another corpse had been discovered near the estate; I was beginning to know his smell almost as well as Mina's. Wherever she'd gone this morning, he had accompanied her. On his visit here, he'd made no mention of Mina accusing me of the attack on her, so I assumed she hadn't. I had all but blurted out a confession before it occurred to me that the truth might sully her in the eyes of the village. *It must be her decision.*

As I sat down with a pot of tea, I stared across the table at her empty chair, wondering how I had so miscalculated. In my laboratory I had let her see what I truly was. I had felt how close she was to fleeing. One more small show of aggression would have sufficed.

I was too weak to do the job properly.

She had a kind heart, and my honesty, instead of making her truly afraid of me, had aroused a compassionate interest. Which had come like an offer of water to a man lost in the desert. I hadn't the strength to refuse it.

Groaning softly, I lifted the pot to fill my cup. Cool air moved through the casement, and I froze.

She's coming.

Stomach dropping, I set the pot down so carelessly tea sloshed from the spout. I started up from the table.

There was nothing I could do to stop her, and I couldn't trust myself to ignore her knock. But I could at least choose the ground we met on.

STONES

As I neared the chapel—winded and weak limbed, though the climb hadn't gotten steep yet—I spotted Mr. Tregarrick coming down the path and stopped. His quick stride set my heart galloping.

I had half turned to escape him, as if such a thing were possible, when he, too, stopped, leaving more than a carriage length between us. His eyes dipped to the bandage around my neck. The rush of heat—the sudden memory of our bodies pressed together—came as a shock. I took a slow and shaky breath, aware my cheeks were apple-peel red.

How these sensations and reactions to him confused and frightened me! One moment I hovered on the point of flight. The next, I longed for him to come closer.

As my eyes moved over him, I noticed the wound at *his* throat, just above the ruffled collar of his shirt—a small cross, charred into the skin. When he'd asked me to wear the necklace, how little I'd imagined I would use it to save myself from *him*.

The change in him took my breath away. The cool tones of his skin had warmed, and there was even a flush in his cheeks. He wore his spectacles, but they rested low on the bridge of his nose, and how his eyes shone! His skin, too, gleamed with youth, and even his hair had lost its ashy tint, leaving a rich, deep brown. Everything about him was brighter and more alive—except his expression.

"Mina." The word was a handful of earth tossed onto a coffin.

"I had not meant to disturb you again, sir," I blurted out unsteadily. "I only meant to leave a note asking you to send your man to me. I've learned things in the last two days that you should know. Things that may help you." I bit my lip. "But it will be much better to tell you directly."

His dismay was plain. "You would put your *life* at risk to help me. Have you stopped to think why?"

His gaze burned into me. Even with some distance between us, I could see his eyes had changed their dusty cast for a glossy midnight purple. I dropped my gaze to the path at our feet, the hem of my skirt draping the rusty bracken on either side.

"I have, sir. I even considered whether I might be under a kind of spell."

"Perhaps you should listen to such thoughts. They might be trying to save you."

I looked at him. "Tell me, then. *Is* it a spell?"

With a glancing shake of his head, he admitted, "Not a conscious one. But there are creatures whose forms are designed to attract."

It would explain much. But I wasn't sure that his *form*, pleasing though it was, could explain my concern for him.

"Well," I said, "my life is hardly more important than anyone else's. I believe you are the only one with even a prayer of stopping this creature before it kills again, and I think I may have found it for you."

His eyes went wide with shock. Slowly shaking his head, he said, "You are remarkable." It didn't exactly sound like a compliment. He tipped his head to my left, where a path branched away from the one we stood on. "Follow me down the heath so we may talk in the open," he said. "Not too closely."

I let out a breath. "Yes, sir."

Footpaths led off in various directions over the estate. From below, you could see them snaking up the hill through the heather and around the dark blocks of granite. The path we walked on now would likely have been the same he'd taken when he carried me, unconscious, from the pool to the chapel.

Though the wall painting at St. Gomonda made it seem even more likely the heath creature had been the one that attacked me and the others, I had to wonder why it hadn't renewed its attack during the close visit to our cottage. The creature had simply watched me and then disappeared with the fog.

We were almost to the pool now, and Mr. Tregarrick's kindness in coming to my aid that day reminded me of another kindness he'd done me.

"I wish to thank you, sir," I said, "for sending your man with your letter and the tasseography book. It was very thoughtful of you."

"Please call me Harker," muttered my companion. "The formality between us has begun to feel silly. And you're welcome to the book. I thought you might get some use out of it."

"Indeed, I already have."

"I appreciated the author's straightforward way of explaining things. Books on alchemy are often opaque and labyrinthine."

"You've read it?" I asked, surprised.

"It *was* in my library," was his puzzled reply.

"Well, yes. But I guess it seems to me your interests are more . . . scientific."

"Alchemists are naturally curious. And alchemy has no contempt for spirituality."

"I see." And mostly I did. Sometimes his explanations went right past me, but the more time I spent with him, the easier I found him to understand. "Did you try it yourself?"

"I did, in fact."

"How did you get on?"

He let out a breathy sound that might have been a laugh. "Not at all. It seems I don't possess the gift for it, despite having a great quantity of spent tea leaves at my disposal."

I laughed, and I took a few quicker steps so I wouldn't have to speak so loudly. "Mrs. Rochester says that besides tea leaves, you only need study and practice."

"I fear my mind may be too busy to really excel. I got the sense a certain sleepy quality of thought was conducive."

I couldn't help it; I laughed again. "Are you saying you weren't quite lazy or simple enough?"

"Not at all, Miss Penrose, only that—"

"Mina," I corrected, because I found I enjoyed teasing him, and also I had no wish to return to "formality."

"Mina. I meant that I struggle to settle my thoughts. You'd think after so many years, I'd run out of things to think about."

"I'd expect rather the opposite."

"Mmm."

We'd come to the pool, and I looked around with new eyes after what Mr. Hilliard had told me. There was the wide slab where I'd often sat, and where I'd hit my head, but the ground here was also littered with blocky stones of varying sizes, their lines softened by time. Especially telling were the small mounds with edges and corners of stones showing. I guessed that earth and grasses had gradually filled in the crevices among piles of masonry bricks.

Moving to stand beside the slab, I noticed a dark stain on the granite that hadn't been there before. *My blood.* Harker stood a few arm lengths to my left, avoiding my eye. I tried to conjure the missing memory—him lifting me in his arms, carrying me to the chapel. Would he have scooped me up without thinking, then realized the risk, or the other way around?

Harker is always thinking.

Yet how well I knew that he could be taken by the moment.

Shivering, I glanced up at the sky—evenly gray now, with no breaks, the air cooler than it had been. Mist almost completely hid the surface of the pool, as if the water were hot rather than cold. Mysterious patchy fogs were common on the Tregarrick estate. Sometimes you could watch them gather here when there was no fog to be found in the village. Da once told me it likely meant the land was more bog than heath—even more reason to stay off it—but I'd crossed it enough times to know better.

Finally I looked at Harker. He stared into the mist, lost in his thoughts. "The constable told me these stones are all that remain of the old manor," I said. "Is that true?"

His gaze flitted in my direction. "So said my father. All but the moorstone burned, and much of *that* was carted away for other uses over time. The house was never rebuilt."

"Do you know why?"

He took a slow breath. "While the chapel was under construction, laborers claimed they'd seen a devil on the estate." I half gaped at him. "Things began to go wrong. Worker injuries and missing tools. My ancestor's wife fell ill while she was carrying his child, and shortly after the chapel was completed, she died in childbirth. The chapel was to have been a gift to the church, but the bishop refused it, ruling officially that there was a demonic presence here. Then the manor burned, and my ancestor and his motherless son moved into the chapel. There was no talk of rebuilding after that, whether because my ancestor was too bereft after his wife's death or because no workers would set foot on the place, I cannot say."

My next question came out in a rush. "Have you seen the wall painting in St. Gomonda's bell tower?"

He looked at me, brows lifting. "Of the saint slaying the demon?"

"I was looking at it today with Father Kelly. You remember what the demon looked like? The thing with tree branches growing from its head?"

His gaze drifted again as he sifted through memories. "It's been many long years since I set foot in the church. My father told me it wasn't safe for us, and we never attended services. But as a boy I was curious about the other tower that we could see from ours." He smiled faintly. "I wondered whether another boy might live there. Roche Rock was not an easy place to be a child."

"You were lonely even then."

"I was." The matter-of-factness of the reply tugged at my heart. How well I knew that loneliness, like a ghost that met you each morning and followed you through your day. I couldn't imagine decades of it.

"My father left the estate very rarely, but one night he had some business with his steward, and I made up my mind to visit the other tower." Sighing quietly, he looked down. "It crushed me to discover it empty. I had brought a lantern with me, and I climbed up to the bell, just to be sure. I noticed the painting as I was leaving, though I wasn't tall enough to see it well. I recall the 'demon' better than anything else about it. Years later, when my father told me the story of our chapel's construction, it seemed to me that the story of St. Gomonda had likely provided inspiration for the church's belief that an evil presence dwelled here."

"It's real, Harker. I've seen it."

I watched the small movements of the muscles in his jaw before his head slowly turned. "Seen what, exactly?"

"The demon, or whatever it really is. I've seen it at least twice, but I think three times. First, the day I found Mr. Roscoe. I glimpsed it in the mist on the other side of the wall. I saw the branches and thought it was a stag. Since then I've seen it twice from the garden behind our cottage."

His gaze remained fixed and flat. When he spoke, his tone was quiet, but I had learned by now that this meant the inside of his head was anything but. "You've always seen it on the estate?"

I nodded. "I think it might be the creature that attacked me. And the one that's done the killings."

Brow furrowing, he said, "What makes you associate the creature responsible for the attacks with the one in the painting? That bell tower is centuries old."

"I know how it sounds. But I *saw* it, Harker. In the painting there's a woman with a wound in her neck, and her blood is pooling on the ground. Maybe the creature is a kind of vampire."

His fingers trembled as he reached up to touch the burn at his throat. "That is a detail I missed."

"You and your ancestors are—forgive me—blood-drinkers who've lived unnaturally long lives. Could this creature and your family be connected somehow?"

His expression was one of wonder and shock. I tried to give him a moment to think. But my own brain was still working, and patience wasn't exactly my strength.

"There was something else, too. Someone had scratched a word into the wall, just above the door arch. 'Goosevar.' Does it mean anything to you?"

For a moment, he seemed not to react. Then his eyes locked on mine. "You're certain that was it? 'Goos-evar'?"

"I made a point to remember in case it was important."

"It's important," he said softly, and I caught a quaver in his voice.

"You know what it means?"

"You said it just a moment ago. 'Blood-drinker.' But in Cornish."

No wonder I hadn't recognized the word. No one spoke Cornish anymore. *No one who isn't nearly a hundred years old.*

"It seems you may be right about the connection with my family," he said. "*How* it is connected is something I would very much like to know. Yet if this creature has been on the estate for centuries, why has no one seen it before now?"

I frowned. "We don't really know they haven't. People might make the same guesses I did—a deer, or a trick of the fog. Or they'd keep it to themselves, afraid no one would believe them. And Harker"—he looked at me—"the face of the creature in the painting has mostly chipped away, but the jaw is long with pointed teeth, like a *wolf*."

His eyes shone above the smoky lenses. "Goosevar could be the source of the old stories."

"The real Wolf of Roche Rock."

He raised his hand, fingers gliding along his own jaw. "And these killings . . . Heaven knows the Tregarricks before me were not always careful. But it's been more than five decades since my family was responsible for a death, so it's hard to imagine that these recent attacks and your sightings of the creature aren't connected. Especially considering you found a victim . . . and then became one."

At that moment a bird fluttered down to the slab—another magpie—startling me.

"I imagine all these recent shocks are taking a toll on you," said my companion, noticing.

"I suppose they are." Though in that moment I felt safe. With *him*. Even if not entirely safe *from* him. Which made no sense at all. "I saw a magpie in that same spot before I was attacked here. I saw one in Mr. Roscoe's leaves, too." *One for sorrow . . .*

"As a tasseographer, you must be a believer in signs."

I slowly shrugged. "I don't know that I ever was until recently, though my mother often spoke of them." I looked again at the bird, whose head tilted from one side to the other as it watched us. "A magpie is said to be a messenger from the spirit world."

"Perhaps it's your mother looking out for you."

My eyes drifted back to his face. His words had been soft, and his eyes were kind. "I hadn't thought of that. I do believe it tried to warn me before it flew off, though I didn't understand it at the time."

A tapping noise drew our attention—the bird had gotten hold of a snail and was knocking it against the rock. When finally the shell broke, the bird nipped the creature out and flew away.

"I know you think me reckless," I said, looking at him. Again I watched a movement in his jaw. "Jack does, too. He speaks to me like I'm a child who ought to know better. But I have no wish to die."

"It had occurred to me to wonder." My raised eyebrow brought a slight smile to his lips, and I felt a tickle of warmth in my belly. "But I believe I'm coming to understand you. You're simply comfortable taking risks to help others."

Heat rose to my cheeks. "No more so than anyone else, I don't think."

"On that, we may have to agree to disagree."

His gaze wandered back to the pool, and I was able to breathe again. "Well, none of this means I'm not frightened. I still see Mr. Roscoe's face when my eyes are closed."

"I can imagine. My violence must have frightened you, too, though you seem to have forgotten it."

My heart drummed. "I was frightened at first. But it wasn't what you might expect. After a few moments, I began to feel . . . calm." It wasn't quite the right word, but I found I couldn't speak of the other sensations that had come with that calm feeling. Not to him.

"I think that's meant to happen," he said grimly. "A spider injects a venom that paralyzes its prey."

I shivered, not caring for this picture. "Do you realize that when you talk about . . . about your nature, you don't describe it as if it were a disease? You compare yourself to creatures. To animals that hunt."

He eyed me. "You're thinking again of Goosevar, and how he might be connected to my family."

"I guess I am. It does feel as if there's something we need to uncover there, though I'm not sure how to go about it."

He stiffened. "You must leave that to me."

Silence filled in between us like fog, and I began to dread his leave-taking. I had never expected to see him again, and I feared this time might really be the last. I had helped him all I could. It was for *him* to find the creature on the heath. My presence would only distract him.

If this was the last time, I'd have nothing to lose by asking a very personal question that had been turning in my mind the past few days.

"What does it feel like to *you*?"

I watched his chest rise and fall slowly, and he clasped his hands behind his back. I wondered whether I would have to explain what I meant, but he said, "I don't like speaking of it, though I suppose I owe you an answer."

"Well," I replied mildly, "*I* have spoken of it."

His gaze drifted to the birch coppice a short distance away. I heard the infant-like cry of a rabbit, caught by a fox or snare.

"I don't know if I have the words," he said. "It feels like . . . *everything*. Or like the only thing that matters. I hope that you have never gone hungry, but if you have, it's really the only thing I can think of to compare it to. Food to a starving man. Yet it's not at all like eating. It's more like breathing, where breathing is . . . an act of worship."

I stared, feeling the hot surge of blood beneath my skin—knowing he must feel it, too. His eyes came again to my face, fevered, like in the moments before the attack.

But his voice was even as he said, "Yet there is nothing reverent about it. It is a violent, selfish, unforgivable act."

"I forgive you," I said faintly.

His brows knit, and he quickly looked down.

"I'm frightened for you, Harker."

There was an edge of disbelief to the dry laugh that escaped him.

"Now that they've found another body," I went on, "I worry what people will be saying in the village. Jack is the worst of them all. There's no question in his mind you are to blame for these attacks."

Harker let out a long breath. "In this century, I'm more concerned about the views of the constabulary than the mob. And I don't think Mr. Hilliard believes I'm his murderer."

"Has he been to see you again?"

"He came yesterday, after they found the other victim. He's a reasonable and intelligent man, but people are pressing him for answers and action."

Feeling fatigue catching up with me, I sat down on the edge of the slab. Its cold seeped through my layers of clothing, just as Harker's had when he'd held me.

"What will you do now?" I asked.

Stooping to pick up a stone, he said, "I must find this creature before he kills again."

"But you thought you were looking for a man like you before. Someone you could reason with."

He frowned, turning the stone in his fingers. "If Goosevar is somehow connected with my family, that may still be possible. I don't see another option except to go to the constable with the truth."

"I fear that instead of believing you, he'll think you're the madman he's looking for. Or—"

"He *will* believe me and think I'm the madman he's looking for."

I gave him a hopeless nod.

He threw his stone, and we watched it skip a couple of times on the pool's dark surface before the fog swallowed it.

"The creature I saw was larger than a man," I said. "I know you're fast and strong, but could he hurt you if he wished to?"

Harker looked at me, the softness in his eyes causing a now-familiar flutter. "It's kind of you to worry. You needn't."

"But *could* he?"

"If you're asking whether Tregarricks are invincible, the answer is no. I have cut and burned myself many times in the laboratory. Though my wounds healed very quickly before I began denying myself blood."

This did nothing to ease my worry. "Do vampires have blood of their own?"

"We do. But it's dark and sluggish. 'Dead' blood, my father called it."

Catching a low murmur of voices then, I glanced toward the birchwood.

"They sneaked in from the other side to retrieve a snare," Harker said quietly.

His young poachers. I forgot sometimes how aware he was of everything around him. "You should frighten them," I said.

He shot me a questioning look.

"They aren't scared of you. Or at least not scared enough. You should do something to change that before your monster gets them. They're sweet boys."

"I wouldn't like to see them harmed," he agreed. "But I'm not sure how I'm to frighten them when I can't even frighten you."

I failed to hold back a little snort of laughter, which made him laugh, too—a real laugh this time, one that escaped before he could crush the life out of it.

"You must try harder, sir."

He bowed his head. "As you wish, madam."

A giddy warmth that had no place in this discussion bubbled up from my belly. I felt like I had at The Wolf's Head, forced to drink a glass of sherry.

As I watched Harker stoop to pick up another stone, something occurred to me.

"Do you suppose Goosevar is somehow bound to the estate? The victims were found just along the edges of it. And of course there are the wolf stories."

He rubbed his thumb over the stone, considering. "It might explain why he hasn't tried to attack you again in his recent visits. The cottages in Carbis are just beyond the boundary of the property, though of course the Tregarricks once owned all of the parish."

"It might be that Mum's cross has protected me."

He looked up, holding my gaze, and my breath stopped. "I will forever be grateful to you for wearing it."

His attention drifted back to the pool, and my chest filled again.

"I can't help feeling it's more than chance that you keep seeing him," he said. "If we don't count the shadow I saw before you were attacked, I haven't seen him once in eighty years. It's as if something has been drawing him to you since the night you found Mr. Roscoe."

His whole body turned toward me now, eyes pinning me to the spot. "Promise me, Mina, that you will never approach him."

I nodded. "Yes, I'll stay away from him. Except . . ."

Harker's jaw clenched, and he tossed the skipping stone aside.

BAIT

"Hear what I have to say," I quickly continued. "You said yourself that Goosevar comes to me, not to you. You can see for miles in every direction from the chapel, yet you've glimpsed no more than his shadow. I'm only wondering if—"

"I am NOT going to use you as bait."

His voice boomed like thunder in the stillness. Before I could compose myself enough to answer, another angry voice sounded.

"Devil take me, Mina!"

I jumped to my feet. It was a sign of just how badly I'd upset Harker that he hadn't sensed Jack coming.

"Why did I *know* I'd find you here?" he demanded. "What in God's name do you think you're doing?"

I could almost see smoke coming out of him, he was that hot. Harker, who was closer to Jack, stood with his back to me now. Yet I felt him tensing. *His anger is the cold kind.*

"Calm down, Jack," I pleaded. "I only—"

"No more of your excuses!" he barked before I could spin out another lie. I had no new ones to tell him anyway. I had defied him, plain and simple.

I'm a grown woman, and I shouldn't have to answer to him.

But that wasn't how the world worked.

"Do I have to set a guard on you?" he continued. His eyes jerked to Harker, his tone threatening violence as he said, "I want you to keep away from my sister, you devil. You have no business with her, hear me?"

"I think—" Harker began, but now *I* was smoking.

"You leave him be, Jack! This isn't his fault. I came bothering him, not the other way round. What are you doing here, anyway? Have they let you go at the mine?"

His eyes bored into me, and he moved closer, edging around Harker. "If they do, it'll be on your head! Mr. Hilliard told me you left home this morning, and I asked for leave to come after you." His hand struck like a snake, catching hold of my wrist and leaving me stunned. He tugged me toward him. "I'll have no more of this. You can't—"

"That's enough," rumbled Harker. In a blink, my wrist was free—and Jack was splayed on the ground.

Now *Jack* was stunned silent, and Harker turned to me with a stricken look. He took my wrist gently in his hand, his fingers cool against the smarting flesh.

"Are you safe at home, Mina?"

Trembling, I frowned at him, unsure what he meant. Then it came to me—*safe from Jack*. It broke my heart, him seeing Jack this way, suspecting him of something that had never been true. I felt ashamed, too, at him seeing Jack and me at our worst.

"It's not like him," I managed, though my voice shook. "He'll calm down."

Harker nodded, eyes still searching mine. "It's best you go home, then. But if something like this happens again, you go to Mrs. Moyle. Promise me."

Tears threatened to choke me, and I could only manage a nod. I turned to go, leaving Jack to clamber up from the mound of dry bracken he'd been tossed into.

I let him trail behind me as I walked down the slope of the heath toward the cottage, and he had sense enough not to try to talk to me before we got inside.

As the door swung closed behind him, I said, "Don't you ever do that again."

"I shouldn't have grabbed you like that," he admitted. He'd simmered down some, but now there was an edge of panic to his frustration. "You've got me at my wits' end. You defy me at every turn, and every day coming home I'm worried I'll find you dead out on the heath. It already almost happened once! How would I bear it, Mina?"

My throat felt thick and hot, and I continued to fight tears. "If I matter so much to you, why don't you come home instead of drinking half the night? My worth doesn't add up to the price of a pint."

His eyes closed, and his hand went to his forehead as he turned his back to me.

"You know it's true," I muttered, starting toward the loft ladder. I was bone tired and starting to see black around the edges.

"Why did you go to him?" Jack called after me. "Are you *trying* to get yourself killed? Because it sure seems that way to me."

I turned. "I can't do this anymore." My voice came out weak as the rest of me. "So here's the truth of it. I went to warn him that people in the village are out of their heads with fear, and they're gossiping about the estate. I told him that he could be in danger."

Jack's eyes went wide, disbelieving. "How could you do something so foolish?"

"Because he's been *kind* to me. Because I *like* him, and I don't want to see him hurt. Because *you're* the ones acting like fools."

"Did you see what happened on the heath? No man moves that fast, Mina."

"Maybe you shouldn't have made him think you were dangerous!"

"Do you even *hear* yourself? You know they're searching all around his estate. Even Hilliard is finally coming to his senses."

My heart turned over, and some of the heat left my voice. "They mean to arrest him?"

Jack grunted. "Hilliard says there's no evidence showing he's done anything. By the time there is, somebody else will be dead. If you know something—if you've *remembered* something—you best not be keeping it to yourself. That would make you an accessory to the crime."

"Those are some fancy words, Jack. Are you sure you know what they mean?"

It was an ugly thing to say, but his talk was scaring me. He knew—or at least sensed—more than I liked. He and the other fools were meddling in a way that could risk not just Harker, but all of us. And like Mr. Hilliard, there was nothing I could say to set him straight that he would actually believe or understand.

Jack's jaw set, and his whole face shut down. "You win, Mina. You've broken me. You go on and do what you like, because I'm done trying to protect you."

He made straight for the front door and walked out of it.

I win. It sure didn't feel like it.

Still recovering, and worn out by the emotion of the day, I didn't wake the next morning until Jack had left for work. I couldn't even have said for sure that he'd come home, except that he'd burned up my best pot while trying to cook porridge. Part of me thought it served him right, and part of me felt sorry he'd gone off to the mine hungry.

Having missed supper last night, I woke with a complaining belly and went out to gather eggs. They hadn't been collected in several days, and I found nearly a dozen in the straw of the nest boxes. Then I made eggs-on-foam, which required whipping the whites and spreading them as a bed for the yolks before baking—a recipe I'd learned from Mrs. Moyle.

Once I'd eaten, I started on *In the Leaves* again, but after the last reading, I found I had no patience for it. The candle for "finding your way in the dark," which I was certainly doing, and not very well, and the cross for "trouble on its way," delivered as promised, and with a vengeance. I wasn't sure what the point of the readings was if they only told you things you'd look back on the next day and say, "It all makes sense now."

Yet by the time I'd boiled water and brewed the leaves, I found myself pouring my tea unstrained. Maybe eventually you got better at making sense of things *before* they happened?

This time when I performed the little ritual, I didn't have to look very hard—a large and clear circle appeared inside the rim to one side of the handle. Mrs. Rochester listed several meanings for circles but only one for a ring, which was how I had read the pattern when I first looked at it.

Marriage. And by the position in the cup, one that would come soon. Which would have to mean it was someone else's marriage, but whose? Jack's? I had always assumed he would marry one day, but to my knowledge he'd never even had a sweetheart. How could he, when he spent all his time at the mine or the tavern? Mrs. Moyle? That seemed more likely, yet I couldn't believe she'd hide a courtship from me.

Sighing, I plunked the cup down and gathered up some stale scones, left from when Mrs. Moyle was here, to carry out to the hens. As I was crumbling them on the ground, I heard someone coming around the side of the cottage.

"Miss?"

Jeremy, the young poacher, appeared. He grinned and held up a fat rabbit. "Got one."

I smiled. "So I see. You gave me a bit of a jump."

He ducked his head. "Sorry, miss. Only you told me to come to the back door."

"I did indeed. Sixpence, I think we agreed?"

He ducked again.

"I'll be right back."

I went inside for his coin, plucking it from an old chemist's tin that I kept in a drawer in my worktable. Going back out, I said to him, "I agreed to buy this one from you, but I won't buy another until they catch whatever is attacking people on the heath. You boys have no business being out there until then, you hear?"

Looking down, he said, "Mr. Tregarrick—he already told us to keep off."

I raised my eyebrows. "You spoke to him?"

"Aye."

"Good." I held back a smile. "Gave you a fright, did he?"

Now a shrug. "The other fellows maybe, on account of him creeping up on us, and those funny spectacles. But not me."

I couldn't keep the corners of my lips down, but luckily Jeremy was still staring at the ground. "I see. What did Mr. Tregarrick say to you?"

"That it was too dangerous, and if we didn't clear off, he'd fetch the constable." Finally he looked up. "But he said we could come back when it was safe."

"That was very kind of him." If memory served, Jeremy's father was Abel Martin, who'd died about a year ago. I imagined the boy poached because his family needed the meat. "I tell you what—you take the sixpence, but keep the rabbit, since you won't get one for a while. Then you bring me one when it's safe again. All right?"

He gave me an eager nod. "Thank 'ee, miss." Then he frowned. "Some folks are saying it's Mr. Tregarrick going after people on the heath, but I don't see how it could be."

I studied him more closely. "Why do you say so?"

"Well, we hardly ever see him outside that black chapel of his. I suppose he could get up to murdering at night, when no one's looking." His eyes dipped to the bandage around my neck. "Do you think he is?"

"I don't, Jeremy. Mr. Tregarrick is going to try to find who *is*, though. Have you ever seen anything strange out there? On the heath, or in that wood where you set your snares?"

"Nay, miss. But my granfer used to say some kind of devil lived there."

"You didn't let that frighten you, either?"

He reached up to touch his chest—a *cross* was just visible between two buttons of his shirt. It looked like it had been made from a couple of small nails bound together with string. "Nay, miss."

"Well, here you go." I handed him the coin, and he slung the rabbit over his shoulder. "You mind Mr. Tregarrick and run on home, now."

"I will, miss."

I watched him walk back around the corner of the house. I'd noticed a limp the first time I met him, and he had it still.

Planting my hands on my hips, I gazed up toward the chapel. Was Harker out searching for Goosevar this morning? It didn't seem that the creature was a threat to Harker—likely he could have killed Harker a hundred times over—but still I worried what would happen if they did finally meet.

And what if they don't? Then Harker was going to have to think again about letting me help him.

I was about to go inside when I noticed a low, woolly cloud creeping past the pool and slowly down toward the cottage. The animals began to fuss and fret again, and soon they had left me alone in the garden.

In spite of yesterday's brave talk by the pool, I stepped to the back door—but stopped with my fingers gripping the handle as an unexpected sound reached my ears. A strange kind of music that seemed to drift on the breeze.

I'd heard music at church from the organ, and though Da had told me it was the same as the angels played in heaven, it had always sounded more like a foretelling of doom. I'd heard music on the green outside the village during fairs and markets, when there was always dancing—lively music, far more pleasing to a child's ear. And I'd heard music right here in our cottage, when Da fiddled or Mum sang Irish airs. This was different from all of these, and I wasn't sure it could even properly be called music. If anything, it was like a blending of out-of-tune fiddle music and Ma's saddest ballad, but also with sounds like birdsong, rustling barley, grasshoppers clicking, and water over stones. It could not be followed or made sense of, yet I stood there trying.

Fairy tricks. These words came to me in Mum's brogue. I squeezed my eyes shut and covered my ears, but it didn't stop the music. And when again I opened my eyes, I found that I'd *wandered out onto the heath*. My heart took off like a hare, yet the rest of me stood frozen. The low cloud drifted over and around me. Cold, damp air kissed my cheeks and hands.

Run!

But as a crown of tree branches floated toward me through the fog, I felt both my mind and body loosening, like my hair falling over my shoulders when I unpinned it at night.

"WHAT HAVE YOU DONE TO HER?"

Harker

I emerged from the chapel onto the battlements under a silver-sulfide sky that seemed not to care the day was young yet. Which was just as well, since my vision was better on dark days.

Atop the tower, I could indeed see miles in every direction. To the south, the heath sloped away toward Pentivale, where springs hidden by willows, reeds, and bracken formed the headwaters of the River Fal. The Fal Valley, which had been mined for tin since medieval times, was also prime farming and grazing land. Lined by willow scrub and slender birch, the river snaked across Goss Moor on its journey toward Falmouth and the English Channel.

The moor spread to the west of my family's estate, and overlooking it from the north was Castle Down with its ancient hillfort, Castle an Dinas. Like many sites in Cornwall, it had associations with Arthurian legend. It was also a ceremonial site of pre-Christian peoples.

In the nearer distance to the northwest was St. Gomonda, the parish church, and across from that The Magpie and the whole village of Roche.

Around the margins of the parish, imposing themselves on the view, were the white conical hills of quartz and mica waste from the china clay operations, the area's most important industry. They were stark and alien interruptions in the pastoral landscape, but without the money from china clay—essentially a decomposed version of the same rock that had built this chapel—a village tearoom in rural Cornwall would be a risky venture indeed.

Mining—whether for tin, copper, or clay—was an integral part of Cornwall's history. Miners worked six days a week in all seasons, and I imagined it wore a man down. Still, I couldn't bring myself to excuse Jack Penrose's behavior toward his sister.

I wasn't sorry for what I'd done, yet it had probably only made things worse between them, and he was all she had left. It also likely reinforced what Jack already believed about me. *You devil.*

If I could put a stop to this creature menacing the parish, Mina could at least go back to her job at The Magpie. Of course the return to her old routine would also mean a return to the daily temptations of her walking back and forth—which would be greater now that I'd given in to the bloodlust.

I will need more vital essence. The process was involved, and the Walachian vintage very difficult to acquire, so I'd kept to small batches up to now. But the outer world was encroaching on my sanctuary, and I could no longer afford to scrimp.

My thoughts were drifting from my intended purpose in climbing up here. Over the quiet decades, my mind had learned a habit of running to extremes. When I studied or worked in my laboratory, I was capable of an intense focus that sometimes kept me going for days without rest. When I was idle, I found my thoughts traveling down strange, forking paths, waking from these mental ambles only to discover I wasn't sure whether minutes or hours (or days) had passed.

Moving slowly along the battlements, I studied the moorstone that littered the ground at the base of this black granite ridge. From the south-west-facing wall, my gaze picked over the ruins of a pre-Christian village and barrow, from which stone for the chapel had been foraged. Due west, almost to the border that the estate shared with parish church property, lay the family cemetery where I'd buried my father and he'd buried my mother. Finally, the oak wood spread north toward the village almost to the road, like a great shawl flung from the battlements. Until undertaking this search, I couldn't have said when last I'd walked among those trees, though I'd played there almost daily as a boy.

Roche Rock was a horrible place for a child, growing up with no one for company save my father and old Mr. Pritchard, who'd served as both my tutor and my father's steward. Before I came of age, I'd sometimes been allowed to accompany my father's agent—one of a long line of Carews—on errands and even trips to Bodmin, and in that way learned something of the wider world that didn't come from books.

Once we went as far as St. Austell, and I saw the sea. The relentless assault of the waves on the strand, the still darkness of the Atlantic, beyond the channel, that seemed to stretch for centuries . . . I had felt a kinship with it that I'd been too young to understand.

These excursions had felt like a game, as I'd been required to pretend I was Mr. Carew's nephew to avoid drawing attention to the estate. How many times had I wished that I was, and that we'd never return to this desolate place?

You were lonely even then. My gaze found the pool on the heath, beetle black under the heavy sky. I closed my eyes, but it didn't prevent her from manifesting in my mind. Yesterday I had studied her profile long enough to paint her, had I the talent for it. The tiniest detail—the outward curve of the Cupid's bow of her lip—was enough to make even the blood of a cold creature like me run hot.

I should have discouraged her pity. I should have discouraged her concern. Most of all, I should have discouraged her presence. Yet Mina Penrose was the only light to have flickered in my far too long shadow of a life.

Glancing down toward her cottage, I noticed a low cloud moving over the ground. My eyes couldn't penetrate the thick vapor. Sudden mists and fogs, lonely clouds like this one—they had occurred on the estate for as long as I could remember. My father once remarked on it, saying my mother had found them unsettling.

My sluggish heart made what passed for a sudden movement. Had I discovered the reason we'd never seen Goosevar?

I was about to hurry down when I noticed the figure of a woman on the heath. The cloud was moving toward her.

"Mina!" I shouted, startling a formation of gray geese overhead.

I ran to the stairway and wound down to the main floor, crossing to the door so quickly I overturned a chair, its back striking the floor with a sound like a shot. The steep entry stairs forced me to slow, but soon I was flying down the hill, dodging the moorstone in my path.

The cloud had reversed course now, and I soon closed the distance. Plunging inside the wall of vapor, I waved my hand as if to clear smoke from my vision.

"Mina?" I called out. Droplets collected on my exposed skin.

No answer came as I moved within the cloud, stumbling over the uneven ground that I could no longer see. I called for her again without result, but then finally the vapor cleared enough that a hulking shadow began to take shape—*along with Mina*, invisible at first against the silhouette.

Goosevar. He had the torso of a tall, broad-shouldered man, back curved like a crescent moon as he hunched over her. The network of branches fanned out from his head, and the bottom half of his torso divided into legs, shaggy with gray lichen. His flesh looked rough like the bark of a tree, including that of the canine face—long snout, ember eyes, and thin lips peeling back over black gums to reveal a gleam of white fangs.

Mina, child-size before him, appeared unharmed, though her eyes were glassy. Her hair hung loose about her shoulders, and her freckles stood out starkly in the strange silver-white light. Her gaze was flat, expression blank. She did not seem to have registered my presence.

"What have you done to her?" I demanded, voice broken by coursing fear.

Goosevar made no reply, but the curtain of fog was re-forming. I lunged for Mina, catching her against my chest. Once again trusting that she was safer with me than this monster.

He stepped back from us, folding himself low to the ground, moving down the heath within the cloud.

Then a series of impossible scenes played before my eyes.

GOOSEVAR

The strange veil fell away, and I felt the body of another person break from mine. *Impossibly cold.*

Harker.

Wind lifting the ends of my hair, I touched my throat, finding the bandage still in place. *He hasn't fed on me.*

Roche Rock loomed before me, its master standing between us. He wore a stunned expression, and his own loose waves blew back from his face.

I hugged my arms around my chest. This didn't feel like a dream, yet how had I come to be here?

Then I remembered the cloud that had seemed somehow alive, and Goosevar waiting inside. *Waiting for me.* I had at last glimpsed his face, with its long jaw and twin flames for eyes. I remembered how fog had rolled from his open mouth.

"What happened?" My voice carried only a hint of the panic I felt. "Where is he?"

"I'm not sure about either," Harker said. "But let us get out of this wind."

I eyed the curving spine of the dark ridge jutting behind him, with its promise of shelter—or possibly death. I looked at him, and he read my question.

"I'm afraid I don't know what else to do," he said, and I could see his desperation. "I have much to tell you. I would far rather take you home. I would far rather you weren't involved. But it seems that you are, whether I like it or not, and I'm beginning to be more afraid for you when you're away from me than when you're with me."

My heart wrenched, and I took a step toward him.

His arms flexed, like he might *reach for me*. Instead, his hands curled into fists.

Breathing deeply, I gazed into the sky. It had gone dark, only a shade or two lighter than the chapel itself. A few cold needles of rain found my cheeks, and soon there were more.

"Yes," I said. "Let us go in."

He followed me up and through the heavy door, and he bade me sit near the hearth while he got a fire going. For long moments neither of us spoke, and the air began to feel thick.

In the silence, I thought about what had happened—the fact I'd been in the power of that creature and had almost no memory of it—and I began to shake.

"I'm frightened, Harker," I said.

Crouched before the hearth, a brick of turf still in his hand, he turned. "Yes," he said softly, "of course you are."

A tear slipped onto my cheek, and I looked down, drying it with the back of my hand.

"Mina."

Breath shuddering through me, I looked up again. Every time our eyes met, I felt that his strange beauty and gentleness might break my heart.

"I won't allow anything to harm you here."

Said the vampire. Yet I believed him. Or at least I believed that if any harm came to me through *him*, it would be the fault of something that was stronger than he was.

I nodded, and he tossed the brick onto the fire. He remained crouched there, just far enough away that I couldn't have touched him without moving closer, and we watched the flames rising.

The room warmed, and the silence grew thick again. Finally, I said, "I don't think I've ever seen a fireplace in a church." It felt like what Jack called "whistling past a graveyard."

Harker turned, and by his expression, I knew he had read me. He saw that I wanted distraction, and room to breathe. Taking up the clumsy change of subject, he said, "This building was originally intended to be used as a hermitage, so this floor would have served as living space for a monk or priest, with the upper floor serving as the chapel. But I do think it likely that one of my ancestors added the chimney system later, to make the tower more comfortable for his family."

I imagined them gathered here as we were. As my own family had gathered around our hearth on cold nights. Then I remembered his family was nothing like mine. Harker and the sons who'd come before him had never known their mothers. *It seems they couldn't survive the birth of a monster.*

"Stay here by the fire," he said, rising. "I'll make tea."

I watched him move in his quiet, steady way up the stairs. I had not expected to find myself here again, drinking tea with a vampire. I thought I had seen the last of Harker Tregarrick. Whatever else this day had brought, or might yet bring, I couldn't help feeling glad that I'd been wrong.

Sitting while others labored wasn't something that came easily to me, so I got up and began moving the furniture around, dragging another chair near the fire before placing the tea table between them. I eyed my handiwork, then moved the chairs farther apart.

I'm sure six more inches will make all the difference.

When Harker came down again, his gaze took in my rearranging as he carried the tray to the tea table. I noticed a plate of biscuits and sliced apple from our tree and managed a smile.

"It seems to be a season for visitors," he said as he filled our cups. Me, the constable, poor Mr. Roscoe. "I confess that visiting The Magpie and having you and your baskets here has made me miss the comforting humanness of the whole tea ritual. I haven't been very deliberate about such things for some time, eating only when I think of it, and whatever is to hand. So I asked Roger to make a few purchases."

You and your baskets. Heat stole into my cheeks as I picked up a biscuit. "It's funny to hear you speak almost fondly of my visits. I truly felt I was the last person you wished to see at your door, though I understand why now."

He studied me across the tea table while my heart flopped around like a fish on a riverbank. "I may not have spent much time around other people, but I've read more books than I can count, and I think if there's anything that defines us as humans, it's wanting things that we shouldn't."

The fish stopped struggling and simply gasped, glassy eyed. I couldn't have said for certain whether he was talking about my blood now or something else. His gaze raked quickly over me, and warmth fountained in my belly. Despite the snug comfort of this room, with its rich furnishings and fire in the hearth, the air around us felt like it did before a lightning strike.

"Harker?" He eyed me through the steam leaving his cup. I thought he looked pleased, as if he liked hearing me say his name as much as I liked saying it. "Will you tell me what happened out on the heath?"

"Mmm." His brow furrowed, and his eyes drifted down.

He sat back in his chair. The turf popped and crackled in the hearth, releasing a scent very like his smoky tea.

"I was up on the battlements looking out over the estate when I saw a cloud moving along the ground, and you standing in its path. Do you have any memory of that?"

I nodded. "I saw the cloud from our garden. But I didn't go out to it. I was going back inside when I heard strange music. Then, somehow, I was out on the heath. I glimpsed the creature in the cloud, but the next thing I knew, I was standing with you at the foot of Roche Rock."

He frowned. "Your story has a familiar ring to it, almost like something from a fairy tale."

"Yes, it reminds me of the stories my mother told us of people taken by the 'gentle folk.'" I shifted in my chair to pour more tea. "Did you get a very good look at him?"

"Oh yes," he said in a low voice. The candle on the tea table guttered. "Did he speak to you?"

I shook my head. "You?"

"No." He blinked a couple of times. "At least not in words."

I waited for him to go on. His eyes reflected a cold dread that caused my heart to thump. "Mina, I've had a kind of . . . vision. I hardly know how to tell you. I keep turning it over in my mind. I don't know what it means, yet it—it terrifies me."

My heart thumped faster. "Maybe we can figure it out together."

I watched his throat tense as he swallowed. Outside, the rain came down harder, heavy drops pelting the windowpanes.

He took a slow breath. "I saw a man and woman. They were standing in a small clearing, surrounded by old oaks. The light of a gibbous moon shone down on their faces. Also on the autumn leaves at their feet, making them glow like coins. Their hands were joined, and a long vine of flowering hedge bindweed twined around their arms. The trumpet-shaped blooms were so bright in the moonlight they hurt my eyes." He hesitated. "Do you know what a handfasting is?"

Entranced by the picture he'd painted in my mind—so different from anything I might have expected him to relate—it took me a moment to respond. "It's an old way of marrying, I think."

"It is, centuries old. It's called handfasting because the couple's hands are joined with a ribbon or cord."

I frowned. "You said the moonlight shone on their faces. Did you know them?"

A heartbeat of silence, then: "It was us."

My mouth hinged open, and my breath stopped. *Us?*

He placed his cup and saucer carefully on the edge of the table, as if he feared he might drop them.

After another moment or two, I recovered enough to speak. "What does it mean, Harker?"

He cleared his throat. "I don't know why I know this, but this vision—I believe it came from *Goosevar*. He meant me to understand that he wishes us to marry. It's the reason he brought you here, to me. It's the reason for his interest in you. What I can't understand, no matter how many ways I look at it, is what kind of sense that makes."

My heart beat quick and light. I sat up straighter.

Marriage.

His eyes came to my face. "I can only imagine how this must—"

"There was a *ring* in my tea leaves this morning," I interrupted. "The symbol almost always means marriage. I thought it must be for Jack, since I don't . . ." Heat stinging my cheeks, I looked down and finished quietly, "Don't have a sweetheart."

He was quiet, and I found I couldn't meet his gaze. Finally he let out a slow breath and settled back in his chair. "Setting aside the obvious impossibility of it, why would Goosevar interest himself in our lives in such a way?"

The obvious impossibility of it. I didn't know why these words should stab at me as they did, because of course it *was* impossible—for so many reasons.

"I can't imagine," I said softly, "but it seems like something we might need to figure out."

He raised a hand to rub his forehead, and I could feel his frustration and fear. My own thoughts were a dizzy, confused mess. But I thought if I could at least anchor *him*, with his decades of stored-up knowledge, we might have a chance.

"What do you do in your laboratory when you have a problem to solve?" I asked. "How do you start?"

I felt foolish talking about his work when I understood it so little, but I could see he was grateful as he replied, "I write down the question or questions that I wish to answer."

"Why don't we try it?"

Nodding, he got up and walked to the dining table. I followed, noticing blank sheets of paper and a quill and inkpot already there. *My letter.*

He sat in the chair with the broken back and took up the quill. I pulled out the chair across from him, saying, "Will it be all right for me to sit with you?" It wasn't much closer than we'd sat by the fire, but the attack had occurred here and was likely still very fresh in his mind—as it was in my own.

He smiled thinly. "I confess the temptation has been somewhat dampened by your resourcefulness the last time you were here."

I didn't grasp his meaning at first, but then his fingers brushed his burn.

I couldn't help a huff of nervous laughter. "I'm sorry!" Feeling for the cross beneath my shawl, I said, "Does it still hurt?"

"Yes, and let us be grateful for that." He took a sheet of paper from the stack and said, "Now, what is Goosevar? What is his connection to my family?" He scribbled down his questions.

"Also, did your vision really come from him?"

"And are the vision and your tea reading carrying the same message?"

"And what *is* the message?"

His eyes touched mine briefly, raising a flutter in my chest.

I took off my shawl and draped it over my chairback while he continued scribbling. Even with the casement partly open, the room had warmed nicely.

When his writing paused, I asked, "How many of your kind have there been through history?"

He touched the black feather to his chin, and the motion drew my notice to the fullness of his dark lips. I couldn't see the deadly teeth, and it seemed to me they came and went—like the way food could make your mouth water.

"To protect the family," he replied, "no written record was kept. But my father said I am the fourth. I'll start another page for known facts." He wrote this down, adding, "Only one child, male, has been born each generation."

"And when each son comes of age, the thirst comes on?"

"Yes."

"You also told me that it's worse at the beginning."

He nodded. "And after many years it begins to diminish, ceasing altogether when the next heir undergoes the change."

"The wives . . ." I hesitated, not wishing to cause him pain.

He looked up.

"All of them have died in childbirth?"

"Yes."

When he'd caught up with his writing, I said, "You've had a vision that seems to mean Goosevar expects you to marry."

"To marry *you*," he corrected, causing my heart to skip. "That was my interpretation, but it is a hypothesis rather than a fact. I'll start another page."

As I watched the black ink bleed onto the pale sheets, an answer to one of our questions came together in my mind. It was obvious, really, with everything laid out this way.

"What if there is a *real* connection between your family and Goosevar?"

He raised his eyes to mine, empty of understanding. It would be harder for him to see it, I supposed, being so close to it.

"If each father goes on to live a more normal life after his son is afflicted . . . That isn't really like a disease, is it?"

"You're right, of course. I imagine we've used the term 'affliction' for lack of a better one. It's more like a 'condition.' Though as my father's thirst lessened, he did grow frailer. When I was a boy, he was youthful, tall, and straight. As my change neared, he grew thin and papery."

I frowned. "I know nothing of science—of any kind—but to me it sounds like maybe Goosevar is connected to one man in each generation.

And when a new connection forms to the son, the father is no longer needed, and he loses his thirst. Grows frail and dies."

Harker sat up, quill dropping onto the table. "A *parasite*, Mina. Moving from one host to the next."

I raised my brows, waiting for him to explain.

"A parasite is a creature that lives off of another creature in some way. A flea on a dog. It bites the dog and drinks its blood, which makes the dog itch. If the flea moves on to another host, no more itch." His fingers tapped the table while he continued thinking. "Maybe the connection—though not so evident as a flea's to a dog—means Goosevar doesn't have to hunt. He doesn't need to drink blood, because *we* do."

Then something else struck me. "But you don't! You don't drink blood." *Usually.*

"I can survive on vital essence, but maybe he can't."

"Or maybe he doesn't want to."

He gave a short nod. "Yes, either way, it's driving him to attack people."

I folded my arms and sat back, glancing out the window at the rain. "It mostly makes sense. But I wonder why Goosevar would use your family to do something he can do for himself?"

Harker slouched and rested his chin in his hand, glancing down at his paper. His loose, windblown hair brushed the edges of his face. It was a charming, boyish posture.

"Without understanding the creature better," he replied, "it's hard to say. Maybe it's simply easier. Or it could be the risk that's involved. Maybe he fears discovery, and men are better at hiding their crimes. Mr. Roscoe's body next to the road being a case in point."

"So it may give him protection. Or it once did."

He nodded, brow furrowing as he continued to gaze down at his notes. Then all the light in his face suddenly went out.

"What is it?" I asked.

One hand moved to his forehead, shielding his eyes from me. "A new host," he muttered.

I waited for more. A turf brick settled in the fireplace, sparks crackling up the chimney.

I tried to fill in for myself the words he couldn't seem to say. When understanding finally came, how it *shook* me.

OPTIONS

"He wants you to marry because he wants you to have a child," I said faintly.

Harker got up from the table, chair digging at the floor. He walked to the hearth and I stared after him, heart beating almost to deafen me.

I recalled how Goosevar had changed. Going from attacking me on the heath to watching me behind the cottage. Enchanting me, and bringing me here.

Slowly I rose from the table. "Why me?"

Harker's head half turned, not quite meeting my gaze. He looked as if he would speak, but instead he turned back to the fire.

After a few moments, he said, "You are only the second woman to have set foot in the chapel since I was a boy."

I let out a laugh that sounded more pitiful than I intended. "In other words, the only option."

More strained silence, followed by, "Something like that."

It shouldn't have hurt. I knew it wasn't meant to. But it did.

Harker took off his fine coat and laid it over the back of one of the chairs. I couldn't help admiring again the draping beauty of his shirt, with its ruffled cuffs and neck. Over it he wore a well-fitted waistcoat the color of wine. I had noticed his old-fashioned way of dressing the first time I came here, though his dress at the tearoom had been modern and very polished. It occurred to me now that this would probably have been the fashion around the time he became a young man. *The same time he stopped aging.*

Though the topic was awkward, the sudden quiet was uncomfortable, and I said, "We've found Roche's killer. We know that he wants something from us. If we were to give him what he wants, would the killings stop?"

Harker looked at me at last, brows drawing down. "Hypothetically, I hope you mean."

I stumbled on the unfamiliar word. "If you're saying that you hope I'm not suggesting we actually marry, of course I know we're not considering that."

My tone carried the barest hint of wounded pride, and I was ashamed to see by the slight softening of his expression that he had caught it.

"If we did, hypothetically, marry," he said, "and we were able to conceive a child"—his gaze flitted down to my belly, kindling a flame there—"it would presumably be eighteen or more years before his change. Would Goosevar go that long without feeding? Before my vital essence, the longest I ever managed to abstain was about a month."

"And how long have you been using your vital essence?"

"Including the less effective formulations, about twenty-five years."

"So it would seem that *he* has also managed to survive on it, and only lately—"

"Reached his limit," Harker said bitterly, glancing down. "I haven't exactly thrived on it myself."

This had been evident from the change wrought in him by my blood. Which brought to mind an obvious solution. I hadn't known him long, but I knew how he was going to feel about what I said next.

"You could go back to what you were doing before your vital essence. Feeding by . . . arrangement. Without killing."

His skin went ashen, and the furrows in his brow deepened. There was gravel in his voice as he said, "It would break me, Mina."

His pain wrung my heart, and I nodded.

He took a breath as he raked a hand through his hair. "If it would stop the killings, I would do it. But only as a last resort."

"It might give us time to think of something better." I walked to my chair by the hearth and sat down. Harker bent and tossed another brick on the fire, and I said, "Do you think it would be possible to destroy Goosevar?"

He sat in the other chair. "I should think it's possible to destroy any living creature. Though after seeing Goosevar, I don't feel optimistic."

"St. Gomonda killed Goosevar," I noted. "Though since he's very much alive, I suppose that's just a story."

"Well, as Goosevar is clearly *not* 'just a story,' I don't think we should be too quick to dismiss anything."

"Maybe there have been others like him?"

Harker nodded. "Though if our Goosevar is only one of a species, the fact they've remained undiscovered for centuries is rather remarkable."

I reached up and gathered my hair over one shoulder, braiding it while I thought over all we'd discussed. Harker's eyes followed the movements of my fingers, causing sparks to dance over my skin. When I finished, I had nothing to bind the plait, so I sighed and let it drop.

"Tell me again about the building of the chapel," I said. "You mentioned that it was meant as a gift for the church. During the construction there were devilish pranks, and the church decided a demon was here—you thought maybe because of the St. Gomonda story—and they wouldn't accept the gift. Then the manor burned down."

"That's it, essentially. After the fire, father and son moved into the chapel instead of rebuilding."

"And the son was the first Tregarrick vampire."

"Thomas, yes."

I looked at him. "What's interesting to me is how all of that happened at once."

His eyes met mine. "Elaborate, please."

Trying not to be distracted by his keen attention, I said, "Father Kelly seems to think the creature in the story might have been some kind of nature spirit or fairy, and my mother believed fairies could live forever. There are banshees in Ireland who follow the same families for generations. What if St. Gomonda only *believed* he had killed him? Maybe instead it was . . . I don't know, a kind of sleep that he woke from? I mean, if you think about what was happening on the estate when the trouble all started . . ."

Harker's face had gone ashen again. "Felling trees, digging up and hauling rocks, setting the granite blocks into the ridge." Something flickered in his eyes. "Some of the rock for this chapel was taken from the ruins of an ancient village on the estate."

My brows lifted. "What in heaven's name could have possessed them to use stones from an old ruin? No farmer or miner or sheepherder would dream of doing such a thing."

His smile was bitter. "But the Tregarricks were none of these. Much of the readily available stone on the estate would have been used in building the manor, and of course the chapel was built *before* the manor burned. Taking it from the ruins probably seemed like a sensible solution."

"In the old stories," I said, "people are tormented and cursed for disturbing fairy homes or sacred places. Your family affliction seems very *like* a curse, though Goosevar also seems to have had a particular use for the Tregarricks."

Harker thought for a moment. Then he stood and walked back to the table, where he took up his quill again and began writing. "We know—or at least believe with a fair degree of certainty—that he requires blood, and he requires the males of my family to consume it for him. We don't know why, but we can probably assume this helps him avoid discovery."

"His hunting might well be what got him into trouble with St. Gomonda. Now the Tregarricks are the ones who take all the risk."

"Or *were*."

As he bent over his paper, the waves of his hair curtained his face. What would it feel like to reach out and push them back? I imagined his eyes lifting to mine as I did it. I imagined his lips curving in a fond smile.

Then his eyes did lift, and there was even the hint of a smile. "I couldn't do this without you, Mina."

His words raised a deep flush, and I let out a sheepish laugh. "It's hard to see things sometimes when you're so close to them."

"No," he said with a firm shake of his head. "It's more than that. You're bright, Mina. You are naturally very logical, and your mind is quick. Had you the advantages I've had—"

"I might be an alchemist too?" I smiled. "Somehow I don't think it's the same for a woman. My brother doesn't even like me working in a tearoom."

His lips pressed together, and he nodded. "You're right, of course. But there *are* women in science and medicine, and one day there will be more."

As much as I enjoyed hearing him sing my praises, the thought of Jack was enough to drag me back to the real world.

"I think I must go home, Harker. I'm worried about the way Jack has been behaving. He won't know I was enchanted and brought here by an ancient blood-drinking forest spirit, and wouldn't believe it if I told him. I don't want to see either of you hurt."

Harker's expression dimmed. "Of course. But how are we to keep you safe after what happened today?"

His anxiety for me lodged like a dart in my heart. "I suppose I must truly keep inside the cottage now. But I wish to continue helping you. Maybe you can send Mr. Carew to me, so we may exchange messages."

Nodding, he said, "I'll also ask him to keep an eye on your cottage." He rose from the table and picked up my shawl from the chairback. "I'll walk you home."

Much as I wished to delay our leave-taking, I said, "I don't think we should take the risk. Jack has been coming home at odd hours lately—remember, he believes you attacked me."

The lines of his mouth tightened. "And so I did, Mina."

Our gazes held, and I said softly, "But it wasn't like he imagines."

Harker came to me, and instead of handing me the shawl, he reached around and settled it over my shoulders. My heart pulsed as the herb-and-brandy scent of him washed over me. His fingers still held the shawl's edges, and I fought my body's wish to lean into him.

When at last he let go, one hand came slowly to the side of my face, stopping an inch away from my skin. "I'll see you to the edge of the estate, at least."

Unsteady from the sudden rush of my heart, I could only nod.

After the comfort of the chapel—and the unexpected moment of . . . *tenderness?*—stepping outside was like crossing from a meadow of spring wildflowers into the deep gloom of winter. The rain drummed steadily down, and I draped my shawl over my head.

"Let me go ahead," he said. "The stairs will be slippery."

We were nearly down safely when a loud voice startled us both. *"I warned you, Tregarrick."*

Raindrops stung my eyes as my gaze swept quickly over the ground at the bottom of the stairs. A lone oak tree, separated from its brethren in the woods to the north, pressed up against the outcrop maybe twenty feet from where we stood, and I made out a figure beneath it.

His light face and hands stood out against the dark trunk, but I knew who it was without them.

He had a *pistol* aimed at us.

"Jack!" I cried. "For God's sake—"

The pistol fired, and I let out a scream.

Harker tumbled down the last few steps, splaying on the ground. Even through the wine-colored waistcoat, I could see the bloom of dark blood.

DEATH

I hurried down to him, then slipped and landed hard on my backside at the bottom of the steps. Pain shot up my tailbone as I crawled to his side.

"Harker," I said, breathless and shaking. The circle of dark blood widened. I pressed a hand to his cold face. His eyes were softly closed, raindrops glistening in his fine, dark lashes. I bent my cheek to his lips. Was there a whisper of breath?

"Mina!" called Jack. I shut out his voice, unbuttoning first the waistcoat, then the shirt. As if I had any idea what must be done! I knew Harker had wound potions in his laboratory, but there was no time for me to search for them. And could they be of any use against a bullet through his chest?

Oh God. His thick blood welled from the hole in time with the slow—and slowing—throb of his heart. It seeped over the smooth flesh of his chest and abdomen. Stifling a sob, I pushed the heel of my hand against the wound, trying to stop the blood.

"Mina!" Jack shouted again. This time he sounded panicked.

"Go for the surgeon!" I shouted back, voice ragged. "If he dies, it will be you that's murdered him!"

Raising my eyes, I saw that Jack had crossed half the distance between us and stopped, his pistol—*who was fool enough to give him that?*—aimed away from the chapel.

Following the line of the barrel, I saw *Goosevar*—crawling slowly from a cluster of jutting rocks. Fangs bared, fog seeped from his peeled-back lips as he straightened to his full height, watching my twin with glittering eyes.

"Jack!" I cried. "Run!"

I jumped as another gunshot shattered the stillness, gray smoke rising from the burnt powder. Again Jack's aim was true; Goosevar let out a snarl and faltered backward. The same thick blood trickled down like sap from the wound in his trunk.

Lowering again to all fours, the monster lunged and then loped, hare-like, over the uneven ground. I shouted another warning as Jack dropped the spent pistol and scrambled away. Goosevar was on him in seconds, catching Jack's ankle in his jaws and dragging him back.

The sound Jack made! *Pain and terror.*

"Please!" I choked out, powerless to do anything else.

Jack squirmed and writhed, and finally he managed to free himself. But as soon as he made it to his feet, the creature swung a branch-like arm, its long-fingered hand knocking Jack to the ground—hard enough that he stayed.

Knotting my skirts in one hand, I dragged myself toward them, but Goosevar bent and hauled Jack up like he was a child. After slinging him over one shoulder, the creature trudged around the southern tip of Roche Rock, mist trailing after him.

Cold rain and hot tears mingled on my cheeks. In my mind, I saw Jack stretched on the heath, drained of blood. The next victim to be found. Our last words to each other had been so angry.

Jack was beyond my help now.

Dress soaked through and heavy, I crawled back to Harker. So much blood! I bent over his mouth and nose again—if there was breath before, there was none now.

"Harker," I sobbed, squeezing his shoulder.

Must I lose everyone?

A host of small moments flitted through my thoughts. Soft glances over cups of smoky tea. The sound of his laughter by the pool on the heath. The first time he'd called me Mina.

The close press of bodies that had nearly ended me.

Something Harker had said now drifted into my mind. *My wounds healed very quickly before I began denying myself blood.*

Then came a desperate, *mad* idea.

I had watched the bloodlust take him. I knew how powerful it was.

Fresh tears streamed down my face. In saving him, if it could be done, there was a very real danger I would lose myself. But in that instant, I found that I had no very strong will to preserve my own life. Not in a world where monsters were real, and my twin brother was one of them. Where he had most likely died because of his decision to murder a man who had struggled his whole life *not* to be a monster.

Fingers trembling, I reached up and fumbled with the rain-soaked bandage around my neck, then unwrapped it and tugged it free. I untied the ribbon that held Mum's cross, closing the small piece of silver in a fist. Finally, I bent over him and pressed my barely closed wounds to his cold lips.

"Harker," I murmured, fingers slipping over his chest until I found the bullet wound. It still seeped, and again I pressed my palm there.

My heart bounced at a small movement against my throat. I felt the quick prick of his teeth and let out a sob of relief. His hand came to the back of my head, and his lips slipped like silk over my skin.

With a sudden gasp, he sat up and dragged me onto his lap. One hand held my throat to his mouth while the other locked around my waist. My warm life flowed into his cold body. I let my arms coil around him like a lover's. If this was my death, I wanted to feel every moment of it. Let that delicious current wash over and through me, carrying me down, down, down into the quiet darkness, until I ebbed and ended.

Then light bloomed behind my closed eyelids.

Autumn leaves. The waning moon. Light and shadow beneath the trees.

Our hands are fasted with bindweed. He bends and presses his lips to mine, and the kiss goes round me, warm as a blanket. Someone calls my name, and I look up. In the distant shadows, I see the silhouette of Goosevar, Jack *in his arms. The creature sets Jack on his feet.*

Jack steps into the moonlight and smiles at me.

"THE OTHER WAY ROUND"

HARKER

This was how it ended. I was an anchor, sinking slowly to the bottom of a dark and lonely sea, echoes of my long life drifting around me. Some memories were brighter than others, like coins winking among the flotsam. One coin was especially bright, and I reached for her, but she slipped through my fingers.

Among this wreckage were many memories I did not recognize, as if they belonged to some other drowned soul. A silver bowl drew my eye, and this I managed to catch. It was highly decorated with both faces and figures, some animal and some human.

One creature had the face of a wolf and antlers like tree branches.

Voices chant around me.

I stand at the foot of a black granite outcrop, my thoughts a tangle of rage and confusion.

I don't know who I am, or how I have come to be here.

I see the blood, and smell it, too. Hot, vivid, sweet, with its copper tang. It fills a silver vessel before me like an offering. One I cannot refuse. I plunge my snout in and lap at it, filling my throat and my belly.

When the vessel is empty, I want more. Beside it lie the broken bodies of three hares, but they are bloodless.

Looking up now, I see the owners of the chanting voices ranged before me, enclosing me against the stone in a half circle. They are cloaked and draped such that I can see no part of them but their hands and faces. Some faces are mostly covered in hair; some are bare and smooth. There are males and females, all holding long staffs. The racket of their chanting stokes my growing rage. I smell their blood and bare my teeth.

An oak tree grows against the outcrop a short distance away, and I notice more figures beneath its branches. Two of them are like the others. They hold the arms of a bound man who is different. The hair of his head is cropped short, with none on his face, and his drapery only reaches his knees. I can smell his fear and his blood. Some of it is smeared across his forehead.

"Bring him!" calls a man standing just opposite me inside the half circle. He has a long red beard threaded with white, and piercing blue eyes. The men holding the prisoner drag him from under the tree, the half circle dividing enough to allow him to be led inside.

"Ancient spirit of the oak forest," calls Red Beard in a deep and grating voice, "we have summoned you so that we may beg your protection. We offer you the blood of three hares, sacred to us, and now the blood of our enemy, who has burned our villages and our forests, and murdered and enslaved our people. We offer him so that you may know him. We ask that you destroy him and his kind, and chase them from our lands and yours."

The men holding the prisoner release him and step away, joining the others. For a moment, he stands frozen before me, eyes wide and round. I can hear the thunderous beating of his heart. I can see his lips working as he begs some outland god to save him. But he is alone. I and my *kind are gods here.*

Then suddenly he bolts like a hare. The half circle divides again, allowing him to pass—and me to follow. The maddening chants resume, but soon I am free. All I can hear or smell or taste is the terror of my prey.

My prey stirred quietly in my arms. I raised my head from her throat, eyes falling on her still features.

Oh God, Mina!

A half-choked sob escaped my lips. I lifted her and pressed my ear to her chest. Beneath the soft swell of her breasts, I could hear it. *Her heart still beats.*

Relief flooded me.

"I am well," came her broken voice.

"You are *not*," was my broken reply.

"You stopped, and both of us live."

A few last vestiges of the memory I'd visited before waking—one I was sure rightfully belonged to the being who'd cursed my family—finally cleared from my mind. Then my *own* memory returned.

Jack Penrose shot me.

My gaze dropped to my bared chest, where Mina was pressed, watching me through heavy-lidded eyes, a faint smile on her full, purpling lips. My wound had closed, though my dark blood smeared us both. The leaden ball had been ejected, rolling free to lodge between her body and mine.

"I—I don't remember attacking you," I stammered.

"It was more the other way round." Her voice was like a child's, dropping off to sleep. "You were dying, and it was the only thing I could think of."

"The only thing . . . ?" Suddenly I understood. *To save me.* "Oh, Mina. Oh, *God.*" The world seemed to tilt, as if to tumble the rock monstrosity that had been the cause of all this suffering and bury us both.

Her cheek rolled against my chest, and she closed her eyes. Her rain-soaked skin was cold as bog water.

Gathering her in my arms, I got my feet under me and ran up the stairs to the chapel.

TANGLED

When I woke, I stubbornly kept my eyes shut, choosing comfort and warmth over the facts that I must face when I stepped back into the world.

But the smells wafting through the room were a very strong temptation. Roasting meat. Harker's smoky tea. Harker himself, and the smell I'd come to know as his—herbs, brandy, old books.

It was the tea—and my desperate thirst—that finally coaxed my eyes open. I found myself for the second time on his comfortable reading chair. A teapot rested on the nearby table, as did a bowl of the same medicinal water. I worked a hand free of the blankets I'd been wrapped in and touched my neck; a fresh bandage covered my newly opened wounds.

My chair had been moved near the hearth, and there I saw a rabbit roasting on a spit before the fire. My mouth watered.

I tried to sit up, but between snugly wrapped blankets, weak limbs, and a bruised tailbone, it proved beyond me. I was about to call out for Harker when I heard boots on the stairs.

"You're awake," he said with relief, coming to me.

I eyed him helplessly. "I'm afraid I'm tangled."

He knelt beside me, a soft smile on his lips as he gradually unwrapped me. My eyes followed his movements. He had put on a clean shirt and rolled the cuffs, exposing the smooth skin and lines of muscle in his forearms, and the knobs and ridges of bone in his wrists and hands.

As the last blanket was peeled back, my breath caught. I was wearing only my shift and corset. My laces had been loosened, too, revealing the curve of my breasts and some of the valley between them.

"Forgive me," he said, his eyes touching mine as he raised the edge of the blanket to cover me. A flush stained his cheeks for the first time since I'd met him. "Your dress was rain soaked and . . . bloodstained. Your breathing was—"

"Thank you," I said. Our fingers brushed as I pressed the blanket in place.

He reached for the teapot and filled a cup, placing it in my hands. "Are you warm enough?"

I was indeed. It was a mystery how the nearness of Harker's cold body could raise such heat in mine. "Yes. I feel much better."

"Good."

I blew steam from the cup and drank. Mrs. Moyle was fond of saying, "Tea sets everything right." Maybe not everything, but it at least gave you a moment to rest and think.

"Where did you get the rabbit?" I asked, a tremor in my voice because of the way he was looking at me. Like I might break, and like that might break *him*.

"In the oak wood. The poachers aren't bold enough to set snares so close to the chapel, and the rabbits are prolific."

"How did you . . . ?" I trailed off, realizing what a silly question I was about to ask. He'd probably chased it down and caught it with his bare hands. "I see," I finished lamely.

He raised one of those hands in the air between us, hesitating a moment while my heart jumped out of rhythm. *Will he touch me this time?* My eyes flicked to his lips, and then realizing there was no way he could have missed that, I let my gaze drop, swallowing dryly.

A lock of hair fell in front of my face, and with his raised hand, he pushed it back.

"Mina, you saved my life."

I gave a shaky nod.

"I might have killed you."

I looked up. "Aye. But you didn't."

He closed his eyes, and I watched the wave of pain wash over him. "I would have placed no value on the life you saved, had I taken yours. I place little value on it as it is."

"And if *you* had died, I would have blamed myself. I . . ." I took a breath, hoping to steady my voice. "I don't think I would have gotten over it."

We eyed each other, and I became aware of a desire I'd never felt before. I wanted—more than anything, so hard it ached—to be in this man's arms. Not as his prey, but in the usual way. Afraid he would read this in my eyes, I lowered them again.

He rose quietly, moving to an armchair opposite the tea table. Some of the wholeness I felt when he was close now seeped away, and fatigue from loss of blood crept back in.

I was trying to understand why he should have this effect on me when he asked, "Where do you suppose Jack has gone?"

My belly twisted. There were things I needed to say to him that I feared might revive the old distance between us. But I couldn't put it off any longer.

"After Jack shot you," I said, "Goosevar came. Then Jack shot him, too—full in the middle of the chest."

Harker's eyes rounded. "Killed?"

I shook my head. "Goosevar just knocked him down and carried him off."

Harker searched my face. "Is he—do you think he's still alive?"

"I believe he is. I've had a dream—a kind of vision, much like yours—and I think we may yet save him." I took a deep breath. "Though maybe you wouldn't choose to."

"The only thing I blame Jack for is his roughness with you. If you were my sister and I thought a man had hurt or compromised you, I would put a bullet in him, too."

Though I was relieved Harker hadn't lost all compassion for Jack, I hesitated, dreading how he might react to the rest of what I had to say. Before I could go on, he said, "We'll discuss this. But first I would like you to eat something."

He moved to kneel beside the fire, where he carved off a hunk of crisped meat and placed it on a costly-looking dish that rested on the hearthstones. Then he spooned something lumpy and glistening from a pot that hung over the flames. *Stewed apples.* Again my mouth watered.

He handed me the dish along with a knife and fork. Too hungry to worry over how it looked, I pulled meat from the delicate bones with my fingers, licking away the grease. Once I'd cleared the plate, he filled it again. I ate that, too, and drank two more cups of tea.

Sinking back with a sigh, I said, "That may have been the best thing I've ever eaten."

He laughed. "You're just depleted. I'm happy to see your appetite. It will help you get your strength back."

He took the dish and handed me a towel so I could clean my hands and face.

"Do you feel well enough to talk more now," he asked, "or would you rather sleep?"

"I think it best we talk." I knew I wouldn't be able to sleep again until I'd told him everything.

"All right." He sat back down in the armchair. "You said you've had a vision?"

"Yes." The blanket that covered my chest had slipped while I was eating, and I tugged it back up. "It was almost exactly like the one you had, with even the small details you described. But Jack was in my vision, too. After the handfasting, Goosevar brought him to us—*alive.*"

Harker shifted in his chair. "I hope he is," he said carefully. "But do you think it might simply have been a dream? Inspired by my vision, and your fear for Jack."

"I know what a dream feels like, Harker. That's not what this was. It's still so clear and real in my mind that it's like it actually happened. I think it may have come to me through your connection to Goosevar, because of your . . . connection to *me*."

Color stained his cheeks again. The vigor that my blood returned to him had made him easier to read. In the same careful tone, he asked, "What do you think it means?"

I held his gaze. "Goosevar is offering us a way to save Jack. A kind of trade."

His face was still. *Too* still. "You mean to say Goosevar is attempting to use Jack to force our hand. That he will spare Jack if we marry."

". . . Yes?" I was wary of his outward calm. "What I'm wondering is whether we can trick him into thinking we're giving him what he wants."

"Trick him how?"

"If we did marry, *hypothetically*—"

"No." I flinched at the iron in his voice. "I am *not* marrying you, Mina Penrose. Hypothetically or otherwise. I don't begrudge Jack his protectiveness, but neither am I willing to trade your life for his. I very much doubt Jack would want that, either."

"It wouldn't have to be that, Harker. Please hear me out."

Might as well have lit a powder blast in a tin mine. "It would be exactly that! Have you forgotten what happened to my mother?"

"I haven't," I assured him. "But Harker, it needn't be a real marriage." Now *my* cheeks flamed, and I hoped I wouldn't have to explain myself further on that point. "We could speak our oaths and get Jack back. Goosevar need never know anything else about it."

"He will expect a *child*, Mina."

I sniffed and adjusted my grip on the blanket. "He can't force us to make one."

Our gazes locked, and I would have bet all the coins in my chemist's tin that both of us were imagining the same thing. I could almost feel his hands on my skin . . . his breath in my hair . . . his lips on my lips . . .

Was it possible that he wanted to touch me as much as I wanted him to? *Not as his prey, but in the usual way.*

His eyes broke away. "You're not thinking. You couldn't go back home with Jack. The ruse would require you to live here. You would never have a normal life. A real husband, or children of your own. None of the things you deserve."

This last line tugged at my heart. And he was right; I *wasn't* thinking. I hadn't let myself think beyond saving Jack. Because I could never be happy in *any* future life if I had a way to save him and didn't. It didn't matter how Jack had changed since our parents died. It didn't matter that we'd grown apart. Jack was my twin, and he would do it for *me.*

He already has. Continuing in a job that was eating his soul away. Spending his free hours inside a bottle because it was the only way he could bear it. When Da first took him to the mines, he used to talk about running off to seek his fortune. He once told Da he wanted to go to sea. Probably he'd been thinking about the smugglers along the Cornish coast, which people loved to tell stories about. Da told him the work was no easier and the food was worse, and for a week he had hardly spoken to any of us.

What had kept him from just walking away after Mum and Da died?

Me. I had no one else. He stayed because of *me.*

Now it was my turn.

All this was too much to expect Harker to understand in this moment, so I settled for, "There is no happiness waiting for me in a life where I choose not to save my brother."

He closed his eyes, jaw clenching. I took a long breath and glanced at the window. Twilight had fallen, and the clouds had cleared. A bright moon hung in the sky, silvering the heath below.

"Even if we set every other argument aside," said Harker, his tone finally softening, "we can hardly assume this would be the end of it. If we give in to this, Goosevar would likely only keep at us. Find more ways to compel us."

"But it would buy us time," I said. "Everything continues. We keep working together to discover a way to stop him. And Harker, I could help you in other ways. Ways that might make your life easier."

His eyes came back to me, flashing. "You of all people should understand what it means to get that close to me."

Refusing to flinch from his gaze, I replied, "I understand that when we're careful, we make do. You have your laboratory, and I . . . well, I could keep to this room at night. This chair is like sleeping on a cloud compared to my straw mattress at home. And it wouldn't have to all be torture, Harker. Think how we could ease each other's loneliness. Think how we have already."

His eyes narrowed. "You hardly need convince me of what light you would bring to my life. I've gotten a glimpse of that myself these last days. But never mind the bloodlust; have you thought about the normal temptations? Married in the eyes of God, always in one another's company? You might be able to bear it, Mina, but I . . ." He trailed off and shook his head.

He does feel something of what I do. Gazes lifting over open books. Hands brushing as we passed teacups. Huddling before the hearth on cold winter nights.

"It wouldn't be easy," I admitted, trembling now. "For either of us."

Harker raised his hand, thumb and fingers pressing his temples. "Even if we found a way to stop Goosevar—to sever his connection with my family—there is no reason to think *I* would change. There is no reason to think I'd be anything other than what I am now."

"And what are you, Harker?"

He dropped his hand, frustration drawing his brows down.

"A kind man," I continued. "A gentle man. A brave man. A man willing to deny himself for the sake of others. These are things Goosevar has failed to take from you." I held his gaze. "Don't make my sacrifice out to be greater than it is."

His expression one of mild shock, his eyes drifted to the hearth. There were long moments of needed quiet, the soothing sounds of the fire drawing the charge out of the air.

It wasn't nothing, the fact that I might never have a true family of my own. But unless we were children, decisions couldn't only be about what we might like best. Jack had taught me that. And if Harker agreed to my proposal, I would have *him*. I would have Jack. And I would have Mrs. Moyle, because Harker would never ask me to give her up. Did I really need more than that?

Finally Harker shifted, sitting up in his chair. "After what you did today, I would give you almost anything you asked for, and not for that reason alone. But this . . ." He shook his head, and my heart sank. "I know how worried you must be about Jack, but I need to leave it for now. I need time to think. And there's something else we must speak of."

Steadying myself with a breath, I said, "Of course."

He bent toward me, elbows on his knees. "When I was dying, I saw something, too. Different from before—more like a memory. I lived it as if it were my own, but when I woke, I knew it wasn't. It was Goosevar's."

My brows lifted. "Tell me!"

"It began with an artifact that had a likeness of Goosevar hammered into it. A silver ceremonial bowl filled with blood."

The scene he then described sounded very much like it could be the story of Goosevar's beginnings. His history. But I found much of it puzzling.

"Did you understand who any of the people were?" I asked.

"Not at the time. But while you were sleeping, I consulted what books I have on the history of Britannia, and I believe I do now. The robed chanters were druids. Does the word mean anything to you?"

I nodded. "Mum talked of druids sometimes when we left offerings at the sacred well in Coldvreath. She said they were holy men of the old religion, before priests, and that they, too, had once left offerings at the well."

"That's right. Druids were the priests—and priestesses—of this isle before the Roman army invaded."

"Father Kelly talked about the Romans when I looked at the bell tower painting with him. He said they went to war against the old religion and won. Do you think the man the druids gave to Goosevar was a Roman?"

"I do. They wanted the creature they'd summoned to have a taste for their enemy's blood."

I shuddered. "After what you told me about the disturbed ruins, I had thought Goosevar might be a kind of fairy. My mother believed this heath belonged to the fairies, and that fairies could be vicious in protecting their homes."

Harker rubbed his chin, thinking. "That may yet be true. He seems to have his roots in nature and the ancient Celtic people, as do fairies. He also reminds me in some ways of the Celtic god Cernunnos, who was worshipped as the lord of nature."

"Well, whatever he is, it seems he's outlived all of them—druids *and* Romans."

"And he is still what they made him. He might not know how to be anything else."

"A blood-drinker."

Harker got up, stretched his limbs, and tossed more turf onto the fire. The shadows in the room had deepened; outside, night was falling.

"It would be helpful to know whether they had any plan for unmaking what they had made," he said. "But that knowledge seems far beyond our reach."

Holding the blanket in place, I sat up and lifted the teapot. Harker's eyes followed the movement.

"The tea will be cold," he said, "and bitter. I can make more."

I smiled, remembering that this was how our first conversation had begun, at The Magpie. I felt less skittish of him now—in some ways. More so in others.

"I don't mind," I said, filling my cup with the dark brew.

As he stood watching the fire, something occurred to me. "I wonder if your connection with Goosevar becomes stronger when you drink blood. Maybe that's why you can see his memories."

His brow furrowed. "I think that would stand to reason, except that my father never mentioned anything like this. I suppose if he never discovered Goosevar's existence, he would think them no more than strange dreams."

"It seems to me our handfasting visions must be related to the connection, too, though they are not memories of the past but—"

"Expectations for the future," he muttered.

With a sigh he turned and began collecting the dishes, a deep frown on his lips. I finished my tea and handed him the cup. As he took it from me, he froze.

My heart skipped. "What is it?"

His expression flat, he handed the cup back to me without meeting my gaze.

A few leaves had stuck below the handle.

They formed a ring.

VOW

I looked at him. "It's the same as—"

"Yes, I haven't forgotten."

I watched him closely, understanding what kind of fight was going on in his head. I couldn't bring myself to point out that not just the symbol but also its position beneath the cup handle had meaning.

Not only a wedding, but soon.

He set the dishes on the hearth and sank back down in the armchair. "While I'm not likely to assign a shape in a teacup more importance than your logical arguments and earnest pleas, it does begin to feel I'm holding out unreasonably."

"Your hesitation is not unreasonable."

When he looked at me, his eyes were full of the gentle gratitude that was so very Harker. "I don't know how we would even do it, Mina. For a common license we would need to apply to the bishop at Exeter, some seventy miles from here . . . which would be risky for a whole host of reasons. It would be far better to wait out the weeks required for the banns to be read, but I don't know that we can expect Goosevar to understand our modern way of doing things."

I felt a fizzing in my chest as I took in these details. *This is becoming real.* Yet I began to fear that bringing Harker to this point had been easy compared to what was coming.

"I don't think we can," I said. "But we could easily arrange a ceremony that matches what we've seen in the vision."

The sudden flash of his eyes would have caused me to step back had I been on my feet. "That wouldn't be a legal marriage."

I nodded faintly. "We could make it legal once the banns were read."

"And in the meantime," he said, "you will have to remain here with me *as if* we are married. You know what people will say about that. They've always gossiped about me, but I don't want that for you, Mina."

Wringing a corner of the blanket, I replied, "I don't know how it can be helped. My brother's life . . . finding a way to prevent future killings—these things matter more than my reputation."

His gaze fixed on me. "You could lose your job. You might not see Mrs. Moyle again."

I hadn't thought of this, but of course he was right. If I was ruined in the eyes of the village, I could hardly continue working in the tearoom. "Yes," I said softly.

Thankfully he let his head tip against the top of the chairback, so he didn't see my tears pooling. I wiped my eyes and held my breath.

After a few moments, he said, "When?"

I stifled a sob that was equal parts relief and regret. Clearing my throat, I replied, "As soon as possible. Tonight. If we mean to save Jack, we shouldn't wait."

He looked at me, worry lines etched in his fine skin. "What if he's already dead, Mina? What if it's a trick? We've no reason to think we can trust Goosevar."

I nodded, looking down as tears again stung my eyes. "If he tricks us, then we needn't be bound by the handfasting. We needn't go through with the official wedding."

My whole life would be upended either way. Bound to Harker, or, with Jack gone, no way to support myself. Even if what I made at The Magpie had been enough, I couldn't live alone as an unmarried woman (a painful reminder of the sacrifice Jack had made for me). With Mrs. Moyle's help, I might be able to seek out my kin in Yorkshire. But I'd lose what was left of my Roche family—Mrs. Moyle and Harker.

Harker rose from his chair and came to kneel before me, stopping my heart.

"I agree to this on one condition," he said, resting a hand on the blanket beside me. "If Goosevar spares Jack, first thing in the morning, we go to the parish priest and tell him we wish to be married. When the banns are read Sunday, people will at least know we intend to do the honorable thing."

I quietly let out my breath. "I agree. And we can go to The Magpie before it opens, so Mrs. Moyle may see that I am well. I can tell her then that I won't be back. If people aren't seeing me going between here and the tearoom, we might avoid a scandal." I might lose my job, but if we were careful enough, I might keep my friend.

His eyes followed an escaped tear down my cheek. "I have many regrets, Mina. But none so great as you ever becoming involved with the Tregarricks."

I lifted my chin. "I have regrets of my own, but meeting you is not one of them."

The deep, dark purple of his eyes was soft as velvet. He raised his hand and brushed the tear track dry with his thumb, sending a shiver through me.

Then he got to his feet and held out his hand. "Come. I have a trunk full of old things upstairs. There may be something that will suit."

At first I didn't understand. Then it came to me—for the handfasting. Unless I wished to be wed in my shift or my bloodstained muslin, I would need a new dress.

I wrapped the blanket around my shoulders and took his hand. It was warmer than usual.

Because he's feeding.

My steps were stiff and slow on the stairs. "Where will we do this?" I asked.

"The trees in my vision reminded me of the woods below the chapel. Perhaps there."

"Do you think he'll know, or will we have to search him out?"

"I doubt much of anything happens on the estate without him knowing it."

Upstairs, we crossed to the stained glass window and his narrow bed beneath. A heavy trunk rested at its foot.

"Here, sit down," he said, and I sank on the edge of the mattress.

He opened the trunk with a creak of old hinges. It was full of clothing, and the scent of lavender lifted into the air as he dug through it.

"I've noticed that much of what you wear is an older style," I said. "Do you prefer it?"

"It's more that I very rarely leave the estate. I've one suit of modern clothing, and I keep it clean and ready in case I do need to go out." He sat back on his heels, placing a stack of folded men's things aside on the floor. "But I suppose I do feel more myself in the older styles. Does it bother you?"

I shook my head. "It suits you. From studying the finer folk I serve in The Magpie, it seems to me that fashions—ladies' especially—have become stiff and almost like cages. But my own dresses are plain and pretty well worn." I felt my cheeks go pink. "I've almost saved enough money for something fresher in the New Year."

But I'd be living a different life by then. I felt the first of what was sure to be many pangs for the life I'd give up. A true marriage, with a husband in my bed and babes in my arms one day. I'd never really longed for such things until now. It was hard not to think about how that might be with Harker, were things different. What our own children might look like.

He drew out a russet-red gown and laid it over the edge of the lid. "I wish we had time for something that wasn't handed down. But it's in good condition still, and I think it might fit you."

The gown's bodice was long and straight, the waist neatly pleated all the way round, with a bit of padding at the hips to give the skirt lift. The sleeves, too, were straight, and elbow length. A sweet layer of lace peeked out at the neckline and sleeve ends.

"It's lovely," I said, fingering the fine fabric. I wondered if the gown had been his mother's.

"I'm glad you like it. I'll go back down while you dress, but call me if you need me."

To my eye the gown was a little slim, so I stripped off both my shift and corset before putting it on. The bodice fastened in front, and it gave me a squeeze, but I managed to close it all the way. The gown's owner had been a tall woman, and I'd have to keep it off the ground, but the extra length would cover my long feet and battered old shoes.

I knelt beside the trunk, carefully sorting through it until I found a muslin shawl. There was also a brush with an ivory handle, and I worked it through my tangled hair. I had no pins, so I would have to leave it loose.

I put away the brush and then unwound the bandage from my neck. It bore only a slight pink smear, and when I touched the wounds, they felt dry. I laid the wrapping aside with my shift and corset.

"May I come up?" Harker called from below.

"Yes, I've finished." I glanced around for a looking glass, but none was in sight.

He joined me, and I watched him closely as his eyes moved over me, lingering a beat at my neckline, where the tight-fitting bodice had caused me to be higher, rounder, and more exposed than ever before.

"How beautiful you are, Mina."

Heat spread from my cheeks to my chest.

He raised his hand, and I saw that Mum's cross dangled from its ribbon, silver winking in the lamplight. "May I?" he asked.

I nodded and he came closer, moving behind me. I lifted my hair, and his breath against the back of my neck was warmer, like his skin.

"Be careful," I whispered as he threaded the necklace around me.

I shivered as his fingers tickled the nape of my neck. Once the ribbon was tied, I turned, letting my hair fall. We were standing close, the small talisman between us.

"It dropped from your hand as I carried you inside," he said.

"I promise to always wear it."

A sad smile curved his lips. "The vows have begun."

Excitement fluttered through me, despite fears, regrets, and strange circumstances.

Harker went to the shelves on the other side of the room, then took down a wine bottle and two goblets. He returned, handing me one goblet of wine and raising the other between us.

"To your health, Mina. And the success of our endeavors."

"Yes," I said, raising my glass to his. "May we find a way together."

The wine was strong and full of dark, overripe fruit, like late-September blackberries. There was also a cool, stony flavor that made me think of the holy well at Coldvreath. Unused to wine, and weak from earlier, I knew if I finished my glass I would be stumbling down the stairs, so I took tiny sips.

His gaze fixed on me, and my heart somehow sensed what was coming. Raising my glass again, I let the wine fill my mouth this time, fruity and tart on my tongue yet dry as clay dust in my throat.

"Nothing is set," he said. "Nothing has been said that can't be unsaid. I need you to tell me, Mina. Is this really what you want?"

"I WILL END MYSELF"

HARKER

"It's what I want." She didn't look away. She didn't hesitate.

I took the goblet from her hand and set them both on the end of my laboratory table.

As ever, I was acutely aware of the blood throbbing at her throat. And now, too, of the small holes that would open at the merest touch of my lips. Even sated from earlier, I wanted nothing more than to taste her again, though perhaps the need was slightly less frantic. How vigilant I would have to be from now on.

Have I gone mad? Join myself to her, but never taste her? Never touch *her in more than the most glancing way?*

But there had never been anything easy about my existence. And taking her as my wife . . . it would make my life worth living.

I can do it for her.

In truth, I was too selfish to deny her.

I reached out and took her warm hands in mine. "Mina Penrose, will you marry me?"

Her wine-stained lips parted, and I felt her tremble as she answered, "I will."

"Then let us go."

I unfolded and smoothed down my sleeves, buttoned the collar of my shirt, and took my waistcoat and coat from the back of a chair.

Returning to her, I offered her my arm, and together we went downstairs and out into the night.

The air was still and damp, but the rain had stopped, and a gibbous moon shone down from the bejeweled indigo sky. It was a night very like the one in my vision.

Mina was still weakened by loss of blood, which showed in the lost gloss of her skin, the shadows beneath her eyes, and the care she took in her movements.

We followed the path along the edge of the oak wood. When I was a child, there were well-worn paths all through the wood, but on my hunt earlier today, I found they'd mostly dwindled to small game trails. Yet there was one slightly wider, perhaps used by the deer, that led to a small clearing. I watched for the trail entrance, and when we reached it, I parted and held back the dry ferns so she could pass.

She was sylvan in the moonlight. In that dress of autumn russet, with her flowing, dark-red hair, she might have been a dryad, or Titania herself.

The fallen leaves limned the path in bronze and gold, making it easier to find our way. The wood's inhabitants were mostly quiet, either sleeping or hiding from the intruders who crushed acorns beneath their feet. Our steps released scents of decaying leaves, damp moss, and raw, rich earth.

As we neared the clearing, I heard the warning bark of a fox, followed by the reedy call of a tawny owl.

"I think Goosevar is close," Mina whispered.

I glanced back and saw a low, thin layer of mist filling in the path behind her, like spilled milk pooling, almost to the edge of her trailing skirt. I reached for her hand and drew her closer.

The clearing ahead was washed in the light of the moon that hung almost directly above us now. As we stepped into it, Mina pointed and murmured, "Look, Harker."

On the clearing's edge was a dark standing stone. A vine curled around it, moon-colored, trumpet-shaped flowers open toward the sky.

We went to the stone, and I pinched free a length of vine, releasing its bitter scent. I took her hand and began winding the vine around our wrists and forearms, protecting the bright blooms as best I could.

We stood eyeing each other over our joined hands. I had balked at the idea of a wedding that no one but Goosevar would recognize as such. Yet in this woodland chapel, under the watchful moon, regal in her velvet cloak of stars, that notion seemed very small. What need had we of anything more than this ancient rite that had served the inhabitants of this island for centuries?

"Are you ready?" Mina asked. I could feel the quick beat of her heart.

I glanced around the clearing and saw that the mist had filled in to the edges.

"Come, then!" I called out. "This is what you've asked of us! Will you bear witness?"

A shadow shifted in the trees behind Mina. I could just make out the great crown of branches sweeping back from the canine face, eyes glowing like distant flames. Fog shrouded his features with each huff of breath.

"Goosevar is here," I said.

Her grip tightened. "Is Jack with him?"

From behind Goosevar, a smaller figure stepped to one side. A finger of moonlight reached down through the trees, revealing a lock of red hair.

"Yes."

She could bear it no longer; still gripping my hand, she twisted to peer into the trees. "Jack?" I could hear the sob in her voice. "Are you well?"

No response came.

"Shall we do what we've come here to do?"

Her eyes came back to me. She nodded.

I moved closer, sweeping my thumb over the back of her hand. "With moon, stars, and ancient oaks as our witnesses, with bindweed to hold us to our vows, I take you, Mina Penrose, as my wife."

She drew a quick breath. "With Jack Penrose—who came with me into this world—as our witness, I take you, Harker Tregarrick, as my husband."

I smiled to encourage her, though my own heart thudded heavily against my ribs. "I vow to remain yours and yours alone until death shall part us."

She answered with her own sweet smile. "I vow to remain yours and yours alone until death shall part us."

Leaning in, I brought my lips close to hers and made a silent, final vow to us both.

And I will end myself before I let this be your life.

HOME

Though our kiss was a careful one—light and soft as the brush of moth wings—it changed something in me forever. *Yours and yours alone until death shall part us.*

Opening our eyes, we shared a moment of perfect stillness. Our first as man and wife.

Then he began to unwind the bindweed. I felt a tingling warmth where the vine had touched my skin, like magic working.

A slight sound behind me reminded me why we were here, and I turned to find Jack stepping into the clearing.

Lifting my hem from the ground, I was about to run to him when Harker set a hand on my shoulder. "Wait."

As Jack came, Harker's lips parted, exposing the tips of his fine-pointed fangs. He moved to stand in front of me, gaze locking with Jack's.

Heart knocking in my chest, I said in a shaky voice, "It's all right, Harker."

With his wordless threat delivered, Harker moved slightly to one side.

Jack reached out and took my hands in his. "Mina," he breathed, green eyes wide and wild in the moonlight.

"Are you well, brother?" Relief, fear, and worry ribboned through my voice.

He cast a glance behind him, and my eyes followed. Goosevar had left us.

"Can you tell me what happened?" I said. "Where have you been?"

"I . . . don't . . ." His eyes flitted to Harker, pain and confusion creasing his brow.

"Jack," I said, dragging his attention back. "It's all right. Harker has helped me to save you. He's not the killer."

Releasing my hands, Jack glowered. "I don't want—" But after these few words, he broke off with a choking sound in his throat.

"Something is wrong," said Harker.

I moved closer to Jack, gripping his arm. "What's happened to you?"

Panic flickered in his eyes now, and his gaze swung around the clearing again.

"You're *safe*, Jack. Do you hear me?"

His eyes came back to me. His lips parted, and he shook his head. Then suddenly he turned and darted off through the trees.

"Jack!" I shouted after him, my voice breaking. *"Jack!"* Feeling Harker's hand at the small of my back, I cast him an anxious glance. "He seems fey, does he not?"

Harker nodded. "It almost seems a kind of enchantment. Like what happened to you on the heath. Maybe to stop him from speaking about what happened to him?"

I stared after my twin, drying a tear that had slipped onto my cheek. Would he be fool enough to go after Goosevar? The creature had held up his end of our bargain, but future mercies seemed unlikely.

"Maybe he's gone home," suggested Harker. "Shall we go there, too?"

I turned, managing a smile as my heart swelled with gratitude. "Aye. I can make us all supper."

"There may be things you'd like to have from there, as well."

It's no longer my home. That fact had yet to really settle in. But it wasn't for me to feel the happiness and excitement of a new bride.

The bright moon allowed us to find our way down the heath rather than walk on the road, which would help us to keep our business quiet.

We wouldn't be able to avoid our neighbors' disapproval for long, but I was glad not to have to face it on our wedding night.

Mist rose and thickened around our knees, like we were walking on clouds, and I wondered whether we would glimpse Goosevar again. I suspected if we did all that he wished, we might go the rest of our lives without seeing him. But of course that couldn't be.

It was a blow to find the cottage dark and quiet; Harker's idea that Jack might have come here had given me hope. We entered through the back door, and Harker, who saw better than I in the dark, lit the lamp on the table and then went around lighting candles.

"He'll be back," he said. "He's bound to be confused and afraid right now, but he has nowhere else to go."

"Do you think it will wear off, whatever is afflicting him?"

He set the lamp on the table. "I wish I could say. It may be that he'll never be able to speak of what happened to him. But he has survived." He stepped closer to me. "You're not alone, Mina. For good or ill, you never will be again. Whatever happens, we'll face it together."

Warmth pooling in my chest, I nodded.

With a careful smile, he said, "You must be cold. I'll light a fire."

The room *was* cold, and the candles cast long shadows on the walls. Yet in my blood, something was simmering. *You're not alone. We'll face it together.* Harker and I were a "we" now.

As he was turning toward the hearth, I said, "If we light the cookstove, I can make supper and tea. It heats the cottage enough for all but the bitterest-cold days."

He gave me a doubtful look. "Are you sure you wouldn't rather rest?"

"I think it will help take my mind off things. If Jack does come back, he'll likely be hungry."

It turned out Harker had no experience with cookstoves, but I showed him the firebox and the basket of wood and kindling, and by the time I'd changed into a dress that I didn't mind soiling, he had it ablaze.

"This seems a worthwhile apparatus," he said.

He moved to the other side of my worktable and watched as I mixed ingredients for pie dough. I would have to bake from what I had on hand—eggs, potatoes, a few dry crumbles of cheese, and a tin of smoked pilchards.

It felt very strange having him here in our cottage. I wondered what he made of the rough planked floor and plain furnishings. Though I was doing something I'd probably done a thousand times, I was nervous and kept spilling and dropping things.

"Mrs. Moyle gave us the stove when she put a new one in The Magpie's kitchen," I explained. "I've been thanking her ever since by making pasties for the shop." I picked up the rolling pin and flattened my dough. "Jack's always complained about my job, and he certainly wasn't keen about putting in the stovepipe, but he's never complained about going hungry."

"He seems not to realize how lucky he's been to have you."

I smiled. "Maybe. But we've always depended on each other. And I've been lucky, too. He might have left when Da and Mum passed. He hates the mine. But he stayed."

"What would he rather do?"

I turned to prick my boiling potatoes with a fork. They were soft, and I set them off the heat. "I don't know, and I don't think he does, either. Jack's always been a dreamer."

Who is it that's married the mysterious master of Roche Rock?

"What have you dreamed of, Mina?"

Harker's voice was low, and I turned. "Me?"

He held my gaze and waited.

No one had ever asked me this question. Not even dear Mrs. Moyle.

I gave a slow shrug. "People like me don't really dream. Our future is set from the day we are born."

"Not even when you were a child?"

He wasn't going to accept a glancing answer. I folded my arms, considering.

"I suppose I did dream when I was a girl. Twins are close, and my dreams were wrapped up with Jack's. For a time, I wanted to be a Knight of the Round Table." Harker smiled at this. "And for a time, Jack didn't see any reason I couldn't be. We were near grown when our parents died, and soon after that Jack took to the bottle. Then I dreamed of a change. *Any* change, really. I was lonely."

"So you went to The Magpie."

I lifted my piecrust into the tin. "Mrs. Moyle opened the tearoom after losing her husband, and in a way, she and I became family. We enjoy each other's company. She helped me with my reading and writing. She loans me books. My pay from The Magpie makes our lives a little more comfortable." I raised an eyebrow and looked at him. "And I meet interesting people."

He laughed, and the sound lifted my heart.

But he soon sobered. "Did you think of marrying? Of having a family of your own?"

I eyed him, uneasy. "Not in a way of longing for it. I knew it would likely mean giving up The Magpie. But I miss Jack and me and our parents all together. I haven't quite figured out who I am without them."

He nodded and lowered his gaze to my flour-dusted worktable.

"How about you, Harker? What have you dreamed of?"

Eyes still down, he echoed, "My future was set from the day I was born."

I could have asked him what he'd asked me. *Not even when you were a child?* Yet I knew what his childhood had been, and the question felt cruel. No mother, no brothers or sisters. A boy who went looking for a playmate inside the other tower he could see from his window.

I pressed and smoothed the crust into the tin, wishing I were better with words.

Finally, he looked up. He smiled, but there wasn't much warmth in it.

"Once we're legally married," he said, "everything I have will be yours. I'll go over the books with you. We'll find a new solicitor, and

I'll make sure everything is set up just as it should be. There are no Tregarricks left to dispute your claim."

"What are you talking about, Harker?"

"Only that should anything happen to me, the money is yours. You may use it in any way you see fit, even if that means selling the estate. In fact I'd advise you to."

I stared at him, heart thumping. "And where exactly are you going to be while I'm off spending your money?"

I could hear the angry edge to my voice, yet he let out a sound very much like a *chuckle*. It was dry as dust, but my anger burned hotter anyway.

"I don't mean to upset you," he said. "I'm only talking of possibilities. Dangers seem to be hemming us in on all sides. I don't want to leave anything unsaid."

"Well," I said shortly, "it sounds more like leave-taking to me." I eyed him more closely, and he had the decency to blush. "If you've been considering the *possibility* that I might live happier with you gone, I'll remind you that just a few minutes ago you told me I wasn't alone. That from now on we face things *together*."

I spun on my heel and took the potatoes from the stove. I spooned them into a bowl with the fish and whisked eggs, stirring so violently the whole thing turned to mash. Good thing I'd used a bottom crust, or it would've stuck like the devil. I poured in the filling and covered it with the other crust, used a knife to cut a few slits, and then slid it into the oven, closing the door with a loud clang of iron.

When I turned, he was *right* behind me, and I let out a squeal. "You mustn't do that when I come home with you," I snapped. "You'll stop my poor heart."

He raised his hand and lifted my chin. "Why are you crying, Mina?"

"I'm *not*." But I was. I felt the sting of salt on my cheeks. "Only I don't like you talking about dying not an hour after we've gotten married."

"I'm sorry. It was wrong of me."

"Very."

His eyes made tiny movements as they searched mine. "You would miss me, then?"

His thumb glided over my chin, and I felt like I'd had a bellyful of his strong wine—fiery, sharp, and heady. My knees wanted to fold, and maybe sensing this, his arms came around my waist. The fire in my belly spread to lower chambers.

I don't want to leave anything unsaid. "More than miss you," I said, my voice softening. "It would leave a hole in me."

His arms tightened, pressing our bodies together, and I could feel his heavy heartbeat behind his ribs. I whispered, "Is this too much?"

He groaned and closed his eyes, but his arms stayed where they were. "Too much and not enough."

Though it was selfish and reckless and wrong, I found myself asking, "Will you kiss me, Harker?"

He opened his eyes. My gaze dropped to his lips—and I saw the gleaming tips of his wolf teeth. His thirst was roused. I felt the slight but comforting weight of the cross against my chest.

I stood perfectly still as his hand came to my face. My heart raced as his thumb traced my bottom lip. My lips opened to his touch, and I gasped quietly as the tip of his thumb grazed my tongue.

With another groan, one that sounded more like a growl, he let go of me and took a step back.

"Forgive me," I breathed, bracing myself with a hand against the edge of the worktable. "I shouldn't have asked you."

His smile was grim. "You are a bride, and you have every right. Please understand how it pains me not to do as you wish. Especially when I wish it, too."

I shook as I turned and set the teakettle on the stove. I kept my back to him, trying to slow my heart and still the pulse of my desire. I heard him scoot out one of the dining chairs and sit. In the loud silence, I waited for the water to boil, and then I filled the teapot.

Finally, sinking down across from him, I realized how weary I was. Between the moments of roused feeling, the fatigue of the long and eventful day set in. In truth, I was tired enough to forgo supper for bed. But I had held out hope Jack would come home. It wouldn't be like him to spend a night out of doors, especially in October. I worried he wasn't in his right mind.

Guessing my thoughts, Harker said, "Why don't we brave Jack's anger and stay here tonight? I'll watch for him while you sleep. I think for tonight, until I can make some changes at home, you'll be more comfortable here anyway."

I met his gaze. "It's kind of you, Harker. Though I fear he won't come."

"Then we'll ask after him when we go to the village tomorrow morning."

Nodding, I said, "We can try the tavern. That's where he mostly is when he's not at the mine." Yet this time I doubted he was off drowning in a bottle. I'd never seen him so shaken. Not even when Da and Mum died.

"His drinking is hard on you, isn't it?"

I took a breath, letting it out in a sigh. "It's changed him. And I hardly see him now, since he really only comes home to eat and sleep. But I guess it helps him forget."

"It probably feels a little like he's abandoned you."

"It feels a lot like that, usually. At the same time, I think about how maybe he could have had a different life if he hadn't stayed to take care of me. I was lucky to have The Magpie. The work eased my loneliness and brought me some joy." Shrugging, I said, "I shouldn't talk so much of loneliness when you've been truly alone for most of your life."

He frowned. "I probably understand it better than most, and I do envy you your family. Especially Jack. I always wished for a sibling. I think it's unnatural for any creature to be so alone. I suppose it's not surprising that my forefathers all eventually married, even if it was the last thing they intended."

Something occurred to me then. "Have you wondered whether Goosevar might have been involved with that?"

"How do you mean?"

"Well, just that as they got older and the bloodlust lessened, maybe Goosevar gave them visions, too. Even if they didn't understand where they were coming from, the visions may have had an effect. We still don't fully understand his connection to your family."

Not liking the way this felt knocking around in my heart, I tilted my teacup. A single damp leaf—looking like nothing more than that—had stuck to the bottom.

"Mina." Glancing up, I found his eyes fixed on me. "Goosevar may have manipulated us into marrying, but what I feel for you has nothing to do with him. What I feel for you has nothing to do with the bloodlust."

I stared, heart thumping wildly. I swallowed, though my mouth had gone dry. "But he chose me *for* you, Harker. You said it yourself—I was only the second woman to have set foot on the estate since you were a boy."

He grimaced. "I did say that. And it was cruel of me."

"I prefer your honesty," I replied, though my voice broke. "Rank, education, upbringing . . . we are mismatched in every way. Goosevar pushed you to marry me for his own reasons. Then I pushed you to marry me for mine."

A muscle worked in his jaw, but I kept going. "If we somehow manage to free ourselves from him, I will hold you to no vow. I will always have a home here with Jack. He blusters, but I know he'd never turn me out."

There was a blur of movement, and a slight shiver in the air that I realized always came with Harker's vampire quickness.

I found myself suddenly up out of my chair and folded in his arms.

PLEASURES OF THE FLESH

I gasped as he crushed me against him. And again as his hand came to my face and pulled my lips to his.

I felt no needle pricks of pain, only the soft fullness of his dark mouth, like a ripe plum. Unlike when he'd fed on me, I wasn't slipping deliciously into a dream. Awash in fiery new sensations, I clung to his coat lapels, worried that at any moment he would remember himself and this would end.

Our mouths were greedy, slipping against each other and tasting, as if cleaning honey from a spoon. My body shuddered into his, and a sound came from him that was low and almost animal. Our mouths opened wider, tongues probing deeper.

His hands glided down to my waist, fingers pressing into the flesh just above my hips. He tugged my body closer still, kindling flames low in my belly. He stepped me backward until my backside came to rest against the edge of the table.

The kiss broke, leaving both of us gasping. His head dipped to my neck. Feeling the tip of his nose under my ear—just above where he'd bitten me—I froze.

My tensing woke him, and with a last squeeze that let me feel how taut and hard his body had gone, he released me and stepped away.

Drunk on his taste and smell and feel, I stumbled, and he muttered an oath as he reached out to steady me.

Our eyes met. "You're not wrong to question what I feel under these strange circumstances, Mina. But I need you to understand—I've never wanted anything so much in my life. And even so, if my life were to end without me ever having more of you than that, I would die happy."

A nod was all I could manage. It struck me how right he had been. How difficult it would be for us to live together yet never truly be man and wife. I wouldn't be lonely anymore, but how I would burn for him. I now began to see how that could be *worse*. And if his strength failed him, what then? Could mine hold?

And this is Goosevar's gamble.

His fingers came to lightly brush my cheek. Then he let out a breath and moved to the window that faced onto the garden.

The smell of browning crust filled the room, and I went to take out the pie. Still breathless, still holding on to the previous moment while I tried to carry on in the current one.

The pie's filling bubbled as I scooped servings into two dishes—though I'd yet to see Harker eat.

Setting the food on the table, I said, "I'm not sure it will be edible. I'm not used to so much . . ."

He turned. "Distraction."

My face went hot. "Aye."

He joined me at the table. I wondered what he'd do, and he did pick up a fork and take a bite. "It's delicious, Mina."

He was being kind, but it *was* hot and filling, and I found I was famished. "Eat as much or as little as you like. I know our appetites . . . differ . . . and you won't offend me."

But he ate it all, and once I'd had my fill, he stood and reached for my dish. "Why don't you sleep now and let me clear up?"

"Just leave it for the morning," I protested, rising slowly. I knew he was used to doing for himself, but I didn't yet feel comfortable with the lord of the manor washing my supper dishes.

"It will give me something to do," he insisted. "The pump is out front?"

Now that my belly was full, my eyelids were drooping and my limbs felt heavy. So I gave in. "It is. There shouldn't be anyone else about at this hour. Will you not sleep?"

"I think it's best if I don't. I don't need much anyway."

I couldn't argue. If Jack did come home, there might be trouble. I felt a hard pang of regret over the fact we wouldn't share a bed on our wedding night—or, most likely, *ever*.

Reading me again, he came close and pressed his lips to my forehead. "Perhaps we'll meet in your dreams," he murmured.

I made fists to stop myself from reaching my arms around him.

Throat tightening, I said, "Good night, Harker."

I climbed the ladder to the loft with a heavy heart. I undressed and crawled into bed, so weary I thought I'd be asleep in moments. But the sounds of Harker setting the kitchen to rights kept me from drifting off. Once the task was finished, I lay awake wondering what he was doing. What he was thinking. If he was lonely. How it was that longing for someone could cause an actual pain in your chest.

I flopped onto my side, sighing, and then I heard a sound I hadn't in a very long time. Harker must have taken down Da's fiddle. It hung on the wall next to the back door, as far away from the heat of the hearth as possible. The plucking noises of his tuning took me back to my childhood.

I recalled Harker's broken fiddle, and the teacher he'd fallen in love with. *The teacher he may have killed.* It came to rest in my chest, cold like a stone.

Yet as the plucking stopped and Harker began to play, no cold feeling could hold. The melody washed over me like water in the bath. This music was like nothing we'd had at home. Da knew jigs and old ballads, and Mum had taught him sad Irish tunes. Remembering how her sweet voice had sometimes risen to the loft after Jack and I had gone to bed caused the tears to spill from my eyes.

I had no category to place Harker's song in. It wasn't joyful, or sweet, or even sadly romantic. The long, slow, somber notes seemed to contain every sorrow from the history of the world—including mine and his.

Yet somehow it brought me peace.

When the gray light woke me, all in the cottage was quiet but for the wind moving in the thatch overhead.

I got up and quickly dressed, braided and pinned my hair, then paused at the top of the ladder. All of yesterday felt like a dream. Would I find Jack below, instead of Harker, still asleep in our parents' bed? Then my gaze fell on the russet gown, which I'd draped carefully over a chair.

It's all real.

There was no sign that Jack had returned, but Harker was there—asleep, sitting on the floor propped up against the wall. Da's fiddle lay across his lap. I stepped lightly, hoping to let him go on sleeping. But as I began to move around in the kitchen, lighting the stove and putting water on to boil, I heard him stirring.

An unexpected shyness came over me—as if we'd had our wedding night—but I smiled and called, "Good morning."

He raised his hand, rubbing the back of his neck. "Good morning."

"You should have moved to Jack's bed. You can't have passed a very comfortable night." We had a couple of chairs and stools near the hearth, but nothing like what he was used to.

He set the fiddle carefully aside and got to his feet. "So much for keeping watch for Jack."

I frowned. "No sign of him, then."

"None, unfortunately. But try not to worry. He won't be fool enough to go after Goosevar again. He'll be somewhere close."

Grasping at his hopefulness, I replied, "Yes, we'll find him."

He walked to the back door and hung the fiddle on its pegs.

"Your playing last night was beautiful," I said, filling the teapot with hot water.

He met my gaze, a small smile on his lips. "You are kind. The instrument needs new strings, and I haven't played in years. Was it your father's?"

I nodded. "No one's played it since he died." We met at the table and sat down. "It's nice to hear it in the house again."

The porridge I'd made sat cooling on the table. I poured him a cup of tea, my heart thumping as I worked up to what I wished to ask him.

"Would it . . ." His eyes came to my face, and my courage flagged. I spooned the porridge into bowls.

"What is it, Mina?" he asked gently.

I set a bowl next to his teacup, and I picked up my spoon. "Would it cause you too much pain to talk about your teacher? You told me that . . . you said she was . . ." Sighing in frustration, I put down my spoon.

"You have a right to hear it," he said.

My hand trembled as I lifted my teacup. Why should this woman frighten me so?

Because he loved her. And because he might have killed her.

"Mrs. Rowe," he said. "Ruby Rowe. I don't think it was her real name. My father first brought her into our home when I was ten years old, and for a decade I saw her once a week. I knew little of her history, only that she'd worked in a traveling theater company."

Frowning, I said, "Da took us to see theater on the green at midsummer sometimes. Is that the kind of thing you mean?"

"Very likely. Though this was many years before you were born. She left the company to work for our family." He folded his arms and rested them on the table. "It would have been a far better life for her. I wish she'd kept to it."

I took a bite of porridge, not tasting it, as he continued, "Ruby was sometimes ill. I didn't think anything about it at the time. My mother had died young, and so had my father's mother, so I suppose

I had gotten the idea it was normal for women to be unwell. But as I approached my change, my father told me what I was. What I would *become*. And it was around that time I also learned Ruby was being paid for more than teaching me the violin."

His eyes came to my face, and my breath hitched as I saw that they shone with tears.

"One day after my lesson, I had left Ruby and gone out to skip stones on the pool on the heath. I had behaved foolishly that day, taking advantage of an opportunity to steal a kiss."

He hesitated, studying me, and how my heart raced. "Ruby played the violin with passion. Lost herself in it completely sometimes. She was beautiful, and although before my change I was sometimes allowed off the estate, she was the only woman I'd ever been alone with. I believed I was in love with her. That day she had thoroughly rebuffed me, and I stalked off humiliated and ashamed." He took a deep breath. "So I threw stones, and I watched columns of dark clouds massing on the horizon. When my emotions had cooled, I ran back to the chapel so I might watch the approaching storm from the battlements."

His jaw clenched and released. He finished his tea and continued, "I found them there together. My father held her in his arms, pressed up against the parapet, his lips at her throat."

Maybe I should have seen where this was leading, but I hadn't. "Oh, Harker. What a shock that must have been."

He nodded slowly. "Though by then I was nearly twenty-one, my isolation had stunted me in some ways. I couldn't understand what I was seeing. It seemed . . ." He rubbed his lips together. "I thought it was lovemaking. And that was bad enough, after her rejection of me. But there was blood, too. It confused me. *Shattered* me. I fled back down to the heath."

He was quiet for a while, and I waited, unwilling to push him. Even after decades, his hurt was still so raw. *It's the not knowing what happened to her.*

Finally, he looked up, his expression flat but for a thin smile. "That same day, I smashed my violin as if I were a jilted lover. Soon after that the change took me, and I never saw her again."

Carefully I asked, "Your father told you he sent her away to protect her from you?"

"He did."

I knew his doubts. I knew his fears. But after so many years, he would likely never know the truth of what had happened. Dwelling on it would only deepen his hurt. Gently I said, "It would make sense for him to do so."

He looked down. "I think the worst of it is that our eyes met on the parapet. Ruby *knew* I'd seen them. I was too angry to take any notice of this at the time, but it was clear from her expression how it pained her."

"I'm so sorry, Harker."

"You are kind to be sorry for me, but it's not why I told you. So many of my regrets about who and what I am, as well as my anger about the life I've had to live, are tied up in Ruby's story."

"I can see why. I'm grateful to you for telling me."

He ran a hand through his dark hair and let out a sigh. "I'm sick to death of my own melancholy and self-loathing, but I don't know how to leave them behind. And I fear they may make me very hard to live with."

I folded my arms on the table, leaning toward him. "For your own sake, I hope you *may* leave them behind. But you are dear to me as you are, Harker."

His brow smoothed as his gaze lifted. There was something soft and wondering in his eyes.

Afraid I'd said too much, I looked away, my gaze coming to rest on Da's fiddle. "Will you tell me what you were playing last night? I've never heard music like that."

"A sonata by a German composer named Bach," he said quietly. "I imagine it's more formal than what your father played. Bach was a composer at court."

I smiled. "You are very good at talking about the differences in our backgrounds without making me feel small and poor."

His brows lifted. "Probably because I don't think of you as either."

This kind reply, given easily and without forethought, made me wish he were sitting closer, so that I might touch him.

"Did you and Jack learn to play?" he asked.

I shook my head. "My parents thought it unseemly for a girl, and Jack hadn't the patience for it."

"Would you like to learn? I could teach you."

Imagining fiddle lessons would likely involve close brushes of fingers and arms, I said, "I'd like that. Though I wouldn't like to cause you pain."

His gaze drifted to the instrument. "I think it's more likely to relieve pain. Last night I realized how much I miss playing." His eyes came back to my face. "We shall have no shortage of time for it. And if we play together, and cook for each other, maybe read to each other sometimes, there will at least be some sensual pleasures we may enjoy as husband and wife."

All but choking on my last mouthful of tea, I dropped my eyes again. One Sunday after church, I'd asked my mother what "pleasures of the flesh" meant. She went red and told me I was too young to be asking such questions, and we never talked about it again. As I grew older and watched my parents more closely, I noticed that sometimes my father made my mother blush, and those moments became connected in my mind with the priest's mysterious phrase. I came to understand that "pleasures of the flesh" referred to something married people were allowed to do—and later, that it had to do with how babies were made.

As Harker's "sensual pleasures" and the priest's "pleasures of the flesh" knit themselves together in my mind, I thought it wasn't very likely that music lessons or cooking were going to serve as satisfying replacements.

"Regrets, love?"

My breath caught. *Love.*

He stood up and came around the table. I rose to meet him.

He stopped an arm's length away, and with my heart flailing, I reached out and clumsily caught the ruffled front of his shirt in my fingers, giving it a tug. He laughed and stepped forward, hands coming to my waist.

"Mina," he uttered softly into my hair.

I pressed my cheek to his chest, but then I felt his fingers in my hair and at the back of my neck. He cradled my head and gently moved it so that he could look at me.

I thought he was going to speak, but then his mouth was on mine. Pressing firmly. *Insisting.* Lips opening, tongue sweeping inside as something very like a whimper escaped my throat.

Then he pulled back, again looking into my eyes. "You've had a taste of what it will be like," he said, voice low and breathless. "There is yet time to make a different choice."

I raised my hands, closing them over his wrists. "Harker—"

"Jack is free. And no one but him and our enemy know of the vows we've taken. No one knows we've spent a night together."

"No, Harker," I protested over the heat and pressure in my throat.

His face came closer still. "This fire between us will only burn hotter, Mina. Denying ourselves won't make it go out. It doesn't work that way. You understand that?"

"Yes," I breathed. "I'll do better. I'll stay back."

His arms came around me, and he let out a desperate laugh. "It's not you. It's *us*. What we're attempting goes against nature. And the penalty for failure is a higher one than I am willing to pay."

I drew back and looked at him. "Do *you* wish to be released?" The words burned like coals in my chest.

His hand came to my face. "I could more easily release my own heart."

Ribbons of warmth unspooled in my belly. He kissed me again, with tenderness this time. Then he said, "Let us go to Father Kelly.

When we are bound in the eyes of God and the law, we'll see what can be done."

I frowned, not following.

"I will do nothing that carries even the slightest risk of creating a child," he continued. "But there are other ways of giving and receiving pleasure that, if we are cautious and mindful of my thirst, we may be able to attempt. If you wish it."

My heart burst into flame. Whatever he saw in my face made him laugh again and pull me against his chest.

We stood there long moments, breathing each other in, feeling the way our bodies fit together. I felt his hands on my back, at my waist, dipping to my hips. Then at last he released me, sighing as he began gathering our teacups and barely touched bowls of porridge from the table.

I took the stack from him and put it in the washbasin, where I intended to leave it until today's business was finished. How could I turn my thoughts to anything practical after *But there are other ways of giving and receiving pleasure*?

When Harker came back with the teapot, I removed the lid out of habit to empty it.

At its bottom, the leaves formed a rose.

MESSENGERS

"I'm almost afraid to ask."

I looked at him; he was watching me warily.

"I want to believe it's a fair omen," I replied, holding out the pot.

He took it and peered inside, turning it in his hands. "Is it a flower?"

"A rose was what first came to my mind. It reminds me of the one at the top of the stained glass window in your laboratory."

"Yes, a rosette. Roses have strong religious associations. They also have many health benefits, and spiritually they are considered to be protective." His lips curved down as he handed the pot back to me. "They can be used for blood purification, and I experimented with sweetbriar when distilling my vital essence."

"It didn't work?"

"It nearly killed me."

I sighed and let the pot slip into the washbasin.

My cheeks warmed as I remembered *In the Leaves*. "Mrs. Rochester says a rose in a teacup is a symbol of romance. We *are* newlyweds."

"Mmm. Occam's razor." I raised an eyebrow, and he added, "It's a problem-solving principle that says the least complicated explanation is often the preferred one." Gaze softening, he said, "I choose to interpret it as a nudge toward our meeting with the priest. Are you ready to go?"

Fog had settled in overnight, making it easier for a youthful-looking stranger in fine, old-fashioned clothing to escort a plainly dressed, unmarried miner's daughter without anyone taking much notice.

Though the hour was still early, it was late enough that we'd missed the miners' march to Wheal Enys. But a farmer driving a cart laden with pears tipped his hat to us as we set out.

Once he was gone, Harker said, "There's something I need to tell you. I saw another of Goosevar's memories last night."

I turned, eyes wide. "Why haven't you said so?"

"Because this morning it felt more important to speak of us."

My heart skipped, and I squeezed his arm. He covered my hand with his.

"Sometime in the night I started thinking about my memory of Goosevar's origin," he said, "and about the connection between him and me. That memory came to me in a dreamlike state, as I was dying. But I wondered whether it might be possible for me to call up his memories intentionally."

"And you have!"

"I believe so, though I'm not sure whether it has gained us anything. I had seen his beginning, so I tried to see his end, assuming it to be true that he'd been killed by St. Gomonda. I tried calling up *his* memory based on my own memory of seeing the painting in the bell tower as a boy. And fragments did seem to come to me. I saw robed priests, large crosses, and even a man armed with a bow. There was panic and angry shouting in a language I would guess to be Old Cornish."

"Was it like last time? Did it *feel* the same, I mean?"

Harker nodded. "I saw it through his eyes. He was frightened and enraged. My own head was burning with it. Just as an arrow struck us, I lost my connection to the memory. But I felt the arrow's impact anyway, in the same place Jack's bullet penetrated."

I let out a breath. "Well, I don't think I agree with you that it's not important. Knowing that the holy men defeated him, at least for a time, as well as *how* they did it, could help us. But the arrow is hard to understand. Jack shooting him in the chest barely slowed him."

"Maybe they were able to defeat him *because* they were holy men. They had crosses, which we know can cause injury. I wish the memory had come to me more complete."

"Should we have another look at the painting when we get to the church?"

"Yes, good idea."

We heard the clopping of horse hooves, and a gentleman appeared out of the fog. I thought I recognized him from the tearoom, though I didn't know his name. He glanced at us as he was passing, and his gaze stuck on Harker. The man reached for his hat, like he would tip it, but instead he pulled it down lower and clucked to his horse to move on.

Harker seemed lost in thought, and I didn't bring the man's behavior to his attention. But it left me uneasy. Had he guessed who Harker was based on the stories going round in the village? If so, the stories had apparently also convinced him that Harker was best avoided.

"Are you feeling anxious about seeing Father Kelly?" Harker asked as we drew near the parish church.

I glanced at him. "Do I seem so?"

"You've gone unusually quiet."

I laughed. "I wonder whether you've had a chance to think about the effect I will have on your peaceful sanctuary."

He smiled. "Peaceful sanctuaries cease to be either when one wakes up alone in them *every day*."

"So you say *now*. I'm sure Jack would have a word or two to offer that would make you think twice about that."

On that thought, I sobered, and Harker squeezed my hand. "I hope we'll find Father Kelly in," he said. "It's only the middle of the week."

"He's there most days. You can often glimpse him on the grounds through the windows at The Magpie. I think he has a fondness for the dead."

Harker's brows lifted. "Indeed?"

"I can't think why else he would spend so much time among the gravestones. I don't imagine it's a requirement of the position. Mum always believed he could speak to them."

"Interesting."

We had come to St. Gomonda's gate, and we stepped onto the path that led alongside the sanctuary to the main entrance. The churchyard, with its big trees, was all but lost to the thick fog.

Before we reached the entrance, a figure approached us from the grounds. I held my breath, hoping it might be Jack. But we soon discovered it was the other man we were seeking.

"Mina," said Father Kelly as he joined us, eyes moving over Harker with a look of polite curiosity.

"Father Kelly," I said, "this is Mr. Harker Tregarrick, of Roche Rock."

"Ah," he said, smiling, his surprise plain, "Mr. Tregarrick. It's a pleasure meeting you at last. I have often wondered whether you were in fact real."

"Thank you, Father," Harker replied graciously. "I confess I wonder myself sometimes."

The priest laughed, and then his gaze moved between us. "Is there something I can do for the two of you?"

"Indeed, there is, sir," replied Harker. "I know we properly owed you this notice last Sunday, but Mina—Miss Penrose—and I have come to notify you of our wish and intention to marry. I wondered whether you'd be willing to read the banns for us this Sunday, so we might conclude the business before the month is out?"

The priest's brows lifted high on his forehead. "Allow me to congratulate you both."

Harker and I murmured our thanks.

His keen gaze settled on me. "Forgive me, but in situations like these, I feel compelled to ask—is there a particular reason for haste?"

I believed I understood what he meant by "a particular reason," and it brought a rush of heat to my face. I gave a quick shake of my head. "No, Father."

"I'm afraid we haven't been as discreet as we might," added Harker. "I hope to spare Mina from gossip by formalizing my intentions as soon as possible."

This was a clever way of stating things, as it was mostly the truth.

The priest gave us a knowing nod. "In theory, I have no objection. I see no reason to make young people wait when I believe they know their hearts. But the only thing I know of you as of yet, Mr. Tregarrick, is that half the village believes you to be some kind of monster. I don't mean to suggest I agree with them, and I hope you won't take offense at my frankness."

Harker looked down, but he shook his head. "On the contrary. I respect you for looking out for the interests of your parishioners. I am happy to offer any reassurances you require."

"I am a reasoning man," continued the priest, "and you appear to be a respectable and rational gentleman. Nevertheless, I do feel I owe it to Mina's parents, rest their souls, to ask a few questions." His gaze now came to rest on me. "Do you trust me, Mina?"

Rather an odd question. It made me worry about what was coming next. But I said, "I do, Father."

"Good. Now then, is it *your* wish that the wedding be conducted as soon as possible? You're not being forced in any way?"

"No, Father. We made the decision between us."

"And you feel you know him well enough to commit yourself to him for the rest of your life, perhaps even beyond? You are possibly the only person in the village who knows Mr. Tregarrick *at all*. One of the few who've even glimpsed him."

What was I to say? As far as Harker and I were concerned, we had already committed ourselves beneath the oak trees on his estate. And the reasons had not been the usual ones that caused people to marry. I could hardly explain this to Father Kelly, yet I was certain it must be the worst kind of sin to deceive a priest.

But there was a truth I *could* tell him.

I looked at Harker. "I love him, Father."

Harker's spectacles had slipped down, and I saw his eyes widen, then go soft. His lips parted, as if he would speak, but then he glanced at Father Kelly.

"I would ask the same of you, son," said the priest. "You're sure of your reasons for this decision?"

Harker's eyes came back to my face, and he said, "God knows I have never been a religious man, but Mina has made me believe in angels. She has brought light where there was only darkness. I love her, Father."

My heart sang, and the blood hummed in my veins. I longed to feel his arms around me.

This answer clearly pleased the priest, too, who closed his eyes and nodded. When he opened them again, he said, "I will read the banns this Sunday. I feel I must ask, however—have you and Jack quarreled over your engagement? I'm sure you'd prefer that he not speak against you in church."

This brought my feet back to solid ground. "Jack doesn't know yet, Father. In fact, we haven't seen him since yesterday, and we wanted to ask whether you had."

The priest frowned. "I have, in fact." My breath caught. "Yesterday evening, after dark, I saw him cross the churchyard. I wouldn't have known him but for the moon and his red hair. I called after him, but he slipped into the shadows."

Harker and I exchanged uneasy glances.

"I've been worried about Jack since last he was here," continued Father Kelly, "and since you and I talked about the rumors in the village." His gaze brushed Harker.

"We intend to look for him today," I said, "but if you see him again, will you tell him I'm worried about him?"

"I will. Let me know if there's anything else I can do."

Tap, tap, tap.

The sudden noise drew all our gazes. A couple of yards away from where we stood, a very old Cornish cross, about the height of a man, had been planted in the churchyard. A magpie perched on top of it, knocking a hazelnut against the carved stone.

"That's a medieval wheel cross, is it not, Father?" asked Harker, eyeing it with interest.

"It is indeed," replied the priest as the magpie flitted away. "A very early one. In fact . . ." He thought for a moment, rubbing his beard. "That cross originally came from your family's estate, if memory serves. It's carved from the same black granite. It may have been a last remaining marker of a much older church."

Harker and I both stared at him. I recalled how we'd wondered whether Goosevar's burial place might have been disturbed during the chapel's construction.

"Well," said Father Kelly, "I shall see you both Sunday, then, for the reading of the banns?"

"You shall," replied Harker. "Thank you, Father."

The priest gave us a slight bow. "Good day to you both."

We watched him walk to the church entrance and step inside. As soon as he was gone, Harker said, "So maybe this cross served as a kind of grave marker over Goosevar—or even a guardian—after he was killed."

"I was thinking the same. The priests killed and then buried him right there, on what would later become your family's estate."

Harker glanced at the bell tower. "Shall we go have a look?"

The fog, moving and changing like a living thing, formed a patchy veil over the old structure. One moment I could make out only the arched doorway, the next only the upper section with its arched window and parapet.

We crossed to the door and entered, but it was too dark to see—at least for me. Harker removed his spectacles and peered up at what remained of the painting.

After a few moments, he pointed to something and said, "Those look like roses."

My eyes had adjusted enough that I could just make out the blotches of color along the arrow shafts that I'd noticed before. "So they do. You're thinking of the rose in the teapot?"

He nodded and rubbed a thumb over his chin. "I wonder if the story's not literal."

I frowned. "What do you mean?"

"Rose water in my vital essence made me terribly ill," he continued. "Maybe because it's poison to Goosevar. Could be it wasn't arrows that killed him at all. Maybe the priest poisoned him."

This reminded me of something. "When last I was here, Father Kelly told me St. Gomonda was an *apothecary*."

Harker's brows lifted with interest, but then I recalled, "You saw actual arrows, though. In your memory of his death."

His gaze went back to the painting. "Mmm. Let's think it over awhile. We'll make our visit to The Magpie. Once we're home, we'll see if we can work it out."

My heart fluttered. *Once we're home.* Together. Because we were married. It still didn't feel real.

We left the tower and passed back through the churchyard, then crossed the road to The Magpie. The aroma of scones drifted on the air, and I thought it must be close to opening by now.

I led Harker around to the back garden, through the drooping sunflowers and glistening spiderwebs, and tapped on the kitchen door.

My employer appeared, eyes going wide at the sight of us. "Heavens," she said, standing frozen only a moment before stepping back from the door. "Come in out of the damp. So many visitors this morning. Let me get you both a cup of tea."

I started to urge her not to trouble herself, but she went to work quickly, seeming flustered. Her uneasiness had me worrying that some unsavory rumor had reached her already.

While the tea steeped, she arranged scones, cream, and jam on a plate. Finally she set it all before us, pouring our tea before sitting on a stool across the worktable from us.

"I'm so pleased to see you recovered, Mina," she said. "It's been lonely here without you." Her eyes wandered to Harker.

"I've missed you, too, ma'am," I said, adding milk to my tea. "I want to introduce you to Harker Tregarrick, of Roche Rock. We've come to you with some news."

"I'm very pleased to meet you, sir." She smiled, but it was strained. "Before you share your news, I think I best tell the both of you—young Jeremy Martin was just here, and the constable, too. It seems Jeremy was on your estate, Mr. Tregarrick, and . . ." She wiped her hands on her apron. "Well, another body has been discovered."

My hand jerked, tipping my cup and spilling tea over the table.

Jack!

"FARE THEE WELL"

Harker

With practiced speed, Mrs. Moyle grabbed a towel and stanched the pool of milky tea.

"Who was it, Mrs. Moyle?" I asked, knowing what Mina feared.

The lady shivered and shook her head. If she suspected me like others seemed to, she did a fine job of concealing it. Though she clearly wasn't altogether comfortable.

"Jeremy found the body in a pool on the heath," she said. I believed the young poacher I'd spoken to was called Jeremy. The lad had apparently disregarded my warning. "He came here frightened half to death," continued Mrs. Moyle, "and I sent for Mr. Hilliard. The poor boy wasn't making a great deal of sense, but the constable seemed to piece together that by the state of the remains, the death wasn't a recent one."

Mina's posture eased, and she and I exchanged a glance. I said, "May I ask where they've gone?"

"Back out to the heath so Jeremy can show him. They left not ten minutes ago."

To Mina I said, "I should go and meet them there."

She nodded. "We'll both go."

"I'd rather you stayed here with Mrs. Moyle."

"Do, dear," entreated the good lady, and I could see how worried she was for her young friend. "I promise not to put you to work."

If I had entertained any fantasy that marrying Mina would make her more likely to conform to my wishes, that notion was now dispelled. She stood up from the table, fixing her eyes first on me. "I'm sure you would, but I'm coming." Then on her employer, more softly. "Please don't worry. I promise to return as soon as we've seen the constable."

While I was chewing on that, she continued, "I don't suppose you've seen Jack recently? Last night or this morning?"

The lady's forehead creased deeply. "No, I'm afraid I haven't. I hope you don't mean to say he's gone missing!"

"He has. Father Kelly glimpsed him last night. I fear he's not quite right in his mind. Will you keep an eye out for him? And if anyone from Wheal Enys comes in, maybe ask them?"

"Of course, dear."

I drained my teacup in one draught and rose to my feet. Mina picked up a scone, and we started for the door. Before we could take our leave, Mrs. Moyle, eyeing us expectantly, asked, "Was there something the two of you wanted to tell me?"

Mina stepped closer to her. "It's not exactly the right moment for this, but I wanted you to hear it from me. Harker and I are to be married. Father Kelly will read the banns this Sunday."

Mrs. Moyle's brows lifted almost to her hairline, much as Father Kelly's had, and her gaze moved between us. "Heavens!" she said again. "Congratulations to you both."

"I can't imagine what you'll be thinking of me," Mina said, "and I promise to explain better when I have more time."

Mrs. Moyle reached out and squeezed Mina's hand, a smile defeating the worry in her expression. "You finding love is the happiest news I could receive, Mina. I do want to hear all about it, but we'll catch up later."

Mina folded her arms around the lady, and Mrs. Moyle let out a soft laugh as she returned the embrace. "All will be well, my dear," she said. "You'll see."

Once we were out on the road again, I said, "This Jeremy Martin—he's one of the boys who snares rabbits on my estate, isn't he?"

Mina nodded and broke her scone in half, steam rising from its fluffy center. "I know you warned him away, and I did, too, but his father died not long ago, and I think his mother may depend on the meat. He's got a limp, and I doubt they'll have him at the mine."

I wondered if she had any idea how good hearted she was, *or* how uncommon that was. At least based on my limited, book-forged understanding of the world.

"I'm glad he hasn't come to any harm," I said.

"When I spoke to him, I noticed he wore a crude cross around his neck. Maybe it's kept him safe."

"Mmm. When I found him in the birchwood, there were several other boys hiding in the trees. Their numbers may also make them a less-than-ideal target."

We were close enough to each other that I felt her shiver as she looked up at me. "The very idea there's been a body in the pool. You and I stood there together only the other day. You skipped a stone!"

I reached for her free hand. "I can't understand it, either." *And I wonder how many more such surprises are in store.*

"It frightens me that they've found this one so clearly on your estate."

I ground my teeth together. "Yes. The constable will have many questions, and there's very little I can—"

My thought was cut short by the sound of voices. The morning's fog had somewhat thinned, and I glanced up to find that a man and woman had stopped just on the other side of the road and stood watching us.

"God above," the man muttered, "can that be *Tregarrick*? Penrose has been telling anyone who'll listen—that wolf has skulked out of his tower to sniff round his sister. Says it was him that attacked her!"

"That's the miller and his wife," whispered Mina, "from down near Coldvreath. I don't much like the way they're staring at us. Can you hear what they're saying?"

"Yes," I said stiffly.

"That's *her*, sure enough," the woman replied to her husband. "I've seen her at The Magpie."

"Keep walking," I said quietly. We were almost to the path that led through the hedge to the chapel.

As Mina stepped through, the miller said in a louder voice, "If the constable is too much of a coward to do his job, I guess some of us will have to do it for him!"

My blood ran colder, and I stopped and turned.

"No!" Mina said frantically, reaching for my arm. But I pulled away and strode directly into the road, stopping halfway across and lowering my spectacles.

All I did was stare at them, but it made their eyes go wide. The miller pressed a hand to his wife's back, and they moved quickly along.

"That's only going to make things worse," Mina scolded as I joined her.

"It was worth it. I'm not going to allow people to threaten us in the streets. Taking the high road is never going to make the right sort of impression on a man like that."

"While you're sounding rather too much like Jack for my comfort right now, I'll admit I'm worried about the mood in the village. Even Mrs. Moyle, who always thinks the best of everyone until they give her reason not to, seemed unsettled by you."

"She's worried about you," I muttered, "and she should be."

Mina's head lay to one side as she tried to draw my eye. "You're still cross with me for refusing to stay behind. You *need* me, Harker."

"That, my love, is the understatement of the century. But if anything were to happen to you, I might as well give myself over to the mob."

A smile bloomed unexpectedly, raising rosy smudges behind those crimson stars scattered over her cheeks. "Then we best look out for each other."

My poor besieged heart gave a throb of longing as she took my arm, and together we started down the path to the pool.

Mist still blanketed the heath, but as we drew nearer, we could see two figures. The taller of them turned, and one hand moved inside his jacket—where I suspected he'd concealed a firearm.

"Good morning, Mr. Hilliard," I called in as peaceable a tone as I could muster.

His hand remained where it was as he replied, "I'm afraid it is, in actuality, rather a grim one, Mr. Tregarrick. I apologize for trespassing, but police business, you understand. I had intended to come up to the chapel after."

"I understand, sir. What have you found?" My eyes moved to young master Jeremy, whose terror of me was plain on his face. Mina went to stand beside him, and Mr. Hilliard's eyes followed her.

"This is no place for *you*, Miss Penrose," he said.

"That's where you're wrong, sir," she replied in a firm tone that carried a tinge of defiance. "Mr. Tregarrick and I are engaged to be married, so these matters concern me, too, you see."

The constable was now the third person to raise his brows and stare upon hearing this news. "Is that so?"

"It is," I confirmed. "It will be made official this Sunday."

"Mr. Hilliard," said Mina, "might I ask whether you've seen Jack today?"

He blinked a few times, obviously still trying to make sense of what we'd told him. Finally he said, "I'm afraid I haven't been to the mine yet this morning, Miss Penrose."

I was about to ask him again what had been found, when a fluttering motion caught my eye. My gaze followed as the flutterer landed on the reedy bank. Another magpie, or perhaps the same as visited us here before. The bird got hold of something and began tugging. It looked like nothing more than a soggy weed, but the creature flapped about, unbalanced by the weight of the thing.

"Get away from there, now!" called Mr. Hilliard, waving his hat until the bird lifted away with a chittering squawk, dropping its prize into the water.

"May I step a little closer, sir?" I asked.

He eyed me with speculation. Giving me a solemn nod, he said, "A *very* little. Don't disturb anything. And avoid stepping on the soft ground until we've had a chance to look things over properly."

I left the others beside the stone slab and made my way around toward the spot where the bird had landed on the bank. Then I carefully stepped to the edge of the scrubby heath grass bordering the pool. Quite a few recent shoe prints had pressed into the mud at the water's edge. They were all the same size and shape, and I guessed they'd been made by Jeremy.

The sky was uniformly gray, leaving no reflection on the pool's surface. My eyes found the thing the magpie had dropped near the bank in a couple of inches of water. Not a weed, but a *chain*. A silver necklace, I thought, by the dark tarnish. I wondered whether the chain still bore its ornament—and, looking more carefully, I saw that it did. Recognition arced through me like lightning through a Franklin rod.

I began to tremble as my gaze expanded out around the necklace. A few feet away, in slightly deeper water, I discovered what had brought the constable here.

The skull and rib cage rested in soft clay in the shallows, while the lower regions of the remains were lost to the deeper, darker water. The skeleton had been recently disturbed, maybe also attributable to Jeremy. By the ridges in the clay, and various depressions around the rib cage, I thought maybe he'd poked around with a stick until it had lodged somewhere, when he'd dragged it partway toward the shore, abandoning it once he realized what he'd gotten hold of.

My gaze returned to the necklace. Perhaps *it* had been what originally caught the boy's eye, as it had the magpie's.

A cross carved from red jasper.

Peering through a slit, I see a man and woman standing at the water's edge. My hiding place is a cave whose roof is a great stone slab resting at one end of the pool. A void left by the collapse of the burning manor—perhaps a cellar once—its entrance concealed year round by bramble and deer fern.

The woman wears a familiar red cloak. She is crying. Though I am the spirit of the wood, I am also myself, and I know this man . . . my father.

"I'm sorry, Ruby. But you knew this day would come. The boy's time is close now, and you won't be safe here once he's changed. Until he learns control, we will have to manage his thirst in other ways."

"And what of your *thirst, sir?" Ruby asks in a voice breaking with grief.*

"My thirst will wane as his waxes. So it was with my father, and his father before him. It is greatly diminished already, as you well know."

Ruby dabs at her nose with a handkerchief. "When he has . . . somewhat recovered, may I come again?"

"Ruby," *my father gently scolds, "did I not warn you against becoming attached to the accursed Tregarricks?"*

"I suppose it was advice easier given than taken, sir."

"Well, I am sorry for it. Perhaps in five or ten years you might safely return to us. But why not take what you've earned and go somewhere you may start fresh? Go to London, where you may find people more open minded, and make pupils of the children of the ton."

"Perhaps I shall."

Her reply carries a note of defiance, but my father chooses to ignore this. "I'm sure you will make a success of it, my girl."

"I could have been, you know." She looks at him. "Your girl."

He reaches out and touches her cheek. She must be nearing forty now. Her dark curls have begun to thread silver. My father's true age hasn't caught up to him yet.

I hear the pain in his voice as he answers, "Don't make me remind you—remind us both—of the many reasons that may not be. Responsibility for the death of one person I loved is all the burden I'm strong enough to carry."

Ruby looks away, endeavoring to control her emotion.

"Fare thee well, my sweet." My father's hand moves to the small of her back for a moment, and she leans toward him. But he withdraws it quickly and turns from her, facing me briefly—and unaware—before moving out of my view as he starts toward the chapel.

Ruby remains, her back shuddering with each quiet sob. After a few moments, she fumbles with something at her bodice, pulling out a chain with a cross pendant carved from red jasper. She's worn a cross since her first day on the estate, though it wasn't always this one. The jasper pendant was a gift from my father. She lifts it over her head and looks as if she might cast it into the dark water, but I sense she doesn't have the heart.

This moment is a gift—an opportunity to indulge without consequence. The temptation is too great. My father feeds less than he used to, and the taste of Ruby's blood is familiar—almost comforting—to the creature whose memory I am now sharing.

There is no one else about, but there are eyes in the black chapel. I breathe a thick mist into the air to ensure our privacy. I leave the shelter of the cave. I am swift, and she hasn't heard me. But at the last moment she turns, and I see her face. Her wide-eyed terror.

I seize her, lifting her off her feet, and the necklace flies from her hand, splashing into the dark water after all.

HIDING

"Harker?" His back was to us, but I heard him gasp. I thought he must have discovered whatever Jeremy had found. I couldn't see anything from where I stood with the others.

"Mr. Tregarrick?" called the constable.

"I . . . yes." Harker turned; how pale and stricken he looked!

"Do you know anything about these remains, sir?" asked Mr. Hilliard, his voice crisp with the authority of his office.

Harker's gaze was aimed at the ground between us. He kept silent, as if he hadn't heard. Then at last he raised his eyes, and the tension in his expression loosened. *Like he's let go of something, or plans to.*

"I believe I do, sir," he said.

"Well, then?"

I didn't care at all for the edge in the constable's voice. Though with a corpse found on the estate, I could hardly complain that he had no right to his suspicions.

"Her name was Ruby Rowe. She worked for my family."

Ruby!

All these years he had wondered, and she had never left his estate. And yet . . . would there really be anything left to recognize her by? How could he *know*?

If he was the one who put her there.

My heart plunged, and I raised a hand to my chest.

“Can you tell me when it happened?” asked Mr. Hilliard. “I don’t want to anticipate the coroner, especially before we’ve extracted the remains, but I think it’s no leap to say this body is in an extremely advanced state of decay.”

Harker’s shoulders rose as he took a deep breath. “No leap, constable. It was many years ago.”

At last Harker looked at me, and without any forethought, I gave my head a tiny shake. *Don’t tell him the truth.* Even if his memory had returned—even if he knew he was responsible—I couldn’t see how any good would come of his confession. Mr. Hilliard would have even more reason to think he’d killed the others.

Maybe he’s tired of carrying it. A hard, hot knot formed in my throat.

Harker’s gaze held mine, and the smallest, saddest of smiles appeared. Somehow I understood—*it wasn’t him.*

I closed my eyes, relief swelling.

“Mr. Tregarrick,” said the constable, “I’m afraid you’re going to have to do better than that. If you’ll come with me voluntarily to the village, we can sit down like gentlemen and discuss the particulars. I’ll alert the proper authorities and get some men out here to collect—”

Something caught the constable’s attention. Jeremy, once he’d felt safe again, had begun fidgeting next to me, kicking at grass seedheads and dry fern fronds. A moment ago he’d inched around the stone slab to the end farthest from the pool. Reminding me very much of Jack as a boy, he’d picked up a stick and started whacking at the wilting plants at the base of the slab.

“Be still a moment longer, lad,” called the constable. “We’re all going back to the village together.”

“Something’s ’ere, sir,” Jeremy replied excitedly, poking below the slab with his stick. “It looks like a ca—”

“No—no—don’t!” shouted Harker, and the desperate fright in his voice caused me to run toward the boy.

I grabbed him and pulled him against me. I could see movement in the soggy vegetation he’d disturbed. Then a confusing shape, dark and twiggy, began to emerge. I dragged Jeremy back, but my feet caught in the heather and toppled us.

What crawled from beneath the slab looked very much like a thorn tree—bent and twisted, spotted with gray lichen—but I soon realized my mistake. A familiar creature unfolded and towered over us.

Lips peeled back over glistening fangs. Goosevar snarled and Jeremy screamed.

A cry of shock came from Mr. Hilliard, and Harker shouted another warning. But even had I not been frozen with fear and tangled up with Jeremy, there was no getting away from the monster, accidentally cornered and furious.

But Harker's unnatural quickness had already brought him. He stood between us and the beast, looking terrifyingly small. There came a long and low growl—not from Goosevar, but from *Harker*.

Goosevar curled down until his great muzzle was only inches from Harker's face. Fog billowed from parted jaws, his breath loud as storm winds.

I had no confidence Goosevar would spare him, or any of us, now that his centuries-old secret was threatened. And strong though Harker was, his strength came from Goosevar. What hope was there of besting him?

But Harker stood against the Goliath and grated out, "Kill me, then, if you can."

"No!" Hands shaking, fear firing my blood, I unwound my arms from Jeremy and got to my feet. The boy scrabbled and ran for the birchwood.

"Run, Mina!" Harker barked over his shoulder.

Fumbling at my throat for Mum's cross, I caught the cool silver in my palm and yanked it from my neck. *It's so tiny.*

As I quickly knotted the ends of the ribbon together, a shot rang out. I glanced up—Goosevar roared in rage and spun around. I saw the constable behind him—he'd climbed onto the stone slab and aimed a pistol.

Goosevar lunged, swiping at the constable with his long, tapered tree-bone fingers, just as the click before the second shot sounded. Mr. Hilliard was swept off the rock, the pistol firing as he splashed into the pool.

"Harker!" I called, tripping forward and thrusting the cross at him.

He snatched at the ribbon, rounding as Goosevar returned. The beast's jaws hinged open as he let out another howl of rage.

Harker swung the cross by the ribbon and let it go. It sailed directly into the gaping maw.

There came a loud hiss, the smell of singed flesh, and a broken yap of pain. The purple ribbon trailed down over the teeth of Goosevar's lower jaw. As he began to sputter and shake his great head, Harker's hand closed over my arm.

"Run to the village," he said urgently. "Tell them the constable's been attacked by the Wolf of Roche Rock. Bring back help."

I could see the sense in this, yet I stood frozen. What would happen to him?

"Mina!"

"Aye," I said, tears stinging my eyes.

The choking noises gave way to enraged snarls as the shadow behind him rose.

Harker took warning from the look on my face, but before he could act, Goosevar lunged and swung. I heard a loud snap as he flung Harker to the ground several yards away. I let out a coarse, desperate cry as the monster followed, each strike of the trunk-like legs shaking the earth.

Then came more snarling, and barking, too—but this time *behind* me. Something whooshed by my head, followed by a quiet *thunk*.

Goosevar *staggered*, almost falling, an arrow sticking out of the bark-like flesh of his shoulder. It hadn't gone in deep; one brush of the long fingers would likely free it. And it wasn't *much* of an arrow—crude looking, and hardly thicker than the wooden spills I used to light the stove. Where had it come from?

Gazing up the heath, I saw a man walking slowly toward us. He carried a bow with another arrow nocked. *Jack!*

Whoosh. The second arrow curved away from its target, and Jack scrambled to nock another. I ran around behind Goosevar to reach Harker. He'd raised himself on one arm, face gray with pain, but he was *alive.*

"Go, Dolly!" someone shouted, followed by three deep-chested barks.

Trailing Jack, there were others. Father Kelly, holding a great wooden cross before him, and Mr. Couch, owner of The Wolf's Head. And Dolly—apparently the name of his sleepy old wolfhound, who now streaked down the heath like a nightmare come to life.

Teeth bared and snarling, she barreled into Goosevar, closing her jaws over a mossy leg, neck twitching back and forth as she tried giving it a killing shake.

The monster howled and bent to the still-snarling hound, wrenching her free and tossing her away like a sack of grain. She hit the ground with a yelp, and Mr. Couch let out an angry shout as he ran toward her.

Goosevar made a clumsy lunge for Jack, but Dolly had given him time to nock and aim . . . The second arrow whistled through the air and stuck fast in the monster's chest.

After a single frozen moment, Goosevar folded and crashed to his knees.

"Another!" barked Father Kelly, stepping closer. With the big cross held like a shield before him, he looked very like one of the figures in the painting at St. Gomonda.

Jack's next arrow lodged in Goosevar's neck, and his head tipped, tongue lolling as he crashed backward onto the heath. Jack moved to stand directly over his foe's great head, taking aim again.

Goosevar let out a half-choked growl as the arrow sank into one eye socket. At last the beast stilled, the flame of his remaining eye dying to a dark smolder.

"Well, *that's* done for you, hasn't it?" growled Jack. Relief washed over me—how like himself he sounded! Raising his bow to his lips, he pressed a kiss into the wood.

"Thanks be to God," muttered Father Kelly, crossing himself.

"He's gone," I breathed, turning back to Harker. The smile froze on my face.

Harker still rested on one elbow, his other arm wrapped around his ribs. His eyes looked empty and distant, and I felt a wrenching in my chest.

It struck me that although we'd wondered whether Goosevar's death might remove the vampire curse from his family, we'd never thought to question whether any *harm* might come to Harker from it. The two of them shared a connection we still didn't understand. *And likely never will now.*

I moved close, laying a hand against his face. "Harker?"

He gave no sign he'd heard me.

"I HAVE FAILED"

Harker/Goosevar

I see the woman in the bright summer sunshine. She cuts long stalks of lavender, placing them in a basket. She hums quietly.

Her husband is away on the other side of the rock, where they remove moorstone from the old village for the chapel they build. This work has brought holy men onto the heath; I know them by the symbols they wear. It was men like these who slew and entombed me, sealing my grave with their stone monument.

Some days ago that monument, too, was dug up. Today the holy men hauled it away in a cart.

Now I do whatever is necessary to ensure they never return. Though I must be stealthy and clever if I'm to survive.

But in the present moment, I am fascinated by the woman. I have lived for hundreds of years, never encountering another creature like myself. Never mating or producing offspring, as I have observed every other creature around me to do. Yet I've seen this before. I understand that the large, rounded growth at her belly is a child.

It is more than fascination for me. I am drawn to her. I thirst *for her. And it's not only that I must feed soon if I'm to survive. I know from my past life that her blood is different. Rich and potent. Blood that creates life. If I drink this blood, I won't need to kill for a very long time.*

There is nothing so likely to inspire another attempt on my own life as taking the life of a woman with child. And yet, if I can manage not *to kill her—to feed on her but let her live—perhaps no one need know. It's not a thing I have ever attempted. And after sleeping for centuries, I am desperately thirsty. Moderation may not be possible.*

But I must feed. And solitary victims carry less risk.

My jaws open, releasing fog over the heath.

The woman straightens, rubbing her back, and looks around in confusion. Only a moment ago the sun warmed her. Now she can't see beyond her low garden wall.

I move closer, making no sound to warn her.

I am only heartbeats away when she senses something stalking her. Fear brightens her eyes, quickens her breath. She drops her basket, which tips and spills its fragrant contents. She turns for the house.

I burst from the trees and catch her easily, like a fawn. Lifting her in my arms, I dig sharp teeth into her soft neck.

She strikes at me with her small fists and lets out a half-choked cry. I feel it through the frenzy of bloodlust. I try to be careful. I try to slow down. It's not what I was made for.

Suddenly something pierces my side; she still holds the garden knife. Such a weapon is no threat to me. The wound will have sealed by the time I've drunk my fill.

Until my death, no *weapon had threatened me. Everything had been tried, and everything failed, until a holy man and healer made arrows from a thorny bush bearing a delicate flower. I know now that I possess vulnerability.*

Though I am parched like late-autumn leaves, I force myself to stop. I don't need as much of this potent blood as I desire.

She has stilled now; her breathing has gone shallow. My jaws have left an ugly wound on her neck, and it still bleeds.

I have failed.

Despite my intentions, it seems she will die anyway, and the wound will set the others hunting me.

Then I notice the trickle of fluid at my side, where she's stabbed me. My own blood is a bitter, dark sap. On instinct, I use the tip of a finger to scoop some of it up, and then I spread it over the edges of her wound.

The wound begins to close before my eyes, leaving naught but a faint scar.

Her heartbeat is weak, as is the child's, but she may yet survive. Without the wound, no stories of an attack will be given credence, but I leave nothing to chance. Bending close to her ear, I sing a song of forgetfulness.

My thirst is roused again by her close scent, but now come sounds of others approaching.

As my song ends, I hear the echo of it in her blood. And of something else, too. My own ancient magic stirs inside her as my blood sinks into hers. It wends through her, to the child in her belly. Creating a bond between him and me.

Footfalls come heavy through the trees. As I flee, I sense that one day this bond could be made to serve me.

SWEETBRIAR

Voice shaking, I repeated, "Harker?"

Slowly he blinked, and his face came alive again. My chest loosened, and I took in a breath.

"Are you well?" I asked.

He sat up gingerly. "He's dead?"

I looked to where Goosevar had fallen, riddled with Jack's strange arrows. Jack and the priest stood over him. "If my eyes aren't playing a cruel trick."

Harker's hand closed over mine, and I turned back to him. He drew my palm to his mouth, pressing his lips against it. I studied him, anxious.

Finally, he said, "It's gone, Mina." His voice was low but charged with feeling.

"What's gone?"

His chin lifted slightly, and his nostrils widened as the air moved through them. "I can smell *you*, but I can't smell your blood."

The others were stirring out of their shock and beginning to speak to each other—Mr. Hilliard among them—but I shut them out as I strove to understand Harker. "What are you saying?"

"I've lost the thirst, Mina."

My heart leapt. "Are you sure?"

"Since the day I became a vampire, I've never—not for a single moment—been without it. I'm quite sure."

"Oh, Harker." My throat tightened, heart beating fast.

He shifted and reached for me.

"Careful," I said, taking his hands but holding back. "I think you've broken a rib."

"I think I've broken two," he replied with a husky laugh. "But they've partly mended. Come here."

His hands came to my waist, and he pulled me close. He rubbed his nose lightly against mine, sending a ripple of heat through me.

Behind us, Jack cleared his throat. "Mina?"

I moved to speak into Harker's ear. "I think the others need not know *all*."

"I will be guided by your wisdom," he murmured. "In this and in all things."

The two of us got stiffly to our feet, and Jack took a slow step toward us.

"I thought I had lost you," I said carefully.

Studying him, I saw that his face was a picture of boyish puzzlement, lacking the resentment and fear that so often twisted his expressions these days. He looked more like the old Jack than he had since our parents died.

"Much of this I don't understand, Mina," he said, "but I *do* understand what you did to save me." His eyes flickered to Harker, whose hand had come to the small of my back. "I'll be sorry all my days for what I did, and if I could take it back, I would. It was out of worry, and hotheadedness, and too much drink, but that doesn't make it right."

"Harker is not a killer, Jack," I said, raising my voice. It was pretty clear that Jack had come to this on his own, but I felt it needed to be stated in front of the others. Father Kelly and Mr. Hilliard—even Mr. Couch in his own way—were all men whom people in the village listened to.

Jack nodded, seeming to understand my reasons. "I'm only glad my aim wasn't better." His brows knit as his eyes moved over Harker, and I knew he was looking for signs of the injury he'd caused. Jack's aim couldn't have been truer, but it seemed best to let him keep believing otherwise.

"Let there be no bad blood between us, Jack," said Harker, drawing Jack's eyes to his face again. "I know how much you care for your sister, and we have it in common."

Harker put out his hand.

Jack stared at it a moment while I held my breath. "You mean to make an honest woman of her?"

"As soon as I possibly may. The banns will be read this Sunday."

Jack grasped Harker's hand, and once they'd shaken, I put my arms around my brother.

He squeezed me against his chest. "And now I'll lose *you*. Not that I don't deserve it."

"You saved all our lives today," said Harker. "You'll always be welcome at Roche Rock." He glanced at the monster on the ground, an eyebrow lifting. "Sweetbriar rose, was it not?"

I let Jack go, and I noticed Mr. Hilliard had joined us, though he still stood back a little. The man was wide eyed and dripping wet. Father Kelly and Mr. Couch were bent over Dolly a short distance away. Mr. Couch's coat was drawn over her, but small movements of furry limbs and tail confirmed that she had survived.

Jack looked down at his hands, which were covered in small scratches. "Aye. Woody stalks, with the knobby parts carved away. Hen feathers for fletching."

Among the four protruding arrows, three had white feathers and one was Rosie-red.

"We had hints of it," said Harker. "We studied the painting in the bell tower. But I couldn't see it. I had started thinking of poisons I might concoct using roses. The idea that St. Gomonda might have killed Goosevar with arrows from a literal rosebush never entered my mind."

Jack shrugged, a sheepish grin on his lips. "Truth is I couldn't think of any other way to understand that old painting. But I didn't know for sure, and I worried I'd end up only making the thing angry again."

The priest joined us, and Jack continued, "I waited for Father Kelly near the church this morning, until after the two of you had gone. I had a time of it making him understand what I wanted to do. Anytime I tried to speak of the creature, my tongue knotted up. I know he thought I'd gone wrong in my head."

Father Kelly's expression was bleak as he looked at Goosevar. "I'm still questioning whether *I* haven't gone wrong in my head, though I know very well there are things in this world we've yet to discover." Looking at Jack, he said, "I confess I had no clear idea of what this was about. Only that it had to do with the killings, and the old stories of a wolf on the Tregarrick estate. But I could see you were going through with it whether I helped you or not. In the end I came along with the hope I would be able to straighten out your thinking before you hurt anyone."

Jack's brows lifted. "I thought I'd managed to convince you when you insisted on fetching Couch and Dolly."

Father Kelly shook his head. "I only wanted Couch for reinforcement, in case you wouldn't listen to reason. I have never in my life been so surprised as when we walked up on that monster."

Eyeing Jack, I said, "You dreamed all this up last night when you left us?"

He shrugged. "Those wolf stories that started up after the killing had gotten me thinking about that painting. Then when I saw the monster with my own eyes—well, I knew I'd been wrong about the killer." His gaze brushed Harker. "Stayed up half the night wandering the downs in the moonlight, collecting the straightest and sturdiest stalks I could find." He glanced at his bow, on the ground next to Goosevar. With a fond smile, he said, "Made that when I thought I was going to grow up to be Robin Hood."

I laughed. "I almost used it for kindling a hundred times, but I remembered how hard you worked on it and couldn't bring myself to do it."

"It's a good bow. Jenny had gnawed one end of it some, but it really only needed restringing. Once I repaired it and finished the arrows, I spent the rest of the night practicing. Only one of those arrows would shoot straight, so I had to learn how to aim the others."

I smiled. "You ended up a hero after all, Jack."

He chuckled at this, but I could see by his ruddy cheeks and bright eyes that he was pleased. After a moment, he sobered. As he rubbed his jaw, I saw that his hand shook. "I've a lot to make up to you, Mina."

"I think we've been pretty hard on *each other*. I know you've only wanted what was best for me. Even if we didn't always agree on what that was."

"Still, I wasn't easy to live with, and I'm sorry for it."

Smiling, I hooked my arm through his. "Well, make it up to me by giving me away at my wedding."

Before Jack could reply, Mr. Hilliard stepped forward. The look of shock on his face had not lessened, and he held his arm against his chest like maybe he'd broken it. He had a bloody welt on his forehead, too. His voice shook as he said, "What I'd like to know is why no one saw fit to involve the constable in any of this."

My brows lifted. "What would you have said if we'd come to you with a story about a wolf-tree-man monster that lived in the fog on the Tregarrick place?"

"And could only be killed with sweetbriar," added Jack.

"Yet had already been killed by a *saint* centuries ago," put in Father Kelly, shaking his head.

Mr. Hilliard drew a shuddering breath. "Fair points, all. But which of you is going to tell me what I'm to put in my report to the Police Watch Committee?"

The constable was far from finished with his questions, but we could all see he was poorly, and Harker suggested we go up to the chapel and continue our talk indoors by the fire. Which reminded me of something.

Glancing at Harker, I said, "Before we go, maybe we want to make use of that cross Father Kelly brought."

Harker agreed, and I explained what was wanted. The priest fetched the cross, and from the moment he laid it over the monster's chest, smoke began rising. His bark skin blackened around it, and soon flames kindled and spread.

The bonfire drew Jeremy out of the birch copse. He combed the ground for his stick and then used it to poke at the fire. The rest of us—except for Mr. Couch, who wouldn't leave Dolly's side—stood quietly watching sparks shoot into the sky. The clouds had retreated, leaving behind a crisp autumn blue. The sun burned off every last wisp of fog.

As the flames began to quiet, leaving a pile of smoldering ash, Harker stepped away. With an arm around his ribs, he stooped to pick up something from the ground. Then he came and handed it to me—*Mum's cross.* The ribbon was missing, and I quickly took his hand and turned it; the cross had left no burn marks.

Meeting his gaze, I saw his eyes shone with tears. I took his face in my hands and pulled his lips to mine. His arms folded around me, fitting our bodies together.

How warm he was.

We sent Jeremy for the surgeon, and the rest of us made our way up to the chapel. Jack and Mr. Couch shared the task of carrying poor Dolly, who also had broken ribs and whimpered pitifully all the way. They arranged her on the ground near the gap in the hedgerow, until Mr. Couch could come back with his pony cart.

The publican had hardly spoken three words since Goosevar was killed, and it seemed to me that he, too, was in a kind of shock. But he met my eye for a long moment before he left, and I knew he was remembering our conversation at The Wolf's Head.

Though the weather had turned fine, a chill had settled within the stone walls, and Harker set Jack to building up the fire. Then the two of us went upstairs to make tea, and so that I could bind his ribs and hopefully give him some relief.

As Harker was removing his shirt, he said, "There is something I don't think I can wait until later to tell you, Mina."

The seriousness of his tone gave me a twinge of anxiety—even as I found myself transfixed by the baring of so much of his flesh.

"All right."

At the tremor in my voice, he closed the distance between us and put his arms around me. I rested my hands on his rounded shoulders, and my heart began to hammer. I had liked touching him even when his flesh was cold. Now I thought it might be more than I could bear.

His chest expanded against me as he breathed. "Goosevar fed on the wife of my ancestor when she was with child."

My own breath caught. "You've seen another of his memories."

He nodded. "It seems the blood of a pregnant woman is especially potent. He nearly killed her and her child, but he made himself stop. He healed the wound with his own blood to hide what he'd done."

A hard shiver went through me. "Was that what created the connection?"

"With her child, yes. Once I'd seen this, I kept sifting for more. I knew it might be our last chance to learn the whole story. He repeated this with each Tregarrick wife, using an enchantment, similar to the ones he used on you and Jack, to keep her from remembering the attack. Do you understand what this means, Mina?"

I swallowed over a tight place in my throat. "It means . . . it really is over?"

He smiled, reaching a hand to my cheek, and softly repeated, "It really is over. He'll never threaten a mistress of Roche Rock again."

"How can we be sure, Harker? I mean, we burned him. But he came back once before."

"I have an idea about that."

His thumb brushed my cheek, and I nodded. If I'd understood him, he was telling me we could *truly* be man and wife.

"You're trembling, love."

Again I nodded, because it was useless to try to speak, and he gently laughed.

Heat fountained in my belly as our lips touched. His mouth moved over mine, hungry not for my blood, but for *me.* His tongue slipped like silk between my lips, then out again. His teeth—no longer sharp, but blunted like my own—took a gentle hold on my bottom lip, and I softly moaned. He pulled me tight against him—and then gasped.

"Oh, Harker," I laughed, stepping back. "Your poor ribs."

I bent to examine them more closely. Purple bruises were already forming on one side of his rib cage. I could see the lines of bone below his skin, and I gently probed each with my finger.

"We should have the surgeon look, but they feel whole to me. I think the worst damage had time to be repaired before the end." *Goosevar's end.* "I'm sorry if I'm causing you pain."

"I don't think I'll ever feel pain again," he said in a coarsened voice. He covered my hand with his, stilling it against the plane of his abdomen. "But you had best stop now or we won't be going back downstairs."

My face and chest flushed hot. "Shall I bind them for you? If nothing else, it will remind you to be careful."

He squeezed my hand before letting it go. "Thank you."

My shift hung over a chair, from when I'd changed before the handfasting, and I found a pair of shears on his worktable. As I began cutting a long strip, he protested that he had a trunk full of clothing and linen that nobody was using.

To which I answered, "This shift is old and threadbare, and I'll not mistreat any of your fine things to save it."

"Then I shall buy you ten to replace it."

As I knotted strips of cloth together, I said carefully, "When you went down to the water, it seemed you might have learned something about Ruby that gave you some peace."

His eyes came to my face. "My father told me the truth. He dismissed her for her own safety. She didn't take it well; I think she may have been in love with him. When he left her by the pool to recover, Goosevar killed her."

My fingers stopped working as I gasped. "You saw the memory?"

"The complete memory of her murder to go along with the fragments I've been seeing the last sixty years."

"I'm so sorry, Harker. But also glad that . . ."

"It wasn't me? Yes. It's taken a great weight from me."

Once I'd bound his ribs, I made tea while he got dressed and dosed himself with an elixir of willow bark. We loaded a tray with cups, a teapot, and tinned biscuits and went down to join the others.

In the end, we told none of them anything of Harker's affliction. As Goosevar was responsible for the deaths, there seemed no reason to leave doubts in anyone's mind. It still bothered the constable that my own wound had been so different from the others, but again it was suggested that the attack might have been broken off early. That I'd saved myself by wielding Mum's cross, even if I didn't remember it. This was reasonable enough to be accepted by everyone.

Our talk of poor Mr. Roscoe made me wonder about him being left, ravaged, where anyone might find him, despite the fact Goosevar clearly understood that the killings placed him in danger. I supposed there had been desperation in the attack, made in the open and so near the road. My approach might have caused him to flee before he could cover what he'd done. All of which reminded me how easily it might have been *me*.

Mr. Hilliard declared that he was obligated to tell the more senior policing authorities the truth of what he'd witnessed, and I didn't envy him that. I also didn't like that it would probably mean we'd all be answering more questions. But I thought as long as we told them no more than we'd told Mr. Hilliard, we'd be all right. Let them make of it what they would.

Harker would have to talk about Ruby, but here, too, the truth (or almost the truth) would likely serve. She was his long-missing boyhood tutor, whom he'd recognized by her necklace. The timing of things might be cause for concern, except that the constable seemed to think the fact of her remains being long in the water would make further investigation difficult.

The way Jack kept eyeing me during the questioning in the chapel told me he knew that I was hiding something. I particularly felt his gaze when Mr. Hilliard made a teasing mention of "Tregarrick's heroics to save his fiancée." Jack would not have forgotten Harker's unnatural quickness. My twin must also have been wondering about the nature of our strange bargain with Goosevar. Thankfully he raised no questions in front of the others.

But as the two of us walked home together later—with Goosevar gone, there was no reason to invite scandal by living at Roche Rock before the wedding—Jack asked me, "Will you be safe with him, Mina?"

I remembered when Harker had asked me the same question about Jack.

"Anyone can see that he cares for you," he continued, "but I know there's something not quite right about him."

"There *was* something not quite right about him," I admitted. "But that changed when you killed Goosevar."

He blew out a sigh. "I'm not going to ask how that can be. I don't actually think you'd tell me. But if you're *certain* . . ."

I met his gaze. "I'm certain. Can you accept that?"

He laughed and hooked his arm through mine. "I'm finished trying to control you, sister. I almost lost you over it, and it never worked anyway."

"TWO FOR JOY"

Harker

Seventeen days later

The final reading of the banns at last took place, and after the services, Father Kelly and I waited in the churchyard for my bride and our witnesses—Jack and Mrs. Moyle. Mina had asked the priest to marry us beside her parents' grave markers. I had fully expected him to reject the idea as too morbid for a wedding, but Mina knew him better than I did, and he thought it a sweet and appropriate gesture.

While we waited, we watched a group of men from the village digging up the old wheel cross in the churchyard. That, too, I had expected him to resist, but he said the relic rightly belonged at Roche Rock, where it was originally erected. And all agreed it was better to be safe than sorry; the cross would be newly erected over the ground where we had burned Goosevar. And where he had murdered Ruby.

Ruby—after Mr. Hilliard's constabulary colleagues had satisfied themselves as much as was possible in such a strange case—was buried in the Tregarrick family graveyard. I thought it would have pleased her.

Mrs. Moyle was the first to join us in the churchyard, dressed in her Sunday best, glowing with happiness and pride. My relief that Mina would not lose her dear friend due to the unseemliness of our engagement could not have been overstated. In the end, we avoided all appearance of impropriety. Mina, awaiting the day of our nuptials at home with her brother, went to and from The Magpie as usual. The morning after Goosevar's death, it brought a smile to my lips to notice her scent on the breeze just as I had nearly every day for the last two years.

The bloodlust had gone, but my sharpened senses had so far remained. I had given up my vital essence, as it was no longer needed, but the purplish tint to my irises, too, had remained. Perhaps both would fade over time. Perhaps not.

It was of no consequence to me either way. Because I had not once, over all the long decades, thought I would ever look to such happiness in this life. Not only the cessation of the bloodlust, but the prospect of a true marriage to Mina.

The priest, Mrs. Moyle, and I hadn't long to wait. Mina and Jack arrived together, joining us under the hazel trees sheltering her parents' graves.

Though I had suspected my bride of being an angel before, she now seemed to me a goddess. I'd insisted on buying her a gown, paying for both her and Mrs. Moyle to travel by train to London and consult a modiste. Mina was captivated by the city that was the setting in so many of the novels she'd read, and I adjusted our honeymoon plans so that we might spend several weeks there before traveling on to Paris and finally Rome for the winter months. Having led the life of a hermit, I was quite as excited as she was. Many of the volumes in my library had once belonged to Oxford or Cambridge scholars, and I planned visits to both of these schools before we left England.

I have no talent for describing ladies' fashions, but suffice it to say, there were seed pearls and lace and petticoats, layer upon layer. A woman from the village had arranged Mina's fiery locks in a soft pile of curls atop her head.

Jack brought her to me, and the priest did before God what we had done already before the spirits of Roche Rock, and I felt no more bound to her now than I had in that moment. But I was happy for her sake that the village of Roche, even if all didn't smile on us, would accept us as legally, properly wedded. As for me, this moment was a symbol and celebration of my own miraculous transmutation, worked not by potions or elixirs, by learned men or dusty volumes, but by the love of a maiden for a monster.

When the priest pronounced her my wife, a flutter of wings drew our gazes to the Penrose crosses. A magpie had landed on each, watching us a moment with dark eyes before flitting away. Mina beamed, tears pooling, and murmured, "Two for joy."

We all then walked across to the tearoom, where we had the dining room to ourselves for a late-morning wedding breakfast hosted by Mrs. Moyle. When the cold meats, cheeses, scones, clotted cream, and jam had been eaten, and my bride had embraced everyone, I was at last permitted to take her home with me.

It was a golden October day, a nip in the air, but warm enough in the sun. Too fine for anyone but a vampire to spend inside a drafty medieval chapel. So I carried cushions, a rug, and a bottle of champagne up to the battlements while my wife made tea.

Once she'd settled like Venus upon a cloud, we sipped our tea and remarked politely on the wedding and the breakfast while my desire to touch her grew to a fever pitch. But we'd agreed to this small ritual, which I knew made her feel close to her mother, and I wasn't about to deny her.

When at last we'd drunk the pot, she removed the lid, narrowed her eyes, and peered inside. Her brow furrowed as she turned it this way and that, and finally she laughed. "I've no idea. Perhaps we should consult Mrs. Rochester."

"Here," I said, reaching for it. As I looked through the opening, a smile spread over my face.

"What?" she said, excited. "Tell me!"

"I believe these refer to your wedding gifts, Mrs. Tregarrick."

"More *gifts*, Harker!" Her green eyes danced, her charmingly freckled countenance lovelier than ever in her happiness. "Well, what are they?"

Soberly, I handed the teapot back to her. "I expect you to at least *try*. Tell me what you see."

She let out a disgruntled sigh and stared back through the opening. "A crown, maybe, just under the handle? And now I'm thinking that's a house on the bottom. Yes, definitely a house."

"First the crown," I said. "I have donated a great deal of money to Church of England charities with the express view of achieving knighthood so that you may be styled Lady Tregarrick."

Her eyes rounded. "Harker!" She let out another ripple of laughter. "But I have everything I need to be happy right *here*."

"I'm glad to hear it, but it made *me* happy to do it. Of course there are no guarantees, but as we've seen, the leaves are never wrong."

With a wincing smile, she said, "Was it truly a *great* deal of money?"

"It was, but we have a great deal more than we need."

Her brows lifted. "I'm almost afraid to ask about the house!"

"Little mystery there, my love. This chapel will be cozy enough for a while, but it's no place to raise a family. After our engagement was announced, I hired an architect to design a new house. Once the design is complete and we are on our honeymoon, Jack will be put in charge of overseeing the construction."

"Jack!" Her eyes filled with tears again, and from her confectionary cloud, she produced a handkerchief.

Mr. Hilliard had made sure Jack didn't lose his job over his missed shifts, but I had told my bride's brother that there was no need for him to return to the clay pits unless he wished to. That I would be happy to put him to work on the estate, to send him to school, or to send him abroad—as long as he gave up drinking, because it was breaking his sister's heart. (He informed me that he hadn't drunk a drop since the night he shot me.) While he had yet to make up his mind, he had agreed to help us with the construction while he considered.

One sparkling tear avoided the handkerchief and slid down Mina's cheek, and I moved closer. Laughing, I wiped it away and said, "A poor bridegroom *I* make. Half the things I say to you these days make you cry."

"How can I not when I'm so happy?" Her voice was creaky with emotion. "And whatever am I to give *you*?"

I shook my head and put a finger to her lips. "You have taken away my loneliness and given me the world. Everything I have given you is meaningless in comparison."

She took hold of my hand and held it in her lap. "There is something else I wish to give you now. I would have already, the night we were truly wed, had it been possible. And all the nights since then, had we been able to spend them together."

My heart pounded, and I felt the fire in my blood. My voice deepened as I said, "That is a gift I will happily accept."

She frowned, and in a quiet voice she said, "I worry . . . will it be as . . . as pleasurable . . ." Her cheeks went red under the autumn sunshine. "I mean, now that you no longer need . . ."

I raised an eyebrow. "Now that I no longer need worry I might lose control and end your life?"

The edges of her smile reappeared.

I got up and arranged the remaining cushions behind her. While I was there, I began to work at the pearly buttons that ran along her spine, my heart heaving against my healed ribs. After an eternity of slipping fingers and under-my-breath oaths, the top of the dress at last fell away.

I moved around her and took hold of her hands, raising and extracting her from both the dress and the engineering works that supported it. I stepped back, knees almost buckling as I took her in—chest and shoulders bare, corset hugging her waist and framing her breasts.

How many times over these last weeks had I dreamed of this moment?

Her soft smile was beckoning as she kicked free of her shoes and pushed her gown to one side with a stockinged foot.

I moved close again, removing the pins and mother-of-pearl combs from her hair, letting out a long breath as it finally cascaded around her shoulders. Burying both my hands in it—a thing I had longed to do since the first day we met—I bent to her ear and murmured, "Sit down."

We sank onto the cushions together, and I eased her back, lowering over her. I kissed her, a gentle caress that grew harder and more insistent as desire took us both. Her back arched, her chest pressing against me as a hungry sound came from her throat.

Her hands began working, tugging my coat down my shoulders until I cast it off. Then unbuttoning my waistcoat, her eyes never leaving mine. When that, too, was dispensed with, she untied my cravat and worked at my shirt buttons, finally peeling down my braces and slipping her hands inside the white lawn.

"Mina," I breathed, shuddering as I ran a hand up over her corset, tugging at the edge so I might feel one berry-red nipple harden against my tongue.

She gasped and wriggled against me, and I reached down and loosened her corset strings so I could plant a kiss in the valley between her breasts. Then another above it, and another, until I'd left a trail of them up to her chin.

"Will you kiss me, Harker?" she pleaded, echoing a moment I well remembered.

"I intend to spend the rest of my life making it up to you for ever having to refuse such a request."

Our lips came together, swollen with need, bodies aching. I trailed my fingers down her waist, over her hip, and down to the hem of her shift, slowly raising it. She shivered as my fingers traced her thigh, and again she arched against me.

I felt her legs spread beneath me, and her hands worked free my trouser buttons.

"This is new to me," she whispered, hands moving down my back, leaving trails of fire.

I smiled and cupped her cheek, using my thumb to smooth the anxiety from her face until finally she smiled, too.

Settling gently between her legs, I said, "We shall master it together, my love."

Acknowledgments

I LOVE vampires, and for years I've thought I'd like to write about one. There are so many different flavors of them—scary, sexy, somewhere in between—but a lot of what vampires are has become canon, and for years I wasn't sure I had anything new to add to the genre. That changed when I looked at them through the lens of the cozy fantasy worlds I love best.

I drew a lot of inspiration, too, from the real-world location, Roche Rock, with its fabulously mysterious old chapel. I took a bit of artistic license with the place, as it's not fully intact, and really too small for the kind of dwelling I needed. BUT THE VIBES.

I had done research on tea-leaf reading for *Salt & Broom*, and I did more for *Tea & Alchemy*. There are differing interpretations for symbols in tea leaves, and for that I drew on a variety of sources, including the charming book *Reading the Leaves*, by Leanne Marrama and Sandra Mariah Wright. I loved including little references to Jane from *Salt & Broom*!

Huge thanks to Stu Flies Around Cornwall on YouTube for the terrific drone footage of both Roche Rock and the St. Gomonda parish church bell tower. I'm also indebted to D. G. Wilson's *The River Fal*, which describes the history and landscape of the book's real setting. Aaaand to *The British History Podcast* for the ancient history of Britannia.

Also, in researching alchemy, one scholarly article was particularly helpful: Tillmann Taape's "Distilling Reliable Remedies: Hieronymus Brunschwig's Liber de arte distillandi (1500) Between Alchemical Learning and Craft Practice" (via the National Library of Medicine).

Of course a shout-out to Bram Stoker's *Dracula*, which I paid tribute to in the main characters' names. Randomly, while I was working on the book, I learned there's a place called The Magpie Café in Whitby, UK, which is where Dracula first landed in Stoker's novel!

A note on the old magpie rhyme at the beginning of the book—I first heard The Unthanks' musical version of it while watching the folk-horror documentary *Woodlands Dark and Days Bewitched*, and it has LIVED RENT-FREE IN MY HEAD EVER SINCE.

As far as the world of the book goes, I could write ten pages on references and inspiration, but nobody wants to read that. And it's high time I thank the folks who support me at the writing desk.

At Writers House, my agent, Robin Rue, for unflinching support always, and Beth Miller for spot-on feedback and fabulous travel advice.

My 47North editor Lauren Plude, who, along with developmental editor Lindsey Faber, tirelessly cheers me on. Thank you both for all your support and for being quite possibly my biggest fans. Thank you, Lindsey, for your amazing insight into my stories and characters and for helping me MAKE EVERYTHING BETTER.

The 47North copyediting (thank you, Bill and Kellie!), production, and marketing folks, who are terrific to work with and give my books polish, plus get them in front of the readers who will love them.

Colin Verdi for the fabulous cover art for *Salt & Broom* and *Grimm Curiosities* (no cover design yet for this book at the time of this writing).

The terrific voice talent I've had the privilege of working with thus far: Elizabeth Bower, Tim Bruce, Henrietta Meire, and Joshua Akehurst (narrators for this novel not selected at the time of this writing).

My language guy, Jeff Lilly, for coming up with the name Goosevar!

Debbi Murray, who's been a beta reader and fan since the beginning of this journey.

Jason, who provides incredible support, including meal deliveries to my desk, and who read and provided feedback for this book THREE TIMES. Selah and Talia, who encouraged me to write a vampire story. I love you all to the moon and back.

I will close with the same disclaimer as always, no less sincere for being repeated . . . I do a lot of research. Hard as I try not to, I miss things. I make mistakes. A novel is like an octopus, except with hundreds of legs. Where I have erred, I hope you will forgive me.

About the Author

Sharon Lynn Fisher is the author of *Grimm Curiosities*, *Salt & Broom*, and many other novels and short stories set in lush, romantic, and atmospheric worlds. Sharon lives in the Pacific Northwest woods outside Seattle, where she spends her free time looking for fairies and mushrooms. She's married to her beta reader and is mom to two teens, an orange cat, and a handful of chickens. For more information, visit www.sharonlynnfisher.com.